KINGSTON 76

KINGSTON 76

ADAM SNYDER

Wheelie Press
Woodstock, New York

This is a work of fiction. Names, characters, places, and incidents are the products of the author's imagination or are used fictitiously. Any resemblance to actual events or persons is entirely coincidental.

•

FIRST EDITION

Interior design by Jason Snyder
Cover design by Jennifer MaHarry

ISBN: 979-8-218-41431-3

1. Mysteries   2. LGBTQ families   3. 1970s

WHEELIE PRESS
Woodstock, New York

adamsnyder.com

For Jennifer and Elliot

★

PART ONE

★ ★ ★

CHAPTER 1

With his bedsheets tied together into a makeshift rope, Timothy climbed out the window of his second story bedroom.

He'd read the instructions several times. He'd estimated the distance to the ground, tied the sheets at the corners using square knots, and secured one end to his bed frame. The bed seemed heavy enough to hold him, that is, until the full weight of his descending body pulled it halfway across the room, causing him to drop several feet quite quickly.

It was at this point that his neighbor across the street, Mrs. O'Connor, looked out her window and saw a long-haired boy dangling halfway down the outside of his house, and thought it was a good idea to call his mother.

"What on earth are you doing?" his mom yelled as she and Cathryn came running out of the house to see what Timothy was doing now.

"I need to practice," Timothy called back, struggling to snake the bottom of the rope sheet between his feet like the book suggested.

"Practice for what?"

"In case there's a house fire," he said, as if this should be obvious.

"Where's the ladder?" his mom asked Cathryn.

"I don't think it's tall enough," Cathryn said.

But by this point, Mr. O'Connor was already making his way across the street with an extension ladder, having been alerted to the situation by his wife.

Timothy, not wanting to be rescued, gave up on the snaking foot maneuver and commenced to lower his 10-year-old frame to the ground using arm strength alone, which was sufficient thanks to his light weight and daily pull-up regime.

When he got within about five feet of the ground, the bed sheet that was pulled taut over the window sill made an audible *scritching* sound as it began to rip the long way, rapidly delivering Timothy the rest of the way to the ground, where his feet touched briefly before he landed on his ass, no worse for wear.

"Are you okay?" his mom said.

"I'm fine."

"You've got to stop doing stuff like this."

No response.

"Timbo," Mr. O'Connor weighed in, "is it safe to bring my ladder home, or are you going to try doing this again?"

"I'm done for now . . ."

"Righto, see you all later," he said, turning around slowly so as not to clock anyone with the oversized ladder.

"Thanks Jim," Timothy's mom said to Mr. O'Connor, then to Timothy: "Go straighten that mess upstairs then come down and help us clean up, we've got Group tonight."

"Why do we always have to have that thing at our house?"

"Timothy, we are a family who welcomes people."

Timothy flashed a look at Cathryn.

"I noticed," he said, not quite under his breath.

★   ★   ★

The one good thing about Group night was that neither Timothy's mom nor Cathryn had time to cook, which meant Timothy sometimes got to eat frozen pizza for supper.

Frozen pizza wasn't exactly pizza, but it wasn't not pizza either.

With the dining room table arranged with snacks for Group, Timothy was eating quickly, standing up in the kitchen. His cat, Oscar, was likewise eating a rushed dinner, straight out of the can.

Timothy was just noticing he'd scalded the tip of his tongue on a greasy bit of pepperoni when he heard the front door opening and closing. The women from Group had started to file in.

"Save yourself while you still can," he said to Oscar, who didn't need to be told twice, and bolted out the back door.

Timothy peeked into the living room. The throw pillows were already arranged in a circle on the floor, the incense was already burning.

Why did all these women have the same look as his mother and Cathryn? No-nonsense haircuts, no make-up, jeans, leather boots that looked ready for Western ranching even though they were in Kingston, New York. Were they all reading the same manual?

He had to admit that they did have sort of a contemporary look about them, considering it was 1976 and half the other women on Warren Street dressed like it was the 1950s. But still.

When the women greeted his mom, they all called her "Denny." His mom's name was Denise. Where did this Denny business come from? It seemed somehow to confirm his suspicion that his mom had actually somehow become a different person than she was barely a year before.

And then came the hugging.

Everyone in Group always hugged each other when they first arrived. Hugging in itself wasn't so weird, it's just that Timothy had an internal clock that told him how long a normal hug should last, and these hugs seemed to drag on forever.

He was about to retreat to the kitchen counter when his mother said:

"Oh, Jacqui, good to see you, we weren't expecting you . . . Timothy!"

The ten or so women now standing in his living room were all taller than him as he tiptoed among them to see what his mother wanted.

"Can you go upstairs and get your beanbag chair? We don't have enough pillows."

Of course Timothy did not want to do this, because who wants a stranger's butt in your beanbag chair? But he didn't want to make a scene either, so upstairs he went.

As he came back down, the women were all taking their seats on the pillow circle. The beanbag chair dangled from his hand like a giant dried fig as he handed it to the woman who had just arrived.

"Cool chair, thanks," she said.

"You're welcome," Timothy said, trying to be polite.

"Hey Timothy!" said another woman, who was already seated.

"Hi Cara," he said softly.

Cara seemed like she was probably the youngest one in the group, maybe college age? He had committed her name to memory because she was the only one who seemed to know his name and always said hello to him. Also, she had a certain twinkle in her eye and, though he'd never admit it, he thought she was kind of cute.

"Why don't you ever sit with us?" Cara asked. "You can, you know."

"I'm sure he doesn't want to sit around listening to a bunch of women talking," said the woman sitting next to Cara. The woman smiled with her mouth, but shot Timothy the evil eye to make sure he got the point that he was not welcome.

His mom and Cathryn were fussing with something on the dining room table so missed all this, but Cara caught the gist of what was going on.

"Anne, be nice," she said to death ray woman.

"It's okay, I've got homework to do," Timothy said, and exited the circle as quickly as he could without stepping on anyone.

Back in the kitchen, what was left of his frozen pizza was now almost cold. He ate it anyway, chewing almost angrily because it gave his emotions somewhere to go besides the forefront of his mind.

He didn't want to go back through the living room, but he had to in order to get up to his room, so he just made himself do it. The energy in the room had shifted since everyone in the circle had settled down. A couple of the women had lit cigarettes, something his mom and Cathryn would never do, but tolerated because it was Group.

Cathryn took the lead and was saying something like:

"So, last time we were talking about Safe Places . . . "

but Timothy didn't really care to know what they had to say on this topic, he just wanted to be in his own safe place, which at this point had shrunk to the size of his bedroom.

He would have punched the hell out of his beanbag chair but it was downstairs under some strange lady's butt. Instead he sat down hard on his bed and hammer punched the mattress repeatedly with the side of his fist.

Why was he so angry? It was that Anne woman. It's one thing for an undifferentiated mass of women to take over his living room occasionally, but to have someone individually glare at him like that, like he wasn't welcome in his own home? That was just too much.

He would've started breaking things if he didn't think it would draw unwanted attention, and it pissed him off even further that he couldn't even find release in his own room.

"Fucking fuck," he blurted out.

His temples continued to pulse, though he instinctively took some deep breaths, which had the helpful effect of calming him to the point where at least his room felt like his own domain once again.

He turned on his alarm clock radio, the sole source of music in his bedroom. Captain and Tennille were playing. They seemed pretty confident that "love would keep them together," but Timothy had his doubts.

By and by, he went into the "junk drawer" at the bottom of his dresser and retrieved the cigar box in which he stored his most personal things. A keychain from a trip to Lake George with his mom. A black-and-white photo of his parents at their seemingly normal wedding in the 1960s. And, most notably, a book about the size of a Readers' Digest wrapped in brown paper.

He opened the book and the title page was revealed:

The Real Men's Guidebook

It had called out to him from the back of a comic book. After much deliberation, he'd taped a quarter and two dimes to the order form and mailed it to a p.o. box somewhere in the midwest. He'd made sure he was the first to check their mailbox every afternoon for three weeks until it finally arrived.

He began turning the pages purposefully as he'd done many times. He reread the page with instructions on how to turn bed-sheets into a rope ladder, trying to figure out what he'd done wrong. In the photo, the man descending the wall seemed to have no trouble snaking the bed sheet between his feet, why had it been so hard for Timothy?

At any rate, Timothy put a small checkmark on the upper corner of the page, satisfied he'd earned his merit badge for this one. He continued flipping through the pages contemplating his next manly experiment.

There was an unexpected knock, his door started opening.

"Timothy?"

He stuffed the paperback book under his butt as Cara walked into his bedroom. What was she doing up here? She must've been looking for the bathroom and knocked on the wrong door. She couldn't possibly actually be looking for him, could she?

"So, this is your room . . ."

"Uh, yeah . . ."

She looked around with actual interest. He hoped she wouldn't zero in on the poster of Farrah in the red bathing suit, which would be kind of mortifying, you could see her nipples if you looked closely. But no, she was looking at other things.

There was something peculiar about Timothy's room, something different than she'd imagined. She realized it was that instead of toys and games, his room was mostly an odd collection of seemingly more adult possessions.

If she'd known the backstory, she'd see that each object was the result of Timothy snatching something from the donation box at the last moment, as his mother systematically tried to rid their house of things that reminded her of their previous life.

She picked up an old bourbon decanter that was shaped like an old-time gunslinger.

"This is neat, where'd you get it?"

"It was my dad's."

She nodded thoughtfully as she appraised it before setting it back down respectfully. With her attention thus diverted, Timothy stuck his Real Men's book beneath his mattress so he could rise to his feet and join her by the book shelf.

"A lot of this stuff's your dad's, huh."

"Yep."

She nodded like she understood.

"Must've been hard, your dad running out like that."

"It's okay," Timothy lied.

"But you know something, Cathryn's really special, she and your mom make a great couple."

"They're not a couple," Timothy quickly corrected her, "they're roommates."

Surprised by this sudden assertion, Cara scanned his eyes. She couldn't for the life of her tell if this was just his standard story or he really believed this. At this moment she realized maybe she'd been too cavalier coming up here, perhaps she'd overstepped her bounds.

"Yes, roommates," she said, correcting herself.

There were other interesting things on the shelf she could ask him about, but she decided she'd best get back downstairs.

"Anyway," she added, "I just came up to tell you you really are welcome to join us, just so you'd hear it from someone other than your mom and Cathryn, we all really do like you."

Timothy thought two things: one, not everyone down there does actually like me and two, he'd never hear from his mom and Cathryn that he was welcome to join Group. But he supposed it was nice of Cara to come in to say so.

"Thanks, but I still have to do my homework."

Cara shut the door on her way out. Timothy sat back down on his bed. He wasn't going to do his homework, because he never did his homework.

But he did feel less full of rage than he had just ten minutes ago.

When he could hear car doors slamming out on the street and engines starting, Timothy figured it was safe to go back downstairs.

His mom and Cathryn were out on the porch seeing the last of them off.

Cigarette smoke still hung in the air. It would take days for the smell to clear out entirely. The pillows were still on the floor, now in more of a twisted oval, mirroring the dynamics of whatever terribly earnest conversation had taken place.

Timothy picked the pillows up one by one, tossing them into the corner, beginning to reclaim the living room where on most nights he snacked and watched TV.

On the rug beside one of the last pillows, he found a pack of cigarettes just lying there. He picked it up, examined it closely, smelled the rich but pungent aroma of the tobacco. He removed a single cigarette just moments before the woman whose cigarettes they were came bounding back into the living room from the outside.

Timothy deftly slid the loose cigarette into his shirt pocket as he held up the pack.

"Just what I was looking for," the woman said. Maybe her name was Sarah.

"I was just about to bring them out to you."

"You're a star," she said, taking the pack and heading back out, "have a good night."

Timothy threw the last pillow into the corner.

His mom and Cathryn came in at the same time, letting out a collective "Phew!" as if, despite having enjoyed their evening, they were glad to be finished with it.

"Thank you, Timothy," his mom said, "you're a real good sport."

She crossed the room and gave him an appreciative hug, which he sort of wanted to wriggle out of because she smelled like everyone else she had hugged all evening, but it's not like they were in public, so he submitted to it, because, well, she was his mom.

"Yeah, thanks," Cathryn echoed, giving Timothy a respectful pat on the shoulder while his mom was still hugging him, which was about the extent of physical contact she figured he'd allow.

Strangely enough, it was at moments like these, after the house had expanded almost to the breaking point of maximum weirdness and unfamiliarity, that the return to it being just Timothy, his mom, and Cathryn felt some version of "normal," the threesome feeling like a unit of some sort.

"There's still some ice cream," his mom said.

Timothy glanced over at the ice cream, which was just now being lapped up by Oscar who'd leapt onto the table.

"Thanks anyway," he said. "Guess I'll just go back upstairs and get ready for bed."

Grabbing his beanbag chair, he shook it out and pulled it this way and that, trying to get the alien butt print out of it as he climbed the stairs. Throwing it in the corner of his room, he took the cigar box back out of his junk drawer.

Carefully removing the cigarette from the snapped pocket of his western shirt, he laid it gently amongst the photos, keepsakes and brown-wrapped guidebook.

The Real Men's Guidebook did not contain instructions per se about the right way to smoke a cigarette, but there was an ad for Lucky Strikes that provided a good model.

This was an experiment that would have to wait for another day.

CHAPTER 2

O ne of these porches was not like the others.

The Williams' front porch featured two discreet wicker chairs painted white, and a Revolutionary American flag with a circle of 13 stars, mounted proudly on one of the porch columns in honor of the Bicentennial.

The Vanderbeck's front porch also had two places to sit, metal lawn chairs, the kind with a slight bounce when you leaned back. Between them was a milk canister with painted flowers on it, the top just big enough for two glasses of lemonade.

Most other porches on Warren Street were much the same.

Then, there was Timothy's porch.

To begin with, there was the couch. It had lived on the sidewalk for a few days shortly after Cathryn moved in. When no one picked it up, it found its way back onto the porch and was soon draped with a batik cover from an Indian import store. It actually didn't smell too bad, considering Oscar the cat could be found there most days.

The columns were in need of paint, house plants straggled in all directions, and alongside the front door was a faded, tie-dyed peace sign that Timothy's mother had actually carried in a rally when she'd marched on Washington a few years back.

But the biggest challenge to Timothy's sense of dignity wasn't on the porch but parked right in front of it.

The 68 Chrysler had probably been a single color when it left the factory. But it had since been painted so many different shades of Rustoleum that it was impossible to say what color the car now actually was.

Timothy called their car the Calico Chrysler, in honor of his cat, who actually had a better paint job. Thankfully, their neighbor Mr. O'Connor was a long-distance trucker. When he wasn't out on the road, he parked the massive cab of his rig directly across the street, which tended to draw attention away from whatever was parked in its shadow.

This morning, Timothy didn't pay much attention to car, truck, or porch. He was running late for school, as usual.

Bounding out the front door, he soon slowed to a manageable trot. Dating back three centuries, his uptown Kingston neighborhood had once been a colonial village, its uneven bluestone sidewalks excellent for popping wheelies on his banana saddle, but a notorious tripping hazard.

Halfway down the block, he slowed further and, despite the ticking clock, came to a full stop when something curious caught his attention. An invitation, of sorts, from the universe.

As different as Timothy's house may have been from the other houses, the building he paused before was in a whole other realm.

Everyone called it The Green Apartment Building. Basically, because it was painted green, and it was an apartment building.

Unlike the other houses on the street, with slanting roofs and gables, the Green Apartment Building was big and boxy. It housed a whole cast of wayward characters. Overall, it felt like it was from another world, and maybe this was why it had an air of mystery in general.

Timothy had never been inside, or even peered within, the Green Apartment Building. The front door was usually closed tight, probably locked, though Timothy had never dared try it.

But today, the front door was wide open.

Timothy stood out on the sidewalk, looking in.

It appeared kind of dim inside. From where he was standing in the brilliant morning sunlight, he couldn't see much at all. He probably should have just kept running and gotten to school.

But then he remembered the line he'd read in the The Real Men's Guidebook, a motto he was trying to make his own:

"When that little voice in your head says *No*, you say *YES* and double it!"

Timothy meant to challenge himself to do something that scared him every day. Would the door to the Green Apartment Building ever be sitting wide open again?

Cautiously, he made his way up the stairs. He walked through the open door.

The outside may have been bright green, but the inside hallway was a sickly gray. There was a very old smell. Old coffee, old cigarettes, old dust, all mixed together so you couldn't tell what was what, just old. It didn't smell like a home.

The floor was a dingy linoleum, worn enough in places you could see the creaky wooden floorboards underneath. The wainscoted walls were painted the same shade of gray as the chipping tin ceiling, all barely illuminated by a single bare lightbulb hanging overhead.

On one wall, a bank of mailboxes. Timothy counted them.

"Eight apartments," he said to himself, as if this in itself were a revelation.

As he was staring at the boxes, a door at the end of the hallway creaked open slightly and startled him. He wanted to run out, but the woman peering out through the door beckoned him.

"Don't run away, c'mere a sec."

Frozen as if in a dream, it took him a minute to register what she was saying and then get his feet to walk in her direction.

"Here," she said, handing him a dollar bill, "run to the store and get me some milk."

He could see through the slender opening that the woman was wearing some kind of dressing gown, her hair up in rollers. He tried not to look too directly.

"Take it," she said, waving the dollar again.

"I have to go to school," Timothy said.

"It'll only take a minute, I need milk for my coffee. Get me a paper while you're at it."

She didn't seem to be asking him so much as telling him. That didn't mean he had to do it, but what if she asked what he was doing creeping around outside her door? This seemed like it could lead to trouble, which led him to conclude that he should just do what she said and get it over with.

He took the dollar, and ran out the front door. Terri's Deli was only a block away, he got stuff there for his mom all the time, so there'd be nothing unusual about him being in there, except perhaps the time of day.

As he ran, he thought about the woman, who he'd seen walk down the street many times, but always in a dress, always in make-up.

About two years ago, his mother had told him something strange about this woman: she'd said she was what was called a prostitute. When Timothy had asked what a prostitute was, his mother had told him:

"A prostitute is a woman who sells her body for money."

This had perplexed Timothy completely.

"How can she sell her body, doesn't she need it?"

Timothy couldn't remember if his mother had offered any further explanation on that particular day, but he was ten now. He more or less had the gist of what selling your body for money meant, even if he couldn't understand why anyone would want to do it.

"Hey Tim," said Lynn, sliding the quart of milk he'd plonked on the counter toward the register.

"Hey Lynn," Timothy said, hoping Lynn didn't notice it was 8:05.

It seemed to take her longer to punch the numbers into the cash register than it took for him to run all the way here. She started popping open a paper bag for the milk, but Timothy didn't wait, he just took the milk and paper and ran back as fast as he could, uneven sidewalk or not.

The woman at the end of the hall must've heard him running back in, she again opened the door a crack and was waiting for him. As she reached for the milk and paper, the door opened a bit more and Timothy caught a brief glimpse of the wall paper, which had some kind of fake velvet stripes. The woman tightened her dressing gown, which was likewise starting to fall open, then began closing the door.

"Your change," Timothy said.

"Keep it," she said, "you're a doll," then she closed the door all the way.

The milk had been 50 cents, the paper was a quarter. Since his allowance was a quarter, he'd basically just doubled his income this week. Not a windfall, exactly, but not bad.

He looked at the number six on the woman's door. On his way out, he checked the mailboxes again. The name on the mailbox with the number six was L. Collins.

So, the Prostitute's name was L. Collins.

Looking at the other seven mailboxes, each with its own strange surname, he wondered if any other kid on his block had ever made it this far into the Green Apartment Building to access this information.

He really needed to bolt to get to school, he was later than he'd ever been by this point, but he lingered at the mailboxes just a few seconds longer. It seemed, at this moment, like he was on the verge of understanding a mystery that none of the other kids had even thought to investigate.

Coming into George Washington Elementary School 15 minutes after the bell meant having to stop at the office first to get a late pass.

Damn, he was even later than the kid who came to school dirty and was the school's most notorious truant. This kid was *ahead* of Timothy at the front desk where Mrs. Hagen, the school secretary, had just forced him to call his mother from the office phone. You could hear the kid's mother screaming at him over the phone from ten feet away.

Timothy didn't want to have to call his mother on that phone, especially after the dirty kid was just holding it up to the side of his greasy head.

"Go straight to class," Mrs. Hagen said to the kid after his mother finished chewing him out.

When it was Timothy's turn to approach the front desk, Mrs. Hagen looked at him over her reading glasses.

"A little late today, Timothy."

"I was helping my mom with something," Timothy offered.

Not that he was convinced that this excuse would work, he nonetheless figured he could say this without completely lying. He did do a lot of work around the house in general, just not on this particular morning.

Strangely, the incredulous glare Mrs. Hagen had given the greasy headed boy moments before softened somewhat as she looked at Timothy.

While the specifics of Timothy's current home situation weren't entirely known, the basic story that Timothy's father had abandoned the family a year or two back had filtered its way to the office staff.

"Is everything okay at home, Timothy?"

"Yeah, fine, just . . . you know, helping out with stuff."

She nodded her head sympathetically, as if she understood.

Without so much as a finger wag, she reached for her pad, wrote out a late pass, and handed it to Timothy.

"Have a nice day, Timothy."

Timothy thanked her, feeling a little guilty for having sort of gotten one over on her but, considering how challenging things had become at home, he was ready to take whatever breaks the world was prepared to give him.

He might've felt additionally a little bad about having gotten better treatment than the dirty kid, but the dirty kid had actually been mean to him in the past, so he wasn't going to feel too bad about it.

As he walked along the highly polished floor toward his classroom, he noticed that the late pass felt kind of thicker than it should between his fingers. Looking more closely, he realized that there were, in fact, two late passes, the one Mrs. Hagen had filled out, and a blank one that had accidentally gotten stuck underneath.

The honest thing to do would be to hand them both over to Mrs. Brenner, his teacher, when he got to class, but this was just too much of a little trophy to pass up. Plus, it was a potentially valuable resource.

Carefully separating the two passes, he looked both ways in the hallway, took a book from his knapsack and pressed the blank one inside the front cover for safe keeping.

Today was show-n-tell. His friend Brandon was standing in front of the room when Timothy entered. Usually show-n-tell meant a model plane, a bug collection, or something to that effect. Today, Brandon was standing in front of the classroom holding a strange black tube.

Whatever it was that Brandon was holding, Mrs. Brenner was so enthralled with the presentation, she simply waved for Timothy to leave his pass on her desk and take his seat.

"Continue," Mrs. Brenner said to Brandon.

"So," Brandon said, "this drum is from an actual copy machine, manufactured by IPM, right here in Kingston."

IPM stood for International Photocopy Machines, but everybody just called it IPM.

"And what does the drum *do*, Brandon?" asked Mrs. Brenner.

"It's kind of hard to explain, but after the machine takes a picture of what you want to copy, these little bits of ink get stuck to the drum, then it rolls over a new piece of paper and that's how you get your copy."

"And how is this different from, say, the mimeograph machine here at school?"

"Well, I don't really know how a mimeograph machine works," Brandon said, "but you know how the copies you get at school come out all blue and smelly? These copies are, like, black and white, just like the original ones. And they don't smell so bad."

"Fascinating."

Come lunchtime, Brandon continued to hold court. Pulling the long cylinder from his knapsack, he held it aloft so all could behold. When another kid dared reach for it, he said:

"Don't touch it, only I can touch it," which made the black cylinder seem all the more to be filled with some kind of magic power.

Brandon was perceived as one of the cooler boys in a group of six or seven boys who regularly ate together in the cafeteria at lunchtime, Timothy among them. Of the lunch groupings of 4th grade boys, this was probably the coolest. It wasn't just Timothy's long hair that earned him a seat at the table, he'd simply had been eating with these same boys more or less since first grade.

"So, did your dad really take you into the manufacturing plant at IPM?" a kid named Drew asked.

"Yeah, you should've seen it," said Brandon, and he proceeded to describe the fantastic machines, conveyor belts, as well as the sterilized white uniforms and other wonders witnessed behind the scenes at the IPM plant.

Despite being at the cool guys' table, the table itself had a two-tiered hierarchy based on whether or not your dad worked at IPM. It wasn't just that dads at IPM tended to earn more money, which they did. And it wasn't just that the IPM families got to go to the IPM Rec Center, which was the cool place to be over the summer.

There was also something almost futuristic about the IPM plant itself, majestically spread out over hundreds of acres at the edge of town. And there was a certain civic pride about the plant producing a type of technology that the world was clamoring for, even though most people in Kingston in 1976 did not yet have access to a photocopier themselves.

Timothy's dad had worked in a department store uptown, so even before his dad split, Timothy was on the wrong side of the IPM hierarchy. Brandon's tales of IPM glory seemed to reveal there was even a hierarchy within the hierarchy.

"I got to wear a hard hat and a name badge," Brandon continued, the other IPM kids listening intently, wishing their dads could somehow get them behind the scenes to see how these copy machines of the future were being manufactured.

For a brief moment, Timothy considered muscling into this exclusive backstage conversation, inserting something like:

"Well, this morning, I got to see inside an actual prostitute's living room."

There was no doubt in his mind that this juicy little tidbit would generate immediate interest. But, on second thought, this was probably the type of disclosure that could easily lead to trouble, particularly if word got back to people's parents.

Seemed like the better plan, long-term, was to keep quiet about this.

Like so many other things Timothy was learning to keep quiet about.

CHAPTER 3

For most kids on Warren Street, the attraction to the Green Apartment Building had less to do with the building and more to do with the field behind it.

Five times the size of a single backyard, the field was completely unmonitored. Whoever owned the building didn't live there, and whoever lived there didn't care, so an after-school pick-up game with zero adult supervision could be counted on.

Being spring it was usually baseball, played with a yellow whiffle ball bat and a pink Spalding, which was softer than a hardball so you didn't need a glove but it could still really fly.

Timothy arrived at the same time as Christy Vanderbeck, who lived in the house with the floral milk canister on the porch.

"We got Timothy!" Carl called, preemptively so as not to be stuck with the seven-year-old girl, but also because he and Timothy were friends. They usually played on the same team along with Mark Williams, a fairly well-coordinated third grader.

Carl, who was sometimes called Crazy Carl, was in 4th grade like Timothy, but was taller because he'd stayed back once. Or twice, no one was quite sure, maybe not even Carl's parents.

"Okay, we'll take Christy," Robbie the other team captain said, "but we go first."

Terms agreed upon, the game got off to a surprise start when Christy Vanderbeck defied expectations and made it onto first. The top of the first inning was short-lived however. Will from Washington Avenue struck out, then Robbie popped one up which Mark caught then tagged Christy waffling between bases.

The bottom of the inning looked promising. Timothy easily made it to first, then held at second when Mark did the same. You couldn't actually stand *on* second, because it was a lopsided chunk of cinderblock permanently embedded in the field (neighborhood legend was that a dog was buried underneath, but no one had ever dug down to confirm.)

Crazy Carl could generally be counted on to bring runners home, but this came at a price, and today Carl had that certain look in his eye which helped reinforce his nickname.

"Don't do it, Carl!" Mark pleaded from first, even though they were on the same team.

Will and Christy moved back, even Robbie moved back from the approximate location of the pitcher's mound.

There's the pitch. Crazy Carl connects. And it's going, going . . .

Gone.

In this field, *gone* literally meant *gone.* The Green Apartment Building's back forty was an overgrown dumping ground, great for finding rusting car parts and the like, but near impossible to find a lost Spalding when you needed to.

"You had to do that," Mark said, while Carl ran the bases.

Both teams united in the search, six kids in weeds up to their waists. Will from Washington Avenue had kept his eye on the ball and had a vague idea of the vicinity, but it didn't help much.

Catching sight of something in the dirt below, Timothy stooped to part the brambly thistle. It wasn't the Spalding. It looked like a weird hammer at first, but rubbing off the caked-on mud with his fingers, Timothy couldn't believe his luck.

It was a meat cleaver.

The edge was dull and chipped and looked like a tetanus shot waiting to happen. This was Timothy's best find ever.

"You gonna keep that?" Mark asked, eyeing the prize in Timothy's hands.

"Fuck yeah," Timothy said.

"Is that a blood stain on it?"

A real blood stain would definitely be a bonus.

"Yeah," Timothy said, "or brain juice or something."

You couldn't tell the rust from the dirt, much less blood from cranial fluid, but it was obvious that some homicidal maniac had concealed the cleaver in the tall grass after a killing spree. Even if a run-of-the-mill butcher had flung it into the field for some unknown reason in a moment of hysteria, the history of the cleaver had to be grisly.

The only thing Timothy had to figure was how to keep possession of the cleaver and play ball at the same time. This proved not to be an issue as the other kids started giving up the search and heading home, including Robbie, who took his yellow plastic bat with him.

This left Timothy, Mark, and Crazy Carl hanging out with no game to play, but not ready to jump ship. They headed down the embankment to Tannery Brook, the neighborhood stream which flowed alongside the field, separating the Green Apartment Building's property from the rest of the yards on the block.

Chucking rocks into the brook was a reliable diversion when there was nothing else to do and, after Carl and Mark finished examining Timothy's meat cleaver, this is more-or-less what they did.

"Eww, what's that?" Carl said.

A blob of green foam was seen floating its way down the brook. You'd sometimes find an old beer can or something bobbing along, but a foamy blob was something new.

The boys commenced pelting the blob until it dissipated along with the mystery of whatever had caused it. The throwing of rocks slowed to a lazier pace once again.

When Timothy noticed someone walking up the sidewalk toward the Green Apartment Building he looked to see if it was the prostitute, but it was someone else who lived in the building, a guy with blonde feathered hair.

Timothy had seen this guy plenty of times before. He had kind of a well-groomed appearance, which seemed a little out-of-place in the otherwise dodgy apartment building.

"That guy's a queer," Carl said.

"How do you know?" Mark asked.

"My dad says so," Carl said, "he says that guy's a queer."

If Crazy Carl had called the guy anything else, a dick or a fuck face, Timothy wouldn't have given it a second thought. But it was that word, *queer*, and the hateful way Carl spat it out. It sent nervous adrenaline coursing through Timothy's spinal column, made his forehead start to sweat.

From a distance of fifty feet or so, the guy with the feathered hair looked over when he saw the three boys staring at him. Maybe he even smiled.

"Fucking queer," Mark said, not loud enough for the guy to hear at this distance.

Timothy waited maybe a beat too long, then added:

"Yeah."

He felt like if he didn't agree on some level, he'd be lumped in with this guy they were calling a queer. But he still couldn't bring himself to use that particular word, or even any other curse words at the moment, which was unusual since deploying a few choice curse words usually brought him so much pleasure.

The guy disappeared into the Green Apartment Building.

Carl and Mark went back to throwing stones into the brook.

"Well, I guess I gotta go home," Timothy said, picking his meat cleaver up off the ground.

"Okay, see'ya," the other boys said.

Timothy didn't really feel like going home just yet. But for the moment, he didn't much feel like hanging out here either.

Timothy's mom and Cathryn were inside cooking dinner so did not notice Timothy burying the meat cleaver beneath the forsythia in the backyard.

When Timothy went inside, he washed up and set the table as usual. Timothy's mom insisted on eating at the dining room table every night. That's how you kept a family together, she said.

Timothy's mom sat at the head of the table, where his dad used to sit. Cathryn sat at the opposite head of the table, where Timothy's mom used to sit.

This left Timothy on the side, same as always. Sometimes he felt like a spectator at a tennis match, watching the adult conversation being lobbed back and forth.

Tonight, Timothy's mom was quiet at first, distant.

"Is it Greg again?" Cathryn asked her, already frustrated by whatever was not being mentioned.

Timothy's mom waved her hand slightly, not wanting to talk about it. She took up the big slotted spoon and served the meat and noodles.

Meat and noodles was something you could count on at least once a week. It was cheap, easy to make, and there was always enough for a growing boy to have second helpings.

"I can go in there and talk to him," Cathryn said.

Timothy's mom kind of laughed slightly at the suggestion and waved her hand again.

"Five more months," she said.

This wasn't the first time this subject had come up and been quickly dropped at the dinner table.

Timothy's mom worked as a secretary for a law firm uptown. From what Timothy could piece together, there seemed to be an ongoing situation with this Greg guy, one of the lawyers at the firm.

Timothy had met Greg once before. He was actually super friendly to Timothy. Evidently, he was a little too super friendly with Timothy's mom, and this was the issue.

His mom was currently doing a night course at SUNY a couple of nights a week. In five months, she'd get her paralegal certificate, find a new firm to work for, and start bringing home more money. That was the plan, anyway.

Meanwhile, though his mom went to great lengths not to

mention it directly, Timothy knew they had barely enough money coming in. His mom would be keeping her current job.

"So," his mom said to Timothy, changing the topic, "anything interesting happen today?"

Timothy figured neither the morning errand for the prostitute nor finding the rusty meat cleaver would go over well at the dinner table.

"Not really," he said.

"Nothing? Not even anything at school?"

"Well, we got to pick out what report we're doing for the Bicentennial project," he offered.

The country was turning 200 in three months, and everyone was going batty about it.

"Yes? And what did you decide on?"

"Well, I wanted to do something about the Burning of Kingston," he said.

Most Kingstonians knew the basic story, that the British had burned the town down during the Revolution. The subject was of particular interest to Timothy, since it was their neighborhood that had been torched.

"That seems like a good idea," his mom said, "you know a bit about that already."

"Yeah, that's what I thought," Timothy said, "but Mrs. Brenner won't let me do it."

"No?"

"She said I need to do something of national importance."

It seemed absolutely ridiculous to Timothy that here they were, living in a town that was actually affected by the Revolution, but Mrs. Brenner wasn't even teaching about it because it wasn't in their state-sanctioned social studies textbook.

"Well, she probably just wants you to challenge yourself and research something you don't already know about," his mom said. "So what did you choose?"

"The Boston Tea Party," Timothy said, with slight resignation.

"Could be interesting," Cathryn said, trying to add a hopeful note to the conversation.

"I guess so," Timothy said. "Maybe I'll dress up like an Indian."

"There you go," his mom said. Then she turned to Cathryn. "How about you, anything interesting happen at work today?"

"Not unless you find a clearance sale on rock salt interesting," she replied.

Cathryn worked part-time as a cashier in a hardware store in the shopping plaza. Both she and Timothy's mom viewed the job as inane, but harmless and necessary, seeing as every extra penny was necessary to keep the household afloat without a male breadwinner.

Most nights Timothy would be content to make his single conversational offering at the dinner table. But tonight they were only halfway through the meal and had seemingly run out of things to talk about, so he piped up again.

"Brandon Phillips brought a toner drum for show-n-tell today."

"What's a toner drum?" Cathryn asked.

He proceeded to describe, to the best of his recollection, cylinders and toner and how a photocopier worked.

"We have one of those at the office," Timothy's mom said. "I've always wondered how it worked."

The table got quiet again. Having already ruled out other of the day's events as inappropriate for the dinner table, Timothy tucked into his meat and noodles.

He'd contributed two somewhat interesting topics on a night

when both his mom and Cathryn had come up with nothing. He'd take this as a win in the adult conversation department and leave it at that.

Thank God there was no Group tonight so they could all just relax in their own living room.

Mom, Cathryn, and Oscar took up most of the pink sofa, so Timothy propped himself up on a pillow on the floor. The pillow still smelled of Patchouli from the night before, but he didn't feel like going upstairs to get his beanbag chair.

Timothy flipped through the TV Guide, but it was Wednesday night, so it was a foregone conclusion they'd be watching The Bionic Woman.

"I like her hair," Cathryn said during the opening sequence.

Jaime Sommers, the Bionic Woman, had hair that was straight on top but somehow cascaded into perfect waves as it broke around her shoulders.

Timothy supposed he liked the Bionic Man better, but he still kinda liked the Bionic Woman because she was, you know, bionic.

"A woman needs to have bionic legs to run faster than a man," Timothy's mom observed.

Timothy thought on this a moment.

"Technically, Steve Austin could probably still run faster than her, if he could run faster than her before they both got bionic legs."

His mom shrugged, not eager to argue the point.

One thing they all agreed on was that both shows would be way more interesting if you could actually see Steve or Jaime outrunning a car instead of running in slow motion, as if slo-mo somehow conveyed superhuman speed, which was patently ridiculous when you thought about it.

Anyway, like 50 million other families across America, conversation died down shortly after the opening credits, eyes fixed on the unfolding drama, despite the outmoded picture quality of the last black-and-white TV set on Warren Street.

There was a promise in the air to replace the old black-and-white with a new color one, once Timothy's mom became a paralegal.

CHAPTER 4

Next morning it was pouring, buckets of rain.

Timothy's mom was getting dressed for work, running late herself.

"I can drive you," Cathryn said.

"Nah, that's okay."

"Really, it's no prob—"

Timothy was already out the door, cramming a Carnation Instant Breakfast Bar into his face. He'd rather swim to school than have Cathryn drive him in the Calico Chrysler.

He pulled his windbreaker up over his head, exposing his midsection to the pouring rain, but keeping his long hair from getting totally drenched. A block later, a passing car pulled over and honked. He paid no attention at first to whoever was waving at him, then an electric window rolled down.

"Timothy Miller! Get in, we'll give you a ride!"

It was Brandon's mother calling to him from a late-model station wagon, the kind with the fake wooden panelling running along the sides. Brandon was in the back seat.

Timothy fell onto the leather seat next to Brandon.

"Hey," Brandon said.

"Hey," Timothy echoed.

"You look like a wet dog."

Timothy laughed, he supposed he did.

"How come your mom isn't driving you to school, Timothy?" Brandon's mom asked from the front seat.

"She has to go to work," Timothy said.

He pulled at his jacket where he could feel the wet shirt underneath starting to cling to his stomach.

"So, how come you still live in this neighborhood?" Brandon asked him.

"Brandon, be polite," his mom said. She had a contemporary hairstyle with a little flip to it, sort of like the Bionic Woman.

Timothy shrugged. It had not escaped his attention that most of the kids whose dads worked at IPM lived up in Hilltop Meadows, a rolling suburban enclave at the edge of town.

Timothy's neighborhood, while not the worst in town or anything, was nonetheless perceived as beneath consideration, compared to the winding roads and placid cul-de-sacs of split-level ranches where Brandon's family lived.

"This is a lovely neighborhood, Timothy," Brandon's mom reassured him, catching his eye in the rearview mirror. "Brandon's father and I have many happy memories of when we lived here before Brandon was born."

"Then why did you move?" Brandon asked her.

His mom shot Brandon a glance and left the question unanswered.

"We sort of like it," Timothy said, as if remaining in this neighborhood was a conscious choice made by the whole family.

What else was he supposed to say?

Every once in a while, Timothy wondered what his life would be like if they lived in Hilltop Meadows and had money.

But considering his current family situation, maybe it wouldn't make much difference.

It was still raining midday, so they kept them inside for recess after lunch.

By the afternoon, the rain had cleared. Timothy figured there'd be other kids who wanted to blow off steam, but the field behind the Green Apartment Building was muddy, and there was no one else there.

Plan B. He ducked back home to retrieve the single cigarette from his cigar box and swiped the matches from above the stove without Cathryn seeing him.

Back by the Green Apartment Building, the brook was running high because of the rain. Timothy walked along as far as he could before the squishy banks turned to complete muck. There was a single rock on which he'd sat on numerous occasions when he just needed to be by himself and think about stuff. Today, he was on a mission.

He pulled the cigarette from his shirt pocket.

He had practiced holding it like the picture in the Lucky Strike ad. You had to make a sort of backwards peace sign, hold it sideways to your face, a confident gaze looking off in the distance.

But how exactly to light it when you needed both hands to strike the match?

He'd seen enough people do this. With the cigarette clenched more between his teeth than lips, he managed to strike the kitchen match against the box, but when he held it to the cigarette nothing was happening.

Figuring he probably had to breathe in to jumpstart the procedure, he inhaled with the full might of his lungs.

The explosion of coughing caught him so off guard that he almost forgot about the cigarette, but somehow he managed to grab hold of it. It burned slowly as Timothy continued coughing his lungs out.

By the time he caught his breath, the ashen butt of the cigarette was over a half inch long. Looking at the cigarette, he tapped it awkwardly to make the ashes fall off. He wasn't about to give up now.

Taking the smallest of puffs, Timothy drew on the cigarette just enough to make the tip glow slightly brighter. The incoming smoke punched his young lungs and made him start coughing again, but this time the cough was much easier to bring under his control.

Continuing slowly, Timothy managed to take four or five additional puffs, coughing less each time, until the cigarette was down to the filter, which he tossed into the brook. He watched it drift away, like Paddle-to-the-Sea, the film about a carved wooden boat that Mrs. Brenner had shown them once at school.

Standing up from the rock, Timothy wasn't expecting to be as light-headed as he was. He had to sit back down quickly before he fell over.

By and by, letting his lungs rejuvenate and pump fresh oxygen through his body, Timothy got his sea legs and was able to stand up and start walking back along the brook.

He started coughing again and continued along with his eyes half-closed for a stretch. He was startled when he opened his eyes fully and came across someone crouched alongside the brook who he hadn't noticed.

It was the blonde guy from the Green Apartment Building, the one Carl and Mark had said . . . what they'd said about him.

"Are you okay?" the guy asked Timothy, seemingly out of genuine concern.

"Yeah," Timothy croaked, his vocal cords scratchy from the abuse he'd just inflicted upon them. "It's just allergies."

"Oh, okay," the guy said, keeping his eye on Timothy an extra second just to be sure, then turning his attention to what he was holding in his hands.

He seemed to have some kind of scientific-looking beaker, he was taking a sample from the brook and holding it up to the light for inspection.

"What are you doing?" Timothy asked him, actually curious. He had never seen anyone do anything to the brook other than throw rocks into it, or dam it occasionally to cause a flood, just for fun.

"I'm testing for toxins," the guy said.

"What are toxins?"

"Have you seen that green foam floating in the brook lately?"

"Yeah, I saw some green foam just yesterday!"

"Yeah, well, unfortunately I've seen it too. The foam itself is probably phosphorus, but there might be benzene and a few other toxic chemicals in the water too."

"Is that bad?"

"It's not good."

Timothy found all this fascinating. Whatever his conception of the residents of the Green Apartment Building, he certainly wasn't expecting any of them to be scientists.

"So, what are you going to do with these tests?"

The blonde guy looked at Timothy as if he was sizing him up as a security threat.

"Can you keep a secret?"

"Yeah . . ."

"If this is what I think it is, I'm about to send it to the D.E.C."

"The what?"

"The Department of Environmental Conservation. They need to know about this."

The guy put a cap on the first bottle, filled up a second, then put a cap on that one too.

"You're gonna send these bottles to the D.E.C.?"

"No, I'll run the tests myself, then I'll send them the results . . . tell you what, you get your mom's permission, I can show you how to run a water test sometime."

Timothy didn't know if the guy actually knew his mom, or if he was just making a general assumption, either way, he was feeling particularly grown-up, having just smoked his first cigarette, and bristled at the suggestion that he somehow lacked independence.

"I don't have to ask my mom's permission," he said, "I can do what I want."

The blonde guy figured Timothy was probably fibbing, but he also thought he recognized him as the boy who lived with the two women down the street, so maybe the kid's mother really was more progressive than most.

"Okay then, you can come in now and take a look, if you like."

If you'd asked Timothy just days ago if he'd even follow a virtual stranger into the Green Apartment Building, particularly this guy, he'd have said *No Way*. But seeing as he'd been inside the building just yesterday talking with an actual prostitute, it didn't seem quite as risky as it would have. This guy was actually a little less scary than the prostitute.

"My name's Ken," the guy said.

"Okay," Timothy said, accepting this new information without offering his own name in response.

Together, the two of them walked from the brook up the slight embankment, then along the sidewalk to the front door of the Green Apartment Building. Timothy looked both ways to make sure no one was watching.

"It's okay, come on," Ken said, opening the door.

As with the day before, Timothy walked through cautiously, making sure it didn't slam shut again behind him. He paused instinctively in the dingy hallway. The musty smell reminded him that this was an alien landscape.

"Which apartment is yours?"

"That one right there, number five."

If it were upstairs, Timothy might've had second thoughts, but it was right next door to the prostitute's apartment where he'd already stood.

Still, he hesitated when he again recalled what Carl and Mark had said about this guy. Yeah, he seemed friendly, but Timothy also knew that there was such a thing as *too friendly*. What if this guy really was . . . queer? What could happen?

Ken unlocked his apartment and looked back at Timothy still standing there in the hallway.

"I have a meat cleaver," Timothy suddenly blurted out, in all seriousness.

Ken looked surprised at first, then started laughing politely at the ridiculousness of this statement.

"You do, huh?"

"Yeah."

"Well then," Ken said, "I'd better leave this door open . . . for my own protection."

With that, Ken disappeared into his apartment and left it for Timothy to enter on his own will, when or if he felt safe to do so.

After thinking on it further for the better part of a minute, Timothy entered the apartment, leaving the door open as Ken had suggested.

Timothy was surprised at what he found inside. Unlike the dirty floors and walls of the hallway, or the tawdry appearance of the prostitute's living room, what little he had glimpsed of it, Ken's apartment was remarkably light and clean.

The wooden floors were waxed and shiny. The walls freshly painted white. There was framed artwork on the wall, stuff that looked like it could be in a museum or something.

On a formica counter in the kitchen was the testing kit Ken had mentioned. All manner of different beakers, tubes, litmus strips.

But what really caught Timothy's attention was the cork board on the wall, on which was pinned an elaborate collection of diagrams, maps, and snapshots. It looked like a Joe Pro crime investigation right out of a TV movie.

"Are you a private eye?" Timothy asked, looking at the collection of materials in amazement.

"No," Ken laughed, "I'm a chemist . . . well, a chemistry student, anyway. I'm working on my degree at SUNY New Paltz."

That was the same college where his mom was studying to be a paralegal. Maybe they knew each other from there?

"This was all just supposed to be part of my thesis but . . ." he waved his hand over all the charts and diagrams, "it started turning into something else . . ."

Timothy continued to look at Ken's work. The maps were perhaps the most interesting of all, giving him a whole new perspective on his town.

It had never occurred to him how many places the brook flowed before its humble appearance as a place to chuck rocks as it trickled through his neighborhood. Reaching up with his pointer finger, he traced the route of the brook several neighborhoods up to a circled area, on which was written in pencil: *IPM?* with a question mark.

"Isn't this the old quarry?" Timothy asked.

"That's right."

"So how come you wrote IPM on it?"

"I think they might have bought it."

It was a lot of new information all at once, but Timothy was putting it together.

"And you think this green foam might . . . have something to do with IPM?"

Ken hesitated. The kid's questioning seemed innocent enough, but it was probably best to be more judicious with this information. Who knew who the kid could start talking to?

"Well, I'm just putting this all together myself . . . like I said, I really need to run these tests, send it in to the D.E.C. and all that . . . there's probably a simple explanation," he said in a reassuring tone so the kid wouldn't get all freaked out about this.

Timothy looked at the clock on Ken's stove, it said 4:45.

"Well, I gotta go," he said.

"It was nice to meet you . . . do you have a name?"

Timothy hadn't given his name before, but now that he'd been inside this guy's apartment and nothing terrible had happened, it didn't seem as risky.

"Timothy."

"Nice to meet you Timothy."

As Ken walked Timothy back into the dirty hallway, yelling could be heard coming from behind the door of number six, the prostitute's apartment.

It was a male voice, an angry voice. Timothy imagined it was the man who he'd sometimes seen walking up the street with the prostitute. The man was always quiet as they walked along, but if that was him, he sure had a loud, angry voice when he used it.

The angry voice reminded Timothy of something. Something troubling. He tried to remember what it was, but he couldn't put his finger on it.

As Ken looked at the door to number six, his face changed from a smile to one of concern. He shook his head, like he'd heard this yelling before but didn't know what to do about it.

"Well, see'ya," Timothy said.

"See'ya," Ken said, mimicking Timothy, smiling again.

As Timothy ran down the street, there were more things spinning around in his head than he could keep track of. Prostitutes, queers, maps, toxins, IPM—how were you supposed to process all these things at once?

The yelling behind the door of apartment six still rang in his ears, but so did various kind and patient things Ken had said.

He was about to run up his front steps when a voice came thundering from across the street.

"Timothy!"

It was Mr. O'Connor. Being a long-distance trucker, Mr. O'Connor was gone half the time, but when he was home, he had an outsized presence on the street. Even his mom and Cathryn agreed that it was good to have a man like Mr. O'Connor on the street, looking out for everyone.

Timothy ran straight over to see what Mr. O'Connor wanted. He was usually really easy going with Timothy, but now he was dead serious.

"What were you just doing in that apartment building?" he said.

"I was just . . . looking. I got curious."

"You got no business going in there. I catch you going in there again I will have words with your mother, you understand me?"

"Yes, sir."

And with that, the spinning thoughts in Timothy's head suddenly ground to a halt. The mysterious portal that was the Green Apartment Building seemed to slam shut before it could open any further.

CHAPTER 5

The school library was, in practice, an unofficial opportunity to fool around and waste time. Mrs. Brenner brought the class there once a week. Mrs. Stein, the librarian, would read a story aloud for the first ten minutes, then students were each free to find a library book, which they would pretend to read while making fart noises and whispering to friends.

This week, the entire library session was devoted to research for the Bicentennial project. To be sure, there would still be a lot of muted clowning around, but since the prize for best report was a gift certificate to Friendly's, there was incentive to do at least a little bit of work.

Elbowing his way into the gridlocked American History section, Timothy ducked under lunch mate Drew's armpit to scan spines with his finger.

"Boston Tea Party: The Protest That Became a Nation" was the newest book about Timothy's sort-of chosen subject. It had the most pictures, so he grabbed it along with two others for good measure. He headed to the check-out desk with time to spare.

"Mrs. Stein," he asked the librarian, "where would I find a book about . . . camping stuff?"

"Are you going camping?" she asked.

"Maybe?"

"Wonderful," she said.

Mrs. Stein was always thrilled whenever a student wanted to use the library for what it was intended.

"Let's go to the card catalog."

Ach, the card catalog. He was hoping she was just going to show him where to find it. The card catalog was an indecipherable, hulking mass with impossibly long drawers, each chockablock with a confusing series of index cards. Authors, titles, subjects, all mixed together.

Timothy pulled the drawer marked C, hoping it wouldn't detach from the cabinet and crush his foot. Flipping back and forth between cards, he wasn't seeing anything for Camping. Mrs. Stein, seeing that Timothy was trying in earnest, took a quick look herself. She couldn't find anything either.

"So, Timothy, can you think of another way to categorize what it is you're looking for?"

It had already taken a bit of creativity to come up with camping, if he switched to something like butchering now, she'd know something was up.

"Uh . . ."

"How about something to do with the outdoors?" she suggested.

"That sounds good," he quickly agreed.

Mrs. Stein pushed the C drawer back in and tried looking in the O.

"Hmmm, yes, here we go, Outdoor Life, 796.5."

She handed Timothy a scrap of paper and a little pencil, like the ones you got when you played miniature golf. Timothy copied down the numbers 796.5.

"Do you need help looking in the stacks?" she offered.

"Thanks Mrs. Stein, I think I can take it from here," he said, ready to break from the lesson in library competence.

The school library only had five or six stacks, The 700s were free and clear because everyone else was still competing for the 900s. There were three or four wilderness books, maybe one of them would have what he was looking for. Amazingly, the Real Men's Guidebook didn't have anything about sharpening a dull meat cleaver.

The first book had no pictures and the print was very small. Like a lot of the books on these shelves, it had been sitting here since the 1950s, when a fair percentage of upper elementary school students could still read at an adult level. But this was the 1970s.

The next book had also probably been here since the 50s, but it had detailed diagrams of everything . . . including how to sharpen a hand axe. Score!

When Timothy checked the book out, Mrs. Stein beamed proudly as she stamped the due date on the inside front cover. The power of reading was alive and well. She pictured Timothy transported by his newfound knowledge, engaging in a wide variety of wholesome outdoor activities.

"Timothy, what's that scraping noise?"

"I'll be up in a minute," Timothy called from the basement.

He figured he had maybe two more minutes before his mom would stop cooking and come downstairs to see what he was doing. He went back at it with both hands, attempting to sharpen the meat cleaver with an ancient, drop-forged file rustier than the cleaver itself.

To hold it somewhat steady, he had c-clamped the cleaver to a broom handle, the other end of which was wedged inside their top-loader washing machine, onto whose lid he'd piled an overturned chair and half a bag of cement mix to weigh it down.

He paused to cautiously run his finger along the edge of the blade. Not razor sharp, but good enough for now.

Loosening the c-clamp, Timothy took careful aim at the hand-drawn target taped to the face of the Bozo punching bag. Hurling the cleaver halfway across the basement, Timothy missed the clown's face entirely, but the cleaver stuck into a wooden support column with a satisfying thud.

Timothy had to give the cleaver a good tug to get it loose. It may have failed initially to strike dead the intended target, but it was ready for a semi-public demonstration.

The next afternoon behind the Green Apartment Building, whiffle ball was put on hold, the kids all gathering around a medium-sized maple, which seemed a good enough target. All eyes were on Timothy, and the meat cleaver, as he hurled it at the tree.

His first shot tumbled through the air and missed entirely. So did his second.

"Use two hands," Crazy Carl suggested, making a two-handed chopping motion above his own head.

Taking his suggestion, Timothy did manage to hit the tree, twice, but it bounced off both times and fell to the ground without penetrating.

"It worked better in the basement," Timothy said.

He handed it off to Carl, who was waiting eagerly. Carl's aim was slightly more consistent, but he likewise failed to get the tumbling knife to stick.

When it was Mark's turn, despite having made expert recommendations to both Carl and Timothy on *follow through*, he also found it harder to accomplish than imagined.

Amid his friends' hatchet throwing attempts, Timothy's gaze shifted to the Green Apartment Building. Did he just see a curtain move? Was that apartment five or six? Was the prostitute secretly watching them at this very moment? Was it that Ken guy?

Timothy couldn't help but wonder about the investigation that Ken was doing. It's not like he wanted the brook to be polluted, but the possibility for scandal was intriguing.

"This thing's no good," Mark said, dangling it by the handle limply while he handed it back to Timothy.

As the gathering broke for the day, Timothy unconsciously swung the cleaver sideways at a six-foot sapling. The tree cut cleanly in two, the severed top half falling with a crackling thud to the ground.

The thing was deadly after all. You just had to get close enough to your target.

Later that night, coming downstairs to set the table, he found his mom and Cathryn in the kitchen, huddled together, brows furrowed. They were staring at the local paper in disbelief, obviously reading something that concerned them.

"What is it?" Timothy asked.

Neither answered at first, still processing whatever it was they were reading.

"It's nothing," his mom said, after a moment.

Timothy leaned in to see what they were looking at.

"Tell me."

Realizing he would likely find out soon enough, his mom tried to translate the article into language that might somehow soft pedal the situation.

"There was a fight last night, a person was injured," his mom said.

"What kind of fight?"

Timothy took the newspaper into his hands. He would usually flip straight to the comics, but there was theoretically not much in the Daily *Freeman* beyond his reading level at this point.

Turned out his mom and Cathryn had been reading the column called Police Beat. The first listing described a break-in, the second a drunken driving incident. It was the third item that had apparently caught their attention.

> *ASSAULT CHARGE—Tuesday evening, responding to a disruption call at the Oriole Tavern, Kingston Police arrested Kingston resident Lucas "Luke" Grafton. Grafton, who remains in police custody, is being charged with assaulting Kenneth Wilson, also a Kingston resident. Wilson was treated by paramedics at the scene and brought to Kingston Hospital, where he is listed in stable condition . . .*

At first Timothy couldn't figure out why this particular story was so upsetting.

"Wait," he asked, "who is Kenneth Wilson?"

"He lives up the street."

"You mean . . . the blonde guy who lives in the Green Apartment Building?"

"That's him," his mother confirmed, "do you know him?"

"Not . . . really . . . I just . . ."

Cathryn walked out of the kitchen. The story had clearly unsettled her.

His mom remained with him as he finished reading the column, trying to make sense of it.

"What does 'provoked' mean?" he asked his mom.

"It means the other man is claiming that Ken, sort of started the fight."

Timothy couldn't believe this. This Ken guy seemed so soft spoken. How could he possibly have done something like this?

"Do *you* think he started the fight?"

"I . . . don't know, I wasn't there. I just think that . . . bad things happen sometimes. I wish they didn't, but . . ."

Cathryn was sitting on the couch, watching some random game show. She wasn't really even watching it, she was just staring at the TV, like she needed something to help her zone out, the more mindless the better.

"Why is Cathryn so upset?"

"Ken's a friend of hers."

"He is?"

"Well, a friend of a friend, but still . . ."

The sum total of concealed adult knowledge was growing by the minute. What else did his mom know that she wasn't telling him?

Absently, he went to set the table.

"It's okay," his mom said, "We can just eat in the living room tonight."

She put some meatloaf on a plate and delivered it to Cathryn, who held it on her lap while she stared at the stupid game show on the black-and-white TV. His mom sat down next to her and started giving her a little shoulder rub, but for the moment Cathryn could not be reached.

Timothy helped himself to some meatloaf, poured ketchup on it, came in and sat cross legged on the floor. He started to clear his plate as usual, but when he looked over, he saw that neither his mom nor Cathryn had touched theirs, and looked like they might not eat at all.

No dinnertime conversation tonight.

CHAPTER 6

The adults of Warren Street had no direct equivalent of the field behind the Green Apartment Building, but they did have their own means of impromptu socializing.

In the evenings after supper, if anyone were outside sitting on their front porch, this was a signal that anyone else on the street was free to stop by for a little chit-chat.

The kids would continue to play in the street while their parents either sat on their own porches, or walked a house or two away to see what was going on. In general, Timothy preferred to squeeze in a little extra playtime, but occasionally he found it interesting to listen in on adult conversation, which was mainly harmless neighborhood chatter.

On this night, Timothy's mom had wandered across the street to join Mrs. O'Connor as she lightly watered her crocuses with the garden hose.

"Weren't these all yellow last year?" Timothy's mom asked.

"You know, I'd almost forgotten I planted these purple bulbs last fall," Mrs. O'Connor said, "but here they are."

"I almost like them better than the yellow," his mom commented, nodding with approval. For a woman who had an almost radically feminist edge to her voice on Group nights, she could sound down-right provincial when she wanted to.

"I wasn't sure at first, but I think I do too," Mrs. O'Connor agreed.

Timothy had been listening to conversations like these since before he was in kindergarten. He never used to think much of them. But the messier their front porch became, the more he found these inane conversations almost reassuring. They seemed to denote a level of acceptance, or at least denial, of the changes within his household.

"Did you read the Police Beat last night?" his mom asked Mrs. O'Connor.

"What was last night?"

"Fight at the Oriole, someone got beaten up pretty badly."

"I saw that."

"That was Ken from up the street."

"Who?"

"Lives in the Green Apartment Building, blonde hair, drives the Volkswagen."

"That was *him*?" said Mrs. O'Connor. "I didn't know his name."

At this point, Mrs. Williams from next door wandered into the conversation. Mrs. O'Connor quickly brought her up to speed in the who/what/where of what they'd just been talking about.

"Really?" said Mrs. Williams, sort of looking over at Timothy's proximity, as if to question whether this was a conversation appropriate to have in his innocent presence. "Well . . . that's a shame."

"It is," Mrs. O'Connor agreed.

Timothy sensed there was something unspoken here, the other neighborhood mothers seeming to know that Ken existed, even if they hadn't known his name. Perhaps they had some ideas about his character, but were nonetheless startled by what had happened.

"Cathryn and I were thinking of maybe bringing some flowers over to the hospital," Timothy's mom said.

"Do you know him, Denise?"

Both Mrs. O'Connor and Mrs. Williams seemed a bit surprised by the suggestion.

"No, not really. It's just that he seems to live . . . alone," his mom said.

This was clearly a different story than what she'd told Timothy about Cathryn being a friend of his, or a friend of a friend, or whatever.

It was at moments like these, when Timothy observed his mom plainly telling the world something different than she'd say at home, that he seemed to have proof: it wasn't just his imagination, their home life really was different, abnormal even.

"That's very nice of you, but I don't know him," Mrs. O'Connor said, preemptively explaining why she would not be acting in kind.

"Neither do I," Mrs. Williams quickly echoed.

All three women continued to look down the street toward the Green Apartment Building, shaking their heads slowly in unison.

After an appropriate pause, Mrs. Williams said to Mrs. O'Connor:

"Ellen, I was just coming over to admire your purple crocuses."

"So was I," Timothy's mom chimed in, deftly realigning herself with the other mothers in the realm of acceptable conversation on Warren Street.

"I was just telling Denise that I'd almost forgotten I'd planted them," Mrs. O'Connor said, repeating herself, "but I think I might like them better than the yellow."

Both Timothy's mom and Mrs. Williams agreed.

★   ★   ★

The only other thing Timothy heard about a possible hospital visit was a snippet of conversation he caught while coming down the stairs the next day.

"Did you want to go with Sarah?" his mom was asking Cathryn.

"She already went."

"And?"

"No improvement."

A day or so after that, on his way home from school, Timothy rounded the corner to find several police cars out in front of the Green Apartment Building. Of course the neighborhood kids were crowding around, because what could possibly be more interesting than an actual police scene?

"What's going on?" Timothy asked.

"The guy who got his head kicked in the other night," Carl said. "He died."

"What?"

Despite Mr. O'Connor's warning, Timothy broke from the pack and ran straight inside. The other kids marveled, they never would've thought to do this.

In the hallway, a cop was questioning the prostitute, who was weeping in her doorway as she answered his questions.

The door to Ken's apartment was wide open, Timothy went right in. The floors were just as shiny, the walls just as white. The cleanliness of the apartment seemed incongruous to the situation, somehow Timothy was expecting a bloody mess, but there were no signs of violence to connect the place with what had happened at the Oriole Tavern.

Timothy made a bee line for the kitchen, where a gloved police officer was examining the testing kit, carefully placing the bottles and test tubes one at time into a cardboard evidence box before taking it away.

The notes on the cork board, on which Ken's meticulous investigation had been mapped out, had already been taken down as well.

"What are you doing in here? Get out," the cop said, then changed course, "Hey, wait a minute, you know who lived in this apartment?"

"I don't know anything . . ."

Timothy backed out of the kitchen before the cop could ask him any more questions. He ran out of the apartment and down the hallway. Back out on the street, the other kids were desperate for information.

"What'd you see? What'd you see?"

"Nothing, they're just putting stuff in boxes."

He brushed past them and ran down the street. The neighborhood mothers were congregating on the sidewalk at a respectful distance, looking up the street toward the Green Apartment Building, speculating among themselves.

His own mom was still at work, but Cathryn was standing with the others. Timothy looked up at her, trying to find the words.

"I know already," she said softly, "it's in the paper today."

Timothy ran inside his house. The newspaper was there on the table, folded open to the article, which seemed to be buried deeper in the local section than you would imagine, considering the magnitude of such a thing.

Timothy tried to slow down and understand the article, but it seemed to have more to do with legal stuff than anything else, how the charges against Luke Grafton might be changing because Kenneth Wilson had succumbed to his injuries.

None of it made any sense to Timothy, wrestling with conflicting emotions. He felt sad, shocked and afraid, yet also worried what people might think if he appeared connected to Ken Wilson, which made him feel guilty on top of everything else.

The next night, Group met again in their living room. This wasn't their usual night, it seemed to be some sort of emergency meeting.

Tempers were running high. His mom asked him to please stay in his room. With the hall light out, Timothy sat at the top of the stairs, listening in.

"Involuntary manslaughter is bullshit," one woman said.

There was general agreement.

"That's the way the law works, Carla," another woman tried to explain, it sounded like Sarah, who Timothy had taken the cigarette from.

"You think if this happened to a straight guy working at IPM it'd still be involuntary manslaughter? That fucking hillbilly would be looking at a murder charge."

Again, boisterous general agreement.

"Look, I don't like this any more than you do," Sarah said, "but to get a murder charge to stick, Shaughnessy would have to prove intent, which is not going to happen, so Man 1 is probably the most we can hope for. He still might get eight years."

"Eight years is nothing . . ."

The conversation continued in much the same manner, emotional responses bumping up against the improbability of achieving whatever vague kind of justice most of the women in the room seemed to be clambering for.

Timothy retreated to his room and shut the door.

As bad as it was that this Ken guy had been killed, it seemed like their level of frustration was connected to bigger issues that Timothy didn't quite understand.

Whatever it was, based on what he'd been hearing, it didn't seem like the problem was going to be solved downstairs in his living room on that evening.

Timothy's newfound interest in the local paper continued. It wasn't much harder to read than anything they threw at him in school, and you could gain instant access to almost anything adults seemed to know about. Like, who was going to run against President Ford, or how IPM was applying for a permit to expand its local facility.

The one story that seemed to disappear without a trace was what had happened to Ken from the Green Apartment Building. As far as that story was concerned, the town just seemed to put it out of its collective mind and get back to business as usual.

Even Group, when it met on its regular night at their house the following week, seemed to get back to some sort of normal. The incense, the long hugs, the meaningful sharing of female topics, these were all very much in evidence. But the heated debate about the Ken situation, that had blown over, like there was simply nothing more that could be done.

And honestly, Timothy himself had other things to concern himself with. Like how to create a secret compartment in an old encyclopedia using a box cutter and some glue, another project he had gleaned from the Real Men's Guidebook.

Then, one Sunday night, Timothy was sitting in the living room with his mom and Cathryn, watching Columbo, trying not to think about having to go to school the next day.

This week, Columbo was called upon to investigate a suspicious death at a meatpacking plant.

"There's something that bothers me . . ." Columbo said to the owner of the plant toward the end of the show. "Here's a man who'd worked in this plant for what, twelve years? How is it possible he didn't know something so basic like how to open the freezer door from the inside?"

The meatpacking plant owner had a ready explanation, of course, something about the onset of hypothermia having caused disorientation and how, while tragic, there were unfortunately many documented cases of this sort of thing.

Columbo appeared to accept the explanation at face value with his customary droopy-eyed grin.

"You might have a point there, Mr. McGee, maybe he *did* get get disoriented in that freezer," Columbo said. "But he wasn't disoriented two days before, when he mailed *this* to the LAPD."

The gotcha moment. Unclasping the manilla envelope he'd had concealed in his signature raincoat all along, Columbo revealed copies of the damning evidence uncovered by the dead worker of contamination at the meatpacking plant. His untimely demise in the meat locker was not accidental in the slightest. It was premeditated murder.

Sitting there on the floor in the living room, a bell went off in Timothy's head.

Was it possible?

He looked over at his mom and Cathryn who seemed oblivious to the connection. But then, they hadn't seen what Timothy had seen with his own eyes.

The green foam in the stream . . . the incriminating water tests . . . the investigation Ken had mapped out so clearly on his kitchen wall . . .

What if . . . someone at IPM knew that Ken was about to contact the D.E.C.? Could they possibly have hired a guy to do a hit job and make it look like a random bar fight?

And why had the police cleared away the evidence of Ken's investigation so quickly? Was it possible even *they* were even in on it?

It was pretty farfetched, he had to admit, maybe it didn't make complete sense.

But a life had been taken, someone he had just been talking to a few days before. And so far the official explanation was that sometimes these things just happen.

That made no sense whatsoever.

The next day after school, it was gray outside, not enough kids had shown up to play whiffle ball. Timothy, Carl, and Mark stood around waiting, staring up at the back of the Green Apartment Building, as if something else might happen.

Carl threw a rock at one of the trash barrels behind the building, it connected with a loud metallic clang.

"So, you really didn't see anything in there?" Carl asked.

Carl and Mark seemed to have a growing suspicion that Timothy was holding out on something.

"Like, you really didn't see the body?" Mark asked.

"Retard," Carl said to Mark, punching him in the arm, "the guy got creamed in a bar, why would they bring his body back to the apartment building?"

"I just made it as far as the hallway," Timothy said for the twelfth time, "then the cops made me come back out."

"So why'd you run in there?"

"I dunno, I just did."

Carl threw another rock, it missed the trash barrel but smacked into the side of the building. He shrugged his shoulders.

"My dad says that queer got what he deserved," Carl said.

"Don't say that," Timothy blurted out before he could think better of it.

"Don't say what?"

"That . . . word," Timothy said.

"Why," Carl said, "are you a queer too?"

Timothy just stared at Carl, so wanting to hit him in the head at that moment, but knowing that Carl was bigger and would for sure hit him back harder. Mark stood there looking from face to face, wondering what was about to happen.

"Just shut the fuck up," Timothy said, walking away from the two of them in frustration.

"Yeah? Make me," Carl said, but Timothy just kept walking, and Carl and Mark just kept standing there.

Timothy walked down the embankment to the brook. He stood there looking at the water until he began to get lost in its gurgling sound. He knew things about this brook and the life connected to it. As with previous springs, soon there would be tadpoles. Not long after that there'd be frogs.

A bit of green froth making its way along the course of the brook caught his attention. This time, he didn't pelt it with a rock.

If Ken were here, Timothy thought, he'd want to test that foam, use it for evidence.

Timothy crouched down and tried to reach for the foam as it floated past, but he couldn't quite grasp it.

Following the foam, Timothy looked for a forked stick to help grab it but couldn't find one. He could take off his sneakers, but from previous experience he knew the stream bed sometimes had bits of broken glass in it. Without further thought, he waded right into the water with his sneakers still on, reaching down and grabbing the green foam with both hands before it could get away from him.

He lifted the foam to his nose and sniffed at it. It smelled like chemicals.

The icy coldness of the springtime water began to penetrate his ankles. It was almost painful, but something about it woke him up, made him feel more alert, alive. With Carl and Mark still watching him from a distance like he was crazy, Timothy continued to stand there, listening to the water ripple around him.

The foam dripped through his fingers back down into the water. He didn't yet know how to test it himself, how it might be connected to IPM or with Ken's murder. But it was clear to him that this case wasn't closed.

Maybe his own life had become incomprehensible, a mystery that couldn't be solved, but this was tangible, something you could touch.

Somebody had to put these puzzle pieces together.

Somebody had to clean up this brook.

Somebody had to see that justice was served.

And that somebody was Timothy Miller.

PART TWO

★ ★ ★

CHAPTER 7

Converting your bedroom into a Crime Lab in 8 easy steps:

Step 1: Clear space on bulletin board by removing *Farrah* poster (temporarily).

Step 2: Draw map of Tannery Brook's route from memory, tack onto bulletin board, add blank postcards to be filled with new information as investigation proceeds.

Step 3: Commandeer family's Kodak Instamatic, including already-inserted film cartridge with 2 out of 12 shots remaining.

Step 4: Rinse shampoo from Prell bottle, return to stream to capture next available sample of green foam.

Step 5: Keep meat cleaver concealed in closet, but at-the-ready in case needed.

Step 6: Assemble toolkit of additional items, beginning with mom's old reading glasses in case disguise is necessary.

Step 7: Tally coins in Uncle Sam piggy bank. Total available funds: $11.35.

Step 8: Repurpose unused section of three-ring school binder for investigative note keeping. Label new section: *Project X.*

The cubed turkey in the hot lunch at school was suspiciously cat food like, but that would have to be another investigation.

Timothy popped open his half-pint milk carton, took a swig for courage, then launched his first line of inquiry.

"So, Brandon, can you tell us more about this tour your dad took you on at IPM?"

Brandon cocked his head and looked at Timothy sideways. His show-n-tell exhibition had been weeks ago, so this seemed a little out of left field. But he supposed, if prodded, he could continue to display his expertise.

"What do you want to know?"

"You know, like, what kinds of machines did you see?"

"What kinds of machines *didn't* I see . . . there was *everything.*"

Timothy dared to get his hopes up, this could be a watershed moment, right off the bat.

"Did you see the machine that made the toner cartridges?"

"Of course . . . I mean, I don't know which machine was which, there were so many, but I must've seen it."

"And what did it smell like in there, did it smell . . . chemically?"

"Why are you asking all these goofy questions?"

Timothy had a ready answer.

"My mom has an IPM copier at work," he said proudly, as if this sort of put him in the IPM club. "I'm trying to explain to her how it works."

Steven broke in at this point:

"My dad has an IPM copier right in our house, in his study."

"He does?" Brandon said. "What model?"

"The C-210," Steven said.

"That's so cool," Drew said, whose dad also worked at IPM, but it obviously never occurred to him that someone might actually be able to have a photocopier in their own home.

"That is cool," Timothy agreed, desperate not to let the conversation get away from him. "So," he redirected back to Brandon, "what did it smell like?"

"What did *what* smell like?"

"The factory at IPM."

Brandon and the other kids all looked at Timothy like he had two heads, but Brandon tossed off a quick answer anyway.

"I dunno, maybe it sorta smelled like when you get an X-ray at the doctor's office, something like that, I can't remember."

"So Steven," Drew said, "how many sheets can you load into a C-210?"

"You have to load it one sheet at a time," Steven answered, "but you can still make, like, four or five copies a minute if you keep loading it."

"Cool," Drew said.

By this point, Timothy was content to let the conversation wander off where it would. It bought him time to surreptitiously open his binder to the section marked *Project X.*

"Might smell like X-ray machines," he jotted down. "Compare chemical ingredients later."

★ ★ ★

When Timothy got home from school he pulled his banana saddle bicycle up and out of the basement and brushed the cobwebs off it. He hadn't ridden it yet this spring because the tires were flat and he didn't have a pump in the house.

The Gulf Station was just a few blocks away, it wasn't too hard to walk his bike over there. It was a full-service station, with a wire on the ground by the pumps that would *ding* when you drove over it with your car.

Sal, the attendant, would come out, pump the gas, check the oil if you wanted, all that.

Timothy always tried to jump on the wire, but he could never make it *ding*.

"You're about a thousand pounds too light," Sal said to him, coming out of the garage.

"Hey Sal."

"Hey Timothy."

Sal was one of those men in the neighborhood everyone would just call Sal instead of Mr. Whatever, even kids called him Sal.

"Sal, you don't have, like, a local map, do you?"

"I gotta stack of state highway maps on the counter, help yourself."

"Thanks!"

Timothy ducked in to grab one, then rolled his bike over to the AIR dispenser, which was mounted on the outside wall of the garage between two open car bays. Sal never minded if the neighborhood kids filled their tires, so long as he wasn't using it to service a customer at the moment.

Timothy liked the look of the AIR pump. It seemed to match

perfectly the curvy white tile of the garage itself. He couldn't have told you the lettering and chrome accents were Deco remnants of when the garage had been built. He just thought it looked cool, oil smudges at all.

There was a crank on the right side, he dialed it down to 25 just to be safe (he'd gone up to 40 once before and his 20 inch tire had exploded on the way home.)

A shiny new Corvette rolled in, the wire *dinged*. The driver looked familiar.

"How's it going, Sal?" he said as Sal approached.

"Hey there, Mr. Hathaway."

Timothy knew the name and made the connection. Mr. Hathaway, of *Hathaway, Hathaway & Myers,* was also known as Greg, the too-friendly lawyer at his mom's office. Timothy's tires were now full to capacity, but he pretended to keep filling them so he could listen in on the conversation.

"Guidry was looking good last night," Greg Hathaway said.

"On the mound, anyway," Sal said.

"Ah, you can't win 'em all," Greg Hathaway said.

At this point, a set of high heels were heard clicking up the sidewalk and the conversation froze. A woman in an attractively form-fitting red dress stopped at the newspaper box on the street in front of the garage.

Inserting two dimes into the slot, the woman bent over the box to retrieve a paper, giving the men ample opportunity to admire her assets from this particular angle.

Standing back up and catching them staring, she flashed the slightest of smiles before continuing on her way, perhaps because Greg Hathaway was driving a Corvette.

With the sound of her clicking heels fading into the distance, Greg Hathaway said, "Mercy . . ." as if he had been holding his breath.

"People will sometimes ask why I've kept this job so long," Sal said. "I always say, you can't fault the view."

"Brother, I might just try working here myself," Greg Hathaway said, and both he and Sal got a big laugh out of this, as this would obviously never happen in a million years.

Sal walked over to Timothy with his hand extended.

"I need the hose," he said.

"Oh, sorry," Timothy said, handing it to Sal, who cranked the PSI back up to automotive territory like he could do this in his sleep, then continued with his business.

Timothy put the little black plastic caps back on the valves of his inner tubes and pedaled off, keeping his eyes on Greg Hathaway's Corvette, hoping he hadn't been recognized.

The baseball cards in his spokes made a *clickety* sound that he only now realized might draw too much attention. When he stopped at the schoolyard on the next block, he removed the baseball cards, but decided to leave the vinyl streamers flowing out of his hand grips. He worked too hard to get them into the holes and, besides, they looked pretty cool.

Timothy unfolded the map he'd scored at the Gulf Station. Being a state highway map, it did not go into granular detail of local roads, but it seemed a valuable resource anyway. Timothy tried awkwardly to refold the map, somehow unable to make it conform to the creases that were already in it. He finally just folded it any way he could to get it into his knapsack. He didn't have all day to monkey around and still be home in time for supper.

Timothy was basically aware of the route the brook followed for a block or two prior to its appearance on Warren Street. From where it flowed before that, other than having seen it on the map in Ken's apartment, was a matter of conjecture.

The brook cut between yards and behind countless people's houses, there was no way he could follow it directly without trespassing all over the place. He would have to take it on faith that it wound its way from the old quarry like Ken's map said it did, and head straight there.

This is where things got tricky. The old quarry was off Route 32. He'd never ridden his bike on Route 32 before. There was no sidewalk, and half a mile out of town the speed limit jumped to 55. Today would be a first.

It turned out the shoulder was plenty wide enough, so long as you stayed far to the right. The cars started speeding up well before the city limits, but they gave him a wide berth, and riding was just as easy as anywhere else.

Then, shortly after the speed limit ticked up, a southbound Trailways Bus whizzed by so fast that the sideways gust of air blew Timothy and his banana saddle bike clean off the paved shoulder and into the litter-strewn grass.

Timothy brushed the burrs off his pants, more than a little psyched out. After letting himself catch his breath, he continued *walking* his bike along the highway, just in case another bus should pass as closely and knock him on his ass again.

He checked the Timex he'd gotten for Christmas. At this rate, he would definitely be late for supper with explaining to do. Wobbly at first, he got back in the saddle and kept going.

Soon enough he was pedaling normally again. By his estimation, with just a half-mile or so to go, if he could just maintain an achievable three miles per hour, he should still get there in less than 10 minutes.

Approaching the quarry from the north side, Timothy pushed his bike a few feet into the surrounding woods and locked it to a tree. He was pretty sure no one was going to steal it out here in the middle of nowhere, but if they did, it would be a long walk home.

He began his exploration by following the chainlink fence along the old quarry's northern periphery. It was an old rusty fence, but it was obviously being well maintained—any places that had been previously damaged or breached had been patched fairly recently with shiny new galvanized fencing.

It was still too early for poison ivy, but the underbrush was tangly, so Timothy had to tread slowly and carefully. Soon, the ground beneath his feet grew slightly mushy and here it was, the brook, right where he imagined it would be.

A rebar grate was cemented into the culvert that directed the brook under the fence. Sure enough, a big clump of ensnared green foam had accumulated just beyond the grate, trying to wriggle past.

There was no way for Timothy to crawl underneath, but that was okay for now. Timothy took the Kodak Instamatic from his knapsack. The film cartridge only had two shots left on it, so he had to get it right. It took him a moment to find the perfect angle, then he snapped the photograph. He could at least document the spot where the brook flowed indisputably from the quarry in general.

Working his way back to the front gate, he wasn't surprised to find it locked. Mounted on the gate was a big old metal sign reading "Colonial Bluestone," the company that owned a lot of these old quarries encircling the small city.

But in the middle of the bigger sign was pasted a metallic sticker, whose three-letter logo was even more recognizable around here than Colonial Bluestone.

"IPM"

"Ken was right," Timothy said aloud, like confirmation of this fact was too important to just keep it in his head.

He got his Instamatic back out, and took a well-framed photo of the sign.

This was a good start, but he was going to have to get beyond this gate somehow to figure out where the green foam was actually coming from.

He went back into the woods to retrieve his bicycle.

He checked his watch. 4:15. He should have plenty of time to get back into town and be home in time for dinner.

So long as he didn't get creamed by a Trailways Bus.

At the dinner table, Timothy raised his drinking glass. Holding it beneath the overhead light, he appeared to be examining it, seemingly oblivious to the *What's he doing now?* glances going back and forth between his mom and Cathryn.

"What are you looking at?" his mom finally asked him.

"I'm looking at the water."

"I can see that. What about the water?"

Timothy paused a second for effect.

"How do we know what's in it?"

"It's water. Water's in it."

"But, what's *in* the water? Where does it come from? What if there are, like . . . chemicals in it, or something?"

Theoretically, this could be an earnest question that might occur to an inquisitive ten year old mind. His mom tried to think of how best to explain it.

"You know that beautiful lake that we drive past on 212 on the way out to Grandma's?" she said. "That's the reservoir. That's where our water comes from."

"But what if people are dumping stuff in it?"

"Nobody is dumping anything in it, we all have to drink it. The City of Kingston has a very efficient filtration system, that's why we pay taxes."

Timothy continued to examine the water, as if considering his mom's point carefully.

"I still don't trust it," he said, "I think I should start drinking Coca Cola, like you guys."

Timothy pointed to the bubbly brown liquid in both their drinking glasses.

"Coca Cola's not good for a growing boy."

"It's better than drinking chemicals."

Timothy's mom looked to Cathryn, the raised eyebrow based on the assumption that this was yet another ploy so they would let him drink soda.

"We sell a home water testing kit at the hardware store," Cathryn offered, "I can bring one home."

The crease in Timothy's mom's brow softened immediately, gazing at Cathryn like *This is why I love you.* But this still sounded potentially expensive.

"What's a kit like that run?"

"I think maybe six dollars? With my discount it'd be less than five."

His mom looked to Timothy.

"If Cathryn brings home the testing kit, will you drink the water?"

Timothy nodded as he set down his glass.

"That would put my mind at ease tremendously."

The kit Cathryn brought home had enough for more than one test. Timothy figured he'd better at least use the first one to test their home drinking water. His mom and Cathryn would probably expect a report to justify their investment.

It was pretty simple. After letting the tap run for a minute, Timothy filled the plastic sample bottle, dipped the test strip, gave a light shake, then let it sit a few minutes.

Once the strip had a chance to fully absorb the water sample, its color changed from yellow to pale blue. Timothy compared the strip to the color chart which had been included in the kit.

It seemed that their drinking water contained sodium, calcium, iodine, and a variety of other trace minerals, all at acceptable levels. It was interesting to know, actually, and kind of reassuring.

"Excellent news, our water is perfectly safe," he announced at dinner, raising his glass, "Cheers!"

"Cheers!"

They all agreed the test had been a worthwhile endeavor. And Timothy had saved a five dollar investment, which would've depleted his available funds by almost half.

After dinner, he returned to the upstairs bathroom, this time with the Prell bottle containing the sample from the brook. The foaminess had died down by this point, leaving flat water with the slightest green tint.

Timothy repeated the steps he had followed earlier, the test strip, the light shake, the short waiting period.

This time the test strip turned brown.

When he consulted the poster, he was disappointed to discover that the chemicals contained in the sample were beyond the ability of this particular kit to determine. A more intensive, and likely more expensive, test was going to be necessary.

There was, however, a clearly printed message associated with brown test strip results:

"Do Not Drink This Water."

CHAPTER 8

The FotoMat in the Kingston Plaza had at various times been the source of much speculation among Timothy's friends. The person who worked in this tiny booth in the middle of the parking lot, how did they go to the bathroom? Was there a trap door leading to a secret toilet underneath? Or did they simply pee in a cup when no one was looking?

Timothy rolled up to the FotoMat drop-off window much like he was in a car, except he was on his banana saddle bicycle.

At first, he couldn't tell if the attendant was a girl or a boy. Looking more closely, Timothy could see she was a girl with a cute face, but kind of a boyish haircut.

She, in turn, looked at the little kid on the bicycle with the long hair, taking a moment to figure out that he was a boy. She continued to stare at him as if he were a mirage, until he held up the Instamatic film cartridge, at which point she realized he was an actual customer and slid open the window.

Timothy sat atop his bike and said nothing at first, so she broke the silence:

"So . . . did you want to develop that?"

"Uh, yes."

The attendant wore an official-looking blue and yellow smock top, which she'd personalized by adding a psychedelic smiley face pin. She reached out through the window and held out her hand, into which Timothy plopped the small plastic cartridge.

While she began to fill out the envelope, Timothy leaned right up to the window and tried to look inside, maybe he could spy the secret trapdoor to the subterranean bathroom.

Was this little boy trying to look at her legs? She wasn't quite sure. Most customers were confined to their cars so this usually wasn't an issue.

"You want one print of each?" she asked, trying to snap Timothy's attention back into the world of the transaction.

"Of each what?"

"Of each exposure. You can get just one print of each, or you can get two if you'd like to share them."

Two prints sounded pricey, plus Timothy wasn't planning on sharing these photos with anyone, at least not at this point.

"One, please," he said. "How much is this going to cost, anyway?"

"A roll of twelve would be $2.40, assuming they all come out."

$2.40 would be almost one fourth of his available funds.

"Actually, I only need two of them—can I just pay for two?"

Who was this kid?

"I can't say I've ever been asked that question before," she said, "but no, we can't go through the roll trying to figure out which ones you want."

"They're the last two, they shouldn't be so hard to find."

"It's kind of an all-or-nothing deal."

Well, it was worth a try anyway. He gave her his name and address and felt very adult about it.

"Here, hold onto this," she said, handing him the receipt. "You can pick them up in two days."

Timothy marveled at the receipt as he steered his bike one-handed from the FotoMat. It was just a tiny strip of paper, but somehow it was an important document. It offered proof from the outside world, in writing, that the investigation was real.

Back at the school library's card catalog, when D for Detective came up empty, Timothy tried M for Murder. He had to start somewhere.

The only thing that came close to what he was hoping for was a book about unsolved murders. Judging from the number of librarian's stamps competing for space on the inside cover, this book was way more popular than the one about camping.

Later, on a lovely afternoon without a cloud in the sky, Timothy lay on his bed, leafing through the morbid book, while the radio played an impossibly whiny pop song about some guy's dog getting lost at sea.

The pages in the unsolved murder book depicting the most gruesome crime scenes were particularly dogeared. There was even one in western Massachusetts involving a meat cleaver, which really wasn't so far from Kingston, when you thought about it.

"What are you reading?" Cathryn asked, peering into Timothy's room, surprised to find him there.

"Oh, nothing," Timothy said, stuffing it under his pillow.

"Why aren't you playing outside?"

"Eh, I don't feel like it."

"What do you mean you don't feel like it? It's a beautiful day."

She had a point. The murder book was creeping him out anyway, it made his hands feel bloody just holding it. Why wasn't he outside?

If he were honest with himself, the minor confrontation with Crazy Carl had psyched him out, just a little. He couldn't say for certain whether a fight was brewing, or if it was a onetime incident that was already forgotten, by Carl if not by him.

Detective work was way more interesting than whiffle ball, but he was running out of ideas for how to go about the investigation. Was he really going to let a single harsh exchange of words keep him inside?

The screen door slammed behind him as Timothy headed down the street toward the Green Apartment Building. Maybe jumping into a whiffle ball game wasn't such a bad idea.

When he reached the field, he found double the kids and a slightly different demographic than usual.

The junior high school boys had come around. These were boys who seemed to have graduated from playing in the field when they'd graduated from elementary, but they all still lived in the neighborhood and Timothy knew them by sight.

At least, he knew most of them. There was a new kid here today who didn't live on Warren Street. He stood out for two reasons, one because he was black and not too many black kids lived in this neighborhood, also because the other three junior high boys were all majorly vying for his attention, like they all really wanted to impress him.

"Man, I used to hit it over the fence every time," said one of the junior high schoolers.

"Yeah, that's 'cause the fence is like, forty feet from home plate," said another.

"It's more than that."

"Okay, fifty feet."

The black kid had an easy going style, he was taking it all in in a good natured way. Timothy was pretty sure he recognized him from the school playground from back when the kid had gone to G.W. Elementary, but of course he hadn't known him personally because he'd been one of the older kids.

"We call this the Green Apartment Building," one of the junior high school boys said. "It's got all these freaks living in it. There's the lady who rides the tricycle, there's a middle-aged hooker, there's Key Man . . ."

"Who's Key Man?" the black kid asked.

"He's a guy who carries lots of keys."

There was the general tendency in uptown Kingston to name the characters for their most obvious defining physical characteristic.

"That queer who got beat up, he lives there too," said Mike, another one of the junior high boys. "Well, used to live there."

"Really," the black kid said, scratching his chin and visually analyzing the Green Apartment Building afresh, like this detail of something he'd read about in the paper had actually caught his interest.

Crazy Carl broke from Mark and went over and whispered something into Mike's ear.

Mike was Carl's older brother, a notoriously tough guy. He squinted over at Timothy, then back to Carl, and said:

"Then what did you say?"

Carl shrugged. "I dunno."

"What do you mean you don't know?"

They were obviously talking about the argument Timothy had with Carl a few days back.

"Hey, queer bait," Mike called to Timothy, "get over here."

Fuck, this was exactly the kind of thing Timothy was trying to avoid.

"You deaf?" Mike said, "Get over here."

Hesitantly, Timothy walked over, not knowing what else to do, everyone was watching.

"You fucking with my brother?" Mike said.

"No."

"No? That's not what I heard. Carl, is he fucking with you?"

Carl didn't like being put on the spot in front of all these bigger boys any more than Timothy did, he was clearly regretting having brought it up. He shrugged, trying to get out of it.

"Look, was he fucking with you or not?"

"Yeah, I guess," Carl admitted, reluctantly.

"Okay . . ." Mike said, like, we're finally making some progress here. "So, kick his ass," he added prescriptively, like, this is simply what is done in a case like this.

"Hey Mike," the black kid said, "let the kids be, they obviously don't want to fight."

Mike waved off this objection as an unnecessary concern. Carl, meanwhile, tried turning away, wishy washy. He had two inches on Timothy, and under normal circumstances could probably do what his brother was telling him to, but the added attention was making him freeze up.

Meanwhile, Timothy's heart was racing. He'd seen Carl fight before, he knew he always just pounded away with his right, so he was prepared to throw up a block, but beyond this he had no idea what he'd do.

"Come on, do it," Mike said, physically pushing Carl toward Timothy.

As the two boys crashed slightly into each other, they pushed back on each other half strength, both reluctant for this to turn into a real fight.

"Don't be a pussy, really do it," Mike said, stepping in, giving Carl a wake-up knock to the temple, then demonstrating by shoving Timothy like he meant it. This of course put Timothy on his butt because Mike was a whole head taller than him.

At this point the black kid stepped in, he'd seen enough.

"Okay, leave the kid alone."

"Ah Charles, I'm just having a little fun, he's just a little queer bait."

As Timothy stood back up, Mike grabbed him and gave him a little shake, like he was just roughhousing, but Timothy was a rag doll in the older boy's grip.

"I said leave him alone," the black kid said.

"What, are you a fucking queer too?"

The black kid spun Mike around so lightning fast, no one even saw it happening, he just suddenly had him in a headlock. Mike squirmed, kicked, and tried to punch his way out of it, but the black kid just stood like a rock, not breaking a sweat in the slightest, continuing to subdue Mike firmly.

"When you let me go, I'm gonna kick your fucking ass," Mike spat out from underneath.

"Who said anything about me letting you go?" the black kid replied calmly, almost humorously. To prove the point, he tightened the headlock effortlessly, sending Mike into a flailing spasm.

"Okay, okay!" Mike gurgled, "I give up, okay?!"

The black kid held on for a few moments longer, to make sure his point was driven home completely. When he released his grip, Mike fell to the ground in a breathless heap.

He looked back up at the black kid resentfully, then over to Timothy.

"What're you looking at?" Mike spat.

The black kid stepped toward Mike again, Mike stood to his feet but backed away.

"Alright, alright . . . Carl, c'mon, let's get outta here."

Crazy Carl followed his brother, looking nervously back at the black kid.

"The same goes for your redneck brother," the black kid called out to both of them, "you leave my little friend here alone."

Did he just call Timothy his little friend? Who was this guy?

"What's your name, partner?" the black kid asked, still confident, but softening his tone.

"Timothy."

"Timothy what?"

"Timothy Miller."

"Here you go, Timothy Miller, you ever need help with anything, you just call me."

He handed Timothy this odd little rectangle of white paper that looked like something an adult should have. It was professionally printed, with embossed letters and everything.

"What's this?" Timothy asked.

"It's my calling card," said the kid, as if it were the most obvious thing in the world that someone as refined as he was would have his own calling card.

As Timothy marveled at the card like he'd just been handed a piece of gold, the older black kid stood up straight and added with confident poise:

"My name is Charles Lambeau, Jr."

hen Timothy pulled back up to the FotoMat, there was a handwritten sign in the window:

"Back in five minutes."

His first thought, of course, was to press his face to the window with renewed vigor to see if the secret trap door could be spied. No luck.

Kickstand deployed, he sat back on his bike. He had a receipt in one pocket and a baseball-sized lump of coinage in the other. He owned the space.

A faux-wood-sided station wagon cruised past. Thinking it might be Brandon's mother, he leaned over and pretended to adjust the dented chain guard on his bicycle, so she wouldn't see his face. The investigation was still top secret.

When the station wagon safely passed, Timothy looked back up again and scanned the parking lot. Man, five minutes was a long time.

When he finally spied the bright blue and yellow smock, it appeared the FotoMat attendant was coming out of the Grand Union supermarket. It was the same gal with the boyish haircut who'd taken his film two days before.

"Sorry to keep you waiting," she said, unlocking the booth and letting herself back in.

"That's okay," said Timothy. "Why'd you go into the supermarket?"

"I was getting something."

"How come you don't have any shopping bags?"

Was this kid really going to make her explain this?

"Let's just say I needed to take a little break, and leave it at that."

"Gotcha," Timothy said.

Bathroom mystery solved.

"Do you have your receipt?"

When Timothy pulled the receipt from his pocket, it was more crumpled and sweaty than he'd intended.

"Sorry it's wrinkled," he said, momentarily afraid it would be illegible or otherwise invalidated.

"I've seen worse," she said, and proceeded to flip through the envelope bin. "Let's see, Miller, Miller, Miller . . . here we go."

She began to ring up the sale.

"Twelve prints, $2.40 . . . did you want another roll of film with that?"

"Uh . . . I don't think so?" he said uncertainly.

"Just 69 cents with developing," she said, "usually set you back $1.29 . . ."

Timothy tried to think fast, would he need more film for the investigation? Likely, yes, but he hadn't planned on spending an extra 69 cents today.

"What would you do?" he asked the attendant.

"I would probably . . . buy another roll now and save the 60 cents."

A car pulled up behind Timothy. It didn't honk, but he could feel the heat radiating off its grill.

"Okay, I'll do it," he said.

2.40 plus .69 plus .22 tax came to $3.31.

Timothy plopped a sprawling pyramid of pocket change onto the small counter. He started sorting out pennies, figuring these had been weighing his pocket down the most. The attendant, fielding an impatient glare from the driver who'd pulled up behind Timothy, airlifted some quarters to speed up the process.

"Okay, we're good," she said, punching the keys of the register to ding the drawer open. She sorted the change quickly and handed Timothy a little bag with his prints and film.

"Make sure you hold on to your negatives, in case you ever want to make any copies," she said. Then she handed him something else.

"What's this?" Timothy asked.

"It's good for fifty cents off your next developing. Our little way of saying Thank you for using FotoMat."

"Wow . . . thanks."

She didn't give a 50 cent coupon to just anyone, but she sorta liked the kooky little long-haired kid on some level. Plus, that'd be 50 fewer pennies she'd have to count if he happened to come back during her shift.

Timothy, happy to have basically made out with a new roll of film almost for free, wobbled off with one hand on the handle bars, the other holding the little FotoMat bag.

He couldn't wait until he got home, so he stopped at a little picnic bench under some trees at the edge of the shopping plaza. He carefully opened the envelope, which contained the negatives in their own little pocket, just like the FotoMat girl had said, the prints themselves were in the larger pocket.

He intended on flipping straight to the crime scene photos, he hadn't bothered to imagine the first ten prints as anything other than padding. But when he saw the photos, he paused to look at them, one by one.

He'd forgotten about this.

Shortly after his dad had left, his mom had taken him on a vacation to Lake George, just the two of them, just for fun.

There was a photo of Timothy gathering firewood, one of him feeding some ducks, another of him playing a carnival game. There were photos of Timothy's mom doing stuff too, she'd let him take the photos.

There was one photo in particular that Timothy focused on. They'd taken a two-hour cruise on one of those old-fashioned steamboats that sail up and down Lake George. Someone had volunteered to take a picture of the two of them, and here they were smiling back at the camera, just Timothy and his mom, happy as could be.

It was a brief period in Timothy's life. His dad had gone, but Cathryn had yet to come into the picture. It was the only time in his life he'd ever really had his mom's full attention.

It seemed like the two of them had made such a good team, just Timothy and his mom. Why did Cathryn have to move in and ruin it? Why did things have to change?

The next few photos were taken shortly after Cathryn had moved in. They were all either of Cathryn, his mom, or the two of them together. Besides a single photo someone had taken of the three of them at the Group Halloween party last October, Timothy was out of the picture.

By the time he got to the last two photos, of the brook flowing out of the quarry and the sign that said IPM, he was pleased they'd both come out, but didn't think much about them beyond that.

For the moment, his mind was on other things.

Timothy's mom would probably appreciate seeing these family photos at some point, but Timothy couldn't explain why he'd commandeered the family Kodak and developed them. For now, he stuck them in his bottom drawer.

The evidence photos from the quarry went up on the bulletin board, then Timothy sat back to admire his own work.

In addition to the photos, there was a better-drawn map of Tannery Brook he'd sketched out after his first epic bike ride. There were also the results of the water test, plus a few choice notes about chemically smells and whatnot.

The arrangement of evidence was starting to look a little like what he'd seen on the wall in Ken's kitchen. Taken as a whole, it looked as though the investigation had accomplished a few things. At the same time, Timothy was well aware that he was also looking at a series of brick walls.

With his available resources, how would he up the ante in the testing department to prove whether or not there was benzene in the water like Ken had speculated? How was he going to get past the locked quarry gate to see where the chemicals might actually be coming from? Beyond that, how could he even begin to connect any of this in the real world to what had happened to Ken?

For all intents and purposes, as far as Timothy's limited detective abilities were concerned, the trail had gone cold, and might have stayed cold, except for an extraordinary occurrence that seemed too significant to be mere coincidence.

Back downstairs flipping through the *Daily Freeman*, Timothy was reading a seemingly unrelated story about how the Midtown Youth Center had been reopened after a series of renovations. The youth center was being renamed in memory of a respected Kingston police officer who had died in a widely reported high-speed chase a year or so ago. The officer's name was Detective Charles Lambeau.

Timothy sat there staring at the accompanying photo. The detective appeared kind, capable, confident, but also . . . white. The Charles Lambeau he'd met the other day was all those things, but black. Perhaps they weren't related at all.

But in the Kingston universe, most recognizable family names tended to have a Dutch ring to them, or Irish or German and the like. Lambeau was a very particular name. How many Charles Lambeaus could there be in Kingston, NY?

With Charles Lambeau, Jr.'s calling card in hand, Timothy stood staring at the beige rotary phone hanging on his kitchen wall.

Taking the receiver in hand, he detangled the coiling cord, then proceeded to dial 339-5997.

One thing about a rotary phone, it not only took a while to dial, but you had to wait for the dial to work its way back after each number. Because Charles' number had so many 9s in it, it took an extra long time, which gave Timothy just enough time to rethink the situation. He hung the phone back up before he finished dialing.

How was he going to begin this conversation? What could he possibly say to Charles Lambeau, Jr. that was going to make this seem like a real case and not just some crazy idea? Would Charles even remember who Timothy was and that he had given him his calling card?

If he could just show Charles the case laid out on his bulletin board it would be much more convincing. But how was he going to get a junior high school boy into his room to show him the work he'd done so far? He didn't even like having friends his own age come over to his house anymore.

A picture, as they say, was worth a thousand words. If he was going to convince Charles to help him, he was going to have to find him and show him what the investigation looked like, then maybe, just maybe, Charles would be intrigued enough to step in and lend a hand.

Timothy looked at Charles' card again. His address was printed in black and white, not too far from Brandon's house.

Looks like it was time to saddle up for a trip to Hilltop Meadows.

CHAPTER 10

Timothy had been up to Hilltop Meadows before, mostly for birthday parties, either Brandon's or one or two other friends. Those times, he'd always been driven there by his mom.

This was the first time he'd ever ridden his bike to Hilltop Meadows.

Distance-wise, this bike ride was more-or-less on par with his ride to the quarry. If anything it was easier, because it didn't involve skirting along the shoulder of a state highway.

Just the same, it felt like a significant journey because here he was, heading to a place previously only accessible via a ride from mom, but now doing it under his own power.

Leaving his own neighborhood of mostly older houses, Timothy was soon pedaling through an adjoining neighborhood more firmly rooted in the 20th century. Not long after that, toward the edge of the city's grid system, the houses became post-war.

This gradual transition from one style of house to another had never been as apparent when his mother whisked him by quickly in the car. At pedal speed, Timothy began to wonder if the gulf between Hilltop Meadows and his own neighborhood was really as wide as he'd imagined. Maybe it was a matter of degrees.

But when the sidewalks petered out, the front lawns expanded with a certain rolling grandeur that matched the gentle curves of the Hilltop roads. No, this wasn't just a slightly better neighborhood. This was a different reality.

Rolling to a stop at the end of a particularly tree-lined cul-de-sac, Timothy double-checked the address on the calling card as he looked up the long driveway. The mailbox read: Lambeau.

Must be the place.

Timothy walked his bike up the drive, then along the walkway that meandered across the well-manicured lawn to the main door. He leaned his bike against the front step, locking it would be presumptuous in a place he was not yet sure he'd be welcome.

Well, here goes.

He rang the doorbell. Somewhere inside was a pleasant chiming.

Catching his somewhat wild appearance in the reflection of the storm door, Timothy patted down his long hair with his palms, pushing it back behind his ears as best as he could.

The woman who answered the door looked vaguely like Brandon's mother in style and appearance.

"Yes?"

She didn't seem overly suspicious, likely she was used to kids Timothy's age collecting for their little league or paper route.

Timothy cleared his throat. He hadn't thought what he might say if Charles Lambeau, Jr. didn't answer the door himself. Asking if Charles Lambeau, Jr. were here would certainly sound weird, he decided to abbreviate immediately.

"Is Charles here?"

"Uh, yes . . . who should I tell him is here?"

"Timothy Miller, Jr . . . I mean, Timothy."

He was not, in fact, a junior, but was more nervous than he thought. The fate of the investigation was hanging in the balance.

"Just a sec," she said, leaving the storm door closed but the inner front door open. Not initially inviting, but not closing him out either. "Charlie . . . Timothy's here."

When Charles arrived at the door, he had a quizzical look at first, but as he opened the storm door he quickly recognized Timothy as the boy he'd stood up for a couple of days before.

"Oh, hey Timothy," he said. "Is everything okay?"

"Yeah I, uh, hello. Everything's fine, I just had a . . . a little project I thought you might be interested in."

"A little project?" Charles said, laughing. Then he looked past Timothy and saw his banana saddle bicycle leaning up against the front step. "You rode your bike all the way up here because you want to do a little project with me?"

"Uh, yeah."

"Well, come on in."

As Charles opened the storm door, Timothy looked back at his bike lying there.

"It's okay," Charles said, reading his mind, "it'll be safe out here."

As Timothy walked into the front hallway, the first thing he saw was a prominently placed portrait of Charles Lambeau, Sr., the same photo he had seen in the paper. It was framed along with a variety of formal memorial tributes apparently connected to his death in the line of duty.

"That's my dad," Charles said proudly. When he saw Timothy continuing to stare at the photo, he added, "I know what you're thinking, why is he white and I'm black?"

"No, I mean yes but, I saw his picture in the paper yesterday."

"Yeah, he did a lot of volunteer work at the Youth Center, that's why they named it for him. Anyway, I was adopted, in case you're wondering. That's why my parents are white and I am black."

Charles said this quite matter-of-factly, as if he'd had to explain this to people twice his age on more than one occasion.

Timothy continued to stand staring at the memorial portrait, not knowing what else to do.

"Come on," Charles said. "Come to my room and you can tell me about your little project."

Unlike Timothy's old-fashioned house, Charle's was a split-level, so you only had to climb six steps to be upstairs. The whole house had wall-to-wall carpeting. Everything looked so new, and there was a very fresh smell in the air from a variety of tasteful cleaning products.

Charles' room was at the end of the hallway. It too was carpeted, and had a very adult look about it. Charles' desk almost looked like a teacher desk. He even had a double bed.

Timothy examined the small collection of sports trophies and academic achievement awards on Charles' shelf.

"You play baseball?" Timothy asked.

"I'm a pitcher," Charles said. "Babe Ruth League, one or two games a week, plus practice here and there."

There were a few more photos of his dad, and some pictures cut out of magazines of bands Timothy was only vaguely familiar with.

"You like Zeppelin?" Charles asked.

"Uh, I don't know them real well . . ."

"What grade are you in?"

"Fourth," Timothy admitted sheepishly.

"Fourth, huh . . . I guess we got a few years to get you up to speed . . ."

Charles walked Timothy through the other band photos, taking him on a quick musical tour. Hendrix, Aerosmith, Sly and the Family Stone . . .

"These here are my personal favorites at the moment," Charles said. "Thin Lizzy, the lead singer is both *black and Irish.*"

Timothy just shook his head.

"How do you find out about all this?" he said, "all I have is an alarm clock radio."

"What station you listen to?"

"WBPM."

The local pop station.

"Timothy, it's not the radio, it's the station," Charles said, and scribbled something down on a piece of notepaper. "Here, you need to start listening to WPDH out of Poughkeepsie."

Timothy looked at the numbers 101.5 like Charles had just written down a top secret code. Who was this magical person and how had he come into his life?

"Why did you stand up for me the other day?" he found himself asking suddenly.

"I don't like seeing people get picked on," Charles said. "And besides, you seem like a cool guy."

Charles had volunteered at the youth center a bit himself, he knew a few tricks about how to make kids younger than him feel good about themselves.

"So," Charles said, "tell me about this little project."

This was the moment Timothy was waiting for and, with Charles' vote of confidence, he was ready to do the job.

Ripping open his knapsack, Timothy removed the exhibits one-by-one and carefully arranged them on Charles' bed, until the assemblage resembled what he'd had pinned to his bulletin board.

"It's an investigation, actually . . ."

"An investigation, really?"

Charles was careful not to sound too condescending, even though this seemed like a highly imaginative game that Timothy was laying out for him.

Timothy just kind of let loose all at once, he really didn't know where to start.

"So, the sample kit wasn't good enough, it couldn't tell me if it was phosphorus or benzedrine, but it definitely said the water was contaminated, and I followed the brook myself just to make sure that it's coming from IPM, and it is, because now IPM owns the quarry . . ."

Charles continued to nod his head thoughtfully, as if he was following all this, as if any of Timothy's crazy story made sense.

" . . . but I can't tell if they're really dumping chemicals because the gate's locked, so I need to get in there, plus I still have to figure out how they murdered Ken, I mean, I know who murdered Ken, but I have to figure out how his murder connects the benzedrine in the water—"

"Wait a minute," Charles cut in, "who's this Ken guy, and what's all this about a murder?"

Now Timothy had his attention.

"Ken is a guy who lived on my street. He's the one who did the water test, the real water test, and figured out there were toxins in it. He was the one who connected it to IPM and was about to contact the D.E.C., that's why they had him killed."

"Okay, slow down here, let's start at the beginning . . ."

Charles had Timothy walk him through the entire story in an order that made a bit more logical sense. It took a bit of redirection here and there to keep Timothy on track, but Charles knew from his dad that you never underestimated the truth of someone's story just because they were in an excitable state.

"So you're saying that this Ken guy had tested the water in the brook and found specific toxic chemicals in it linked to IPM?"

"Yes."

"And Ken was just about to turn the test results in when he was . . . when he died?"

"That's exactly what happened."

The whole time Timothy was talking, Charles had scanned the so-called evidence on his bed that had at first seemed like a fantasy. But using his own imagination to replace each amateurish element with something more professional, he began to see it, the underpinnings of an actual police investigation.

Who knew, maybe the K.P.D. was conducting a similar investigation at this very moment, or perhaps Timothy had a window into something they had missed simply because they weren't in the right place at the right time?

"You know Timothy," Charles said, "you might just have something here."

When Timothy and Charles met up next it was at Dietz Diner, Charles' idea.

Timothy was in front of the diner chaining up his banana saddle when Charles rolled up on an actual 10 speed. It had *two* sets of hand breaks, handlebars that gleamed like metallic ram horns in the sun, and more gears than Timothy could imagine using.

"That's a nice bike," Timothy marveled.

"My mom says I'll grow into it," Charles said, taking a high hop off a frame slightly too large for him. He locked it up next to Timothy's.

Charles and Timothy walked into the diner together.

"Hi Charles," the waitress said. Charles smiled and waved in return.

Man, this guy was like a local celebrity.

Plopping down into a booth by the window, Timothy immediately began flipping through the tabletop jukebox, which he'd had occasion to play, having eaten here before with his mom. Being here in the diner with a friend and no parent was another first.

"You two young men need menus?" the waitress asked. She was wearing a uniform that looked like it was from the 1950s, but without the beehive hairdo that some of the older waitresses still had.

"I know what I'm having," Charles said. "You need a menu, Timothy?"

"No, I know what I'm having too."

He figured he'd just order whatever Charles ordered, but the plan fell flat when Charles waved an open palm toward him, politely suggesting that, by all means, Timothy should order first.

"Go ahead," Charles said.

Timothy looked around the diner. It wasn't exactly mealtime. He saw some men sitting at the counter, they all had coffees.

"I'll have a cup of coffee," Timothy said.

"You will?" the waitress asked, with the same playfully surprised tone Charles had used when Timothy first told him he had a little project.

"Yes," Timothy confirmed.

"Did you want cream and sugar with that?"

"No, I'll take it black."

Timothy had read in his Real Men's Guidebook that real men always drank their coffee black. Charles flashed a brief look of disbelief, but he was starting to learn to take aberrations in stride when it came to Timothy.

"Okay then," the waitress said, "and for you, Charles?"

"I'll have a vanilla ice cream."

"One vanilla ice cream, one coffee . . . black," the waitress repeated, writing it down on her pad. "Back in a minute."

And she was.

As she set the vanilla ice cream down in front of Charles, he made sure to first make eye contact when thanking her, then looked to his ice cream like, *Come to Papa.*

Timothy, meanwhile, looked at the black coffee she set before him like, *What have I done?*

"The first spoonful is always the best," Charles said, savoring a mouthful of ice cream with deep satisfaction.

Timothy needed both hands to lift the heavy white porcelain mug to his mouth. The first sip was hot and bitter, his face contorted as it crossed his lips.

"You sure you don't want milk and sugar with that?" Charles asked.

"It's fine," Timothy croaked, sort of like after he'd smoked his first cigarette. "I drink this all the time."

Charles decided to take him at his word and continued to enjoy his ice cream, pausing to speak again when he was about halfway finished.

"So, did you bring that water sample?"

Timothy had been tasked with getting a fresh sample from the stream. He'd wisely used one of the more professional-looking plastic bottles from his home test kit, instead of the oversized Prell bottle.

"It's right here," Timothy said, producing the sample from his knapsack, handing it across the table to Charles.

Charles held it up to the light.

"The foam's kinda disappeared," Timothy said, "but it's still a little green, if you look hard."

"Yes," Charles agreed, squinting at the sample, "definitely a green tint."

Charles made sure the lid was screwed on tight before putting it into his own knapsack.

"I talked to my science teacher, Mr. Carlson," Charles said. "He's gonna let me use the science lab to run the test. And, get this, he's gonna give me extra credit!"

Timothy hadn't thought much about the specifics of junior high beyond the basic idea that he would be going there one day, but it was starting to sound like a magical place.

He took another few sips of black coffee. It tasted like it was getting more bitter by the minute, but a Real Man certainly wouldn't order a black coffee and then not drink it.

"Another thing," Charles continued, "I swung by the police station to check out the report from that bar fight."

"You can do that?"

"Anybody can. I mean, you can't see the whole police report, but they keep some stuff available for the beat reporter, that's how the paper gets their info."

"This is amazing . . . " Timothy said.

When he asked Charles to help him, he had no idea the world was going to start opening up so vastly and quickly.

He took another swig of coffee, not connecting his consumption of the strong black fluid to the fact that he was wiggling in his seat, his right leg starting to swing back-and-forth repeatedly.

"You mind aiming that foot in another direction?" Charles asked.

"Oh, sorry," Timothy said, not realizing he'd started to kick Charles in the shin.

"No problem. Anyway, you're definitely right, there's something fishy about that case. The report had all this stuff that was scribbled out, like there's something they don't want people to know about."

Unbelievable. If Timothy had any doubts before, he was now absolutely convinced they were onto something.

Charles finished his ice cream. As Timothy painfully downed his coffee to the grounds at the bottom of the mug, the waitress stopped by to see if they needed anything else, then dropped the check.

Timothy emptied the pile of change from his pocket onto the table.

"I got this one," Charles said.

"Oh, thanks," Timothy said, trying to sweep his change pile back into a cupped hand without spilling it all over the floor.

Looking at what was obviously the contents of Timothy's piggy bank, it occurred to Charles that if they were to meet regularly, the diner might not be the most fiscally responsible location from Timothy's perspective.

"You know," Charles said, "we don't always have to meet here, sometimes I can come by your house."

"No, my house is . . . under construction," Timothy blurted out.

"Under construction?"

"I mean we're, like, fixing it up. Stuff all over the place. I can just come to your house."

"That's quite a long bike ride."

"I don't mind, I need the exercise."

"Okay," Charles said, leaving the tip, "we'll figure something out."

Back outside, the pair unlocked their respective bicycles, then rode off slowly together along Green Street to bypass the busier streets uptown.

They rode alongside each other, Charles on the left on his oversized 10 speed, Timothy on the right on his little banana saddle. In this configuration, if they were in a police cruiser, it would almost be like Charles was driving while Timothy rode shotgun.

"My dad used to like that restaurant," Charles said, pointing to the old Hoffman House on the corner, Kingston's oldest restaurant.

Timothy had never eaten there himself, but he figured he'd throw out a little factoid, just to stay in the conversation.

"I think Franklin Roosevelt's family lived there back in the olden days," Timothy said.

"Really?"

"Well, it doesn't say so on the sign, but I read it in a book somewhere."

"How do you like that . . . I didn't know Kingston had any presidential connections."

"Oh, tons, right on this street alone . . . right up here is where George Clinton used to live, he wasn't President, but he was Vice President under Jefferson," Timothy said, "and then of course we have all the Van Burens on the next block . . . "

Timothy proceeded to regale Charles with a whole array of details about the various stone houses on the street, and how the townspeople had fled to Hurley that fateful night in 1777 when the British set fire to the place.

"If the British burned the place, how come all the houses are still here?"

"They're made of stone, they just had to rebuild the insides," Timothy said, "but if you go inside some of them you can still see the fire marks."

Timothy was kind of surprised that Charles didn't know any of this. He figured that because Charles knew so much about other things that he would know everything.

They continued to pedal slowly along, Timothy giving Charles an historical tour, until they hit the red light on Main Street. At this point, it was time for Charles to head up the hill toward Hilltop Meadows, and for Timothy to continue to working class Warren Street.

"Well, see you, Charles," Timothy called out as Charles rode off.

"See you, Partner," Charles replied.

CHAPTER 11

he next time Group met at Timothy's house, it was a little different.

It started with the usual hugs and greetings, but the pillows stayed piled up, and even a few pieces of furniture were moved to make more room.

Tonight was self-defense night. This was the first Group meeting Timothy was even mildly interested in, but he was still on the fence about sticking around.

On the one hand, he was all for watching David Carradine execute a flying kung-fu style high kick on TV. On the other hand, he wasn't so sure he wanted to see his mom or any of the other Group ladies attempting to do the same in his living room.

The class was being led by Sarah, the woman he'd stolen the cigarette from. Turned out that Sarah was both a martial arts expert and a Kingston cop. If he decided to steal another cigarette, it should probably be from someone else.

Often people would bring wholesome snacks that smelled like the health food store, but tonight someone actually brought nacho cheese flavored Doritos, something his mom would never buy.

Timothy hovered by the dining room table, crunching and observing as the class began.

"What is the first rule of self-defense?" Sarah asked aloud.

The assembled ladies looked around at each other—who would dare answer first?

"Keep your hands up in front of your face?" one woman guessed.

"Hit them first before they hit you?" tried another.

This got a laugh, but still didn't seem to be the answer Sarah was looking for. She scanned the faces one last time to make sure there were no other wild guesses.

"The first rule of self defense is," she said, "do not put yourself in a position where you will have to defend yourself in the first place."

Heads nodded in general agreement.

"So, let's talk about some places where we might want to think ahead about our own safety . . ."

Again she opened it up to the Group, but this time everyone had the right answers:

"On the street alone at night."

"In a bar alone at night."

"Passing a group of rowdy young men."

Then Timothy's mom said:

"In my office."

And everybody had a big chuckle about this one, but Sarah cut right in:

"You might laugh, but did you know that 90% of women who are assaulted are assaulted, not by strangers, but by men they already know . . . 90%."

She let that figure sink in.

"So what's the answer to that one?" someone finally asked.

"There's no one-size-fits-all answer but, again, use your head. Don't put yourself in a situation when no one else can hear you if you need help. And, if worse comes to worse . . . hit him first before he hits you."

Biggest laugh.

Timothy was actually fascinated by this conversation. He'd gone out of his way on more than one occasion to avoid a fight. He'd always thought this just meant he was chicken shit, he'd never considered this was actually a sensible self-defense tactic.

Shortly, Sarah broke the women into pairs so they could practice some basic self-defense exercises.

The first exercises were verbal, and mostly involved looking the other person in the eye and yelling something very purposefully. This got loud very quickly.

Then, things started to get physical.

Cara, who'd been practicing with Anne, looked up and saw that Timothy was still watching from the dining room.

"C'mon Timothy, join us, it's fun," she said, which seemed particularly funny because just a moment before she'd been screaming "Back the fuck away from me!" in Anne's face.

That night in his room, Cara had made a generalized invitation, but this was way more direct. She looked over to his mom. "It's okay if Timothy joins in, right?"

His mom, who hadn't fully realized Timothy was still there watching the whole time, was a little on the spot.

"Well," she called over to Timothy, "you've been bugging me for karate classes, now's your chance."

Uh, yes, he had been bugging her for karate classes, but mixing it up with a roomful of angry, screaming women was not what he'd had in mind.

Permission granted, Cara stepped it up a notch.

"C'mon Timothy, you'll like it," she said, came over, took him by the hand, and pulled him into the living room. "You can be my partner."

Sarah, making the rounds, offered to work with Cara's previous partner, Anne, so it was settled.

"Okay, new exercise," Sarah called out, "one person on top, one person on the bottom."

She demonstrated with Anne a move that was designed to get you out from beneath someone if they were on top of you.

"You can be on top first," Cara said to Timothy.

Cara lay down on the oriental rug and Timothy, awkwardly, climbed above, his knees on either side of her hips. Gradually, he shifted his weight, until more of it was resting on her belly instead of on the floor. It was almost like riding a horse, except she was looking up at him the whole time.

"Pin down the shoulders," Sarah called.

Timothy hesitated.

"It's okay," Cara said, cheerful at every turn, "you can't hurt me."

Leaning forward, Timothy placed his hands on Cara's shoulders. This required putting his face much closer to hers. He sensed something vaguely wobbly beneath her shirt. Living with women, he knew just enough about brasiers to guess she wasn't wearing one. He tried not to look too directly into Cara's face as he awaited Sarah's next instruction.

"Person on the bottom," Sarah said, "reach for the elbow . . . the attacker's arm is attached to his torso, this is simple physics . . . use the arm like it's a handle connected to a pot . . . lift up . . . up, and . . . push over."

Cara did exactly what Sarah instructed, she had no difficulty whatsoever getting Timothy up and off her, though she did this gently and non-aggressively.

They practiced this several times.

"Okay, let's make this a little more challenging," Sarah said. "Person on top, pin the arms down."

Timothy looked around the room to see if anyone else was watching this very physical exchange going on between him and Cara, but everyone was concentrating on their own physical exchanges, no one paid any attention to them in the slightest.

Sitting atop Cara, Timothy leaned over a bit further in order to pin down her arms. This meant that their faces were a lot closer, and that their chests were beginning to make contact. It was much like the previous move, but this one was undeniably more intimate. Their breathing was harder from the exertion.

When Sarah gave the next instruction, Cara followed, pressing her pelvis upward. Utilizing her core strength like this would be effective even if Timothy were bigger and stronger. With her back arched she was able to use Timothy's weight against him and knock him off top.

Like the previous move, they practiced several times. It was kind of fun to figure out how this worked, actually.

"Okay, switch," Sarah called out.

Timothy took his place lying on the floor. He was glad for the rest, and also imagined it would be less awkward to be beneath Cara than the other way around. But when Cara climbed on top of him and used her weight to press his hips to the floor, the sensation was equally strange, but from a different angle.

"Pin down the shoulders," Sarah called.

"Ready?" Cara asked, smiling down at him.

"Ready," Timothy said.

As Cara leaned forward, her shirt billowed ever so slightly, but it was just enough to set her breasts swaying freely above Timothy. This was a detail Timothy could not help but notice. The slight loosening of her shirt also seemed to release a fragrance, equal parts perfume and light perspiration.

Timothy thought he felt a drop of sweat fall from her forehead onto his.

"Person on the bottom, reach for the elbow," Sarah said.

Timothy heard Sarah's voice, but it was as if it was coming from a different room, or a different world, even.

For the moment, he just lay there, not doing anything but looking up at Cara, who continued to smile back at him.

Timothy had imagined this experience might be at least just a little bit like the karate class he was not going to get any time soon.

But this wasn't karate.

This was . . .

confusing.

The next afternoon, Timothy stood facing his bedroom mirror, a singularly excellent place for shadow boxing. He'd hung with the self-defense class long enough to pick up a few more techniques, now he had some new moves.

"Silly Love Songs" by Wings was dribbling out of his alarm clock radio. The bass line was catchy, but the song did not exactly pump him up.

Timothy had only gotten into the habit of listening to WBPM because it was the station that announced school closings when it snowed, somehow he'd never thought to change it until now.

Where was that piece of paper Charles had given him? Which jeans had he been wearing that day? Digging through the laundry basket, he found the note with 101.5 written on it in the back pocket of his Lee jeans.

He dialed a few notches to the right to WPDH. The song just starting was one he immediately recognized from Charles' bedroom. Maybe he didn't remember it was the first track on Led Zeppelin III, or that it was called "The Immigrant Song," but the guitar and screeching vocal all but blew his hair back.

The tiny speaker in his alarm clock radio was exploding with images of hammers, gods, and fighting hordes. He faced off afresh in front of his mirror with the energy of a Norse berserker. He could picture Crazy Carl's older brother Mike floating right there in front of him.

Raising his fists, he faked with his right then, with a quick rotation of the shoulders, he jerked his hand back toward his chest and BAM, surprise elbow strike to the face!

"Yeah, I'm a queer bait?" Timothy said to the mirror, "then what does this make you?"

Cartilage crunches, blood splatters everywhere.

"Who's the queer bait now, mother fucker?"

Somewhere downstairs, the telephone rang. A few moments later, Cathryn knocked on Timothy's door as he was wiping the imaginary blood from his elbow.

"Phone call," she called, loud enough for Timothy to hear over the cranked radio.

Turning the music down, Timothy ran downstairs and scooped up the receiver, which was dangling from its twisting cord on the kitchen wall.

"Hello?"

"Timothy, it's Charles. How quickly can you get over to Bailey?"

J. Watson Bailey Junior High wasn't so far away. Although Timothy had never been inside, it was right next to Forsyth Park where he played sometimes, so he knew it was an easy bike ride.

School had ended 40 minutes ago, the buses were long gone. Even the faculty parking lot was mostly empty except for a few dedicated teachers and the custodians.

Timothy pulled hard on what seemed to be the main door. Locked. The place was twice the size of his elementary school, where to begin?

"Timothy!" Charles called from an open window. "Meet me at the end of the building, I'll come down and let you in!"

By the time Timothy reached the stairwell exit door, Charles was holding it open for him. It felt like he was sneaking in somehow as the door slammed shut with finality behind them.

"So this is Bailey," he whispered aloud, as much to himself as to Charles.

The hallways really were lined with lockers, just like in the movies. Timothy could envision a chaos of towering teenagers, bumping from one class to the next with quick stops in between. So much independence, so much intrigue. Even the student artwork hanging on the walls had depth and shading, like it was done by professional artists.

Charles led Timothy up to the top floor and into the science lab.

"Mr. Carlson, this is my partn-, uh, friend Timothy."

Mr. Carlson, who was sitting at his desk grading papers, rose to give Timothy a proper handshake.

"Hello, nice to meet you Timothy, welcome to the science lab," he said. "So, you're interested in hydrology too?"

Timothy looked to Charles.

"The study of water," Charles clarified.

"Yes," said Timothy, "I'm interested in hydrology."

"Excellent, well, welcome welcome . . . Charles is conducting some water analysis over in the corner there, please be my guest, join right in . . ."

Mr. Carlson got back to grading his papers, happy to have students using the lab who actually seemed to love science.

Charles explained the process to Timothy, which was basically a lot like the test Timothy had already conducted, except there was a whole series of litmus-type strips, to test for a much wider range of chemicals.

"We're just waiting for these last strips to soak up the water . . ."

Timothy's eyes wandered around the science lab. Past the beakers and burners, there was a morbidly realistic model of a human being with an open body cavity. Is that really what it looked like? The organs were way more crammed in there and gnarly-looking than he'd imagined.

"I could be wrong," Charles said, looking at the results of the last sample, "but it looks like we've got some toxic stuff in here."

He and Timothy marched the little bottle with the test strip back up to the front of the room along with the corresponding chemical-identifying manual.

"Mr. Carlson, does this water have benzene or toluene in it?"

Mr. Carlson set down his red pen, adjusted his eyeglasses, and compared the test bottle to the small print in the manual.

"Looks like both to me. Where did you get this water from?"

"Let's just say this water sample is from a stream in our area," Charles said. "Would you say these results are . . . concerning?"

Mr. Carlson held the water up for examination again. To the untrained eye, it looked more-or-less innocuous, other than the slight green tint.

"This is water from a local stream?" he asked, incredulously.

"It is."

"Well, if you found benzene in a local stream," Mr. Carlson said, "then yes, I would find this very concerning."

Charles had missed his bus. Timothy volunteered to walk Charles home, at least part of the way, so they could continue conversing about their findings. Timothy would still have time to coast downhill and be home for supper.

"I think it's time to investigate the quarry," Charles said.

"We're gonna have to break in," Timothy said, "the gate is locked."

"Timothy, that's a code 140.05 . . . you're not actually suggesting we break the law, are you?"

The stunned look of guilt on Timothy's face was almost immediate.

"I'm just messing with you," Charles laughed heartily.

Timothy let out a nervous laugh, relieved, mostly.

"Anyway, there might just be another way in," Charles said. "I was in that quarry once."

"You were?"

"A kid I know lives right around there, took me dirt biking all over the place. I'm gonna reach out to him, see what he knows. Maybe he can get us in there."

"That'd be . . . great," Timothy said, still a bit dazzled by Charles' knowhow and connections.

They were about halfway up the hill between Bailey and Hilltop Meadows. Charles was taking the incline in stride, while Timothy leaned in a bit to keep pushing his banana saddle by its curving chopper handlebars.

"Lemme ask you something," Charles said. "Does anyone ever call you Tim?"

"No, just Timothy."

"Not even your mom?"

"She calls me Timothy . . . my neighbor Mr. O'Connor calls me Timbo sometimes for some reason."

Charles gave his chin a scratch, like he was considering the merits of this.

"Timbo's not bad, but we can do better."

"For what?"

"If we're gonna do this thing, you need, like, a really good cop name."

"What's wrong with Timothy?"

"Nothing, for everyday usage it's quite a nice name, actually. But for a detective, Timothy doesn't quite cut it . . . how about T-Bird?"

"T-Bird?"

"You know, like the car?"

Timothy thought about it for a second.

"What's the T stand for again?"

"It stands for Thunder. Thunderbird."

Timothy pondered again.

"I can deal with Thunderbird . . . What are we gonna call you?"

"I'm Charles Lambeau, Jr."

"I know, but what's your *detective* name?"

"Are you kidding, do you not remember who my father was? In this town, you cannot get a better detective name than Charles Lambeau, Jr."

So, with that, the matter of their detective names was decided.

They continued walking together until they reached the spot where the sidewalks ran out.

"Well, I guess you'd best head home if you're gonna make it there by five," Charles said. "I'll talk to that kid with the dirt bike and call you as soon as I know something, okay Thunderbird?"

Timothy did like the sound of that.

"Okay, Lambeau."

Pushing his bicycle most of the way up the hill now paid off, Timothy barely had to pedal once on his way home.

With the wind in his hair, he said the name "Thunderbird" to himself and, for a moment, it really felt like he was flying.

CHAPTER 12

Timothy had deduced he could pretty much count on B's without doing homework. Since B's seemed acceptable enough to his mom these days, the choice not to do homework wasn't a hard one.

This said, the deadline for the Bicentennial report was fast approaching. He'd been so preoccupied with the investigation that he hadn't even started. He didn't care so much about the prize, but the report would have to be read in front of the whole class, no faking that.

Timothy dumped the contents of his knapsack onto the dining room table with a dramatic flair. Whenever he did something academic, he always did it noisily and made sure his mom or Cathryn saw him doing it. This way they might think he actually did some homework once in a while.

"Working on your report?" Cathryn asked, wandering in to look over his shoulder.

"Yup, got a lot of research to do," Timothy replied studiously.

"Well, lemme know if you need any help," she said. "I always hated doing reports."

"Okay, thanks."

He hated to admit that what Cathryn said was actually kind of cool, not so much the offer of help, but that she hated doing reports. You'd never hear his mom admitting anything like that.

Timothy spread out the books he'd taken out of the school library. "Boston Tea Party: The Protest That Became a Nation" was the newest, with the most pictures. Seemed the logical place to start.

Scanning the opening chapter, he sketched out the "Five W's" like Mrs. Brenner had taught them in school:

Who: the colonists

What: dumped tea in the harbor

When: Dec 16, 1773

Where: Boston

Why: something about taxes

That was a pretty good start. Time for a snack.

He went back into the kitchen to see if anything had materialized since the last time he checked. No luck. He settled for a couple of stale cookies shaped like little windmills that tasted vaguely like molasses. Why couldn't his mom just buy Twinkies like all the other moms?

Returning to the table, Timothy procrastinated by skimming through the book and looking at the pictures. There were, of course, the same standard illustrations of the Sons of Liberty dressed up like Indians as they ransacked the old frigate. Mrs. Brenner had shown them these in her general overview of the Boston Tea Party during social studies.

But as he dug deeper into the book, he began turning up some interesting tidbits that Mrs. Brenner had failed to include in her lesson.

For example, Samuel Adams and John Hancock, who led the tea party, were both actually tea smugglers, that sounded kind of cool and dangerous. Also, it wasn't a quick operation like he'd imagined. It took something like three hours to get the job done because there was something, like, a million dollars worth of tea.

And they didn't just throw the crates overboard, either. The men in Indian costumes used tomahawks to hack the chests open individually before dumping their contents into the harbor.

This last detail made Timothy stop to think for a moment.

He was pretty sure tea wasn't toxic, his mom and Cathryn drank quite a lot of it in the evenings while they were watching television.

But wouldn't dumping all that tea at once do something to the water? Did it just float away, or did it brew the whole harbor into a giant vat of tea? Did it turn the shoreline brown? Can fish survive in tea?

There were a lot of questions that had nothing to do with the Bicentennial or the American Revolution. But, given their current investigation of what he knew to be happening to Tannery Brook, could he possibly leave this point unaddressed?

On Saturday, Timothy was helping his mom clean the house while Cathryn was working at the hardware store.

When the phone rang he answered it hoping it would be Charles, but it was Greg Hathaway from his mom's office.

"Hey big guy, is your mom home?" Greg asked.

"Yea, just a sec."

Timothy made like he was going down to the basement to get the sheets out of the dryer, but he hung by the top of the basement steps so he could listen in.

"I'm kind of in the middle of something," his mom said to Greg. "Yes, I know the case is being heard Monday afternoon, but I should have time Monday morning to . . . yes, I know there's more paper-work than usual but . . ."

Timothy couldn't hear the other side of the conversation, but it seemed like Greg must be being particularly pushy.

"Okay, give me a few minutes, I'll come over . . ." his mom finally said, hanging up the phone with resignation.

"What was that about?" Timothy asked.

"It was just Greg, he needs me to come over and make some copies."

"On the photocopier?"

"Yes, on the photocopier."

The last time he'd been to his mom's office and watched her use the copier was well before the dawning of the investigation and he barely knew what he was looking at. Now seemed an excellent opportunity to do some technological research. If he could see the thing in action, maybe he'd learn something important.

"Can I come?"

"No, it's better if you just hold down the fort. I won't be long."

Timothy thought quickly.

"If I could copy just one or two pictures for my Boston Tea Party report, it'd make the whole thing look a lot more professional . . . it'd make a big difference, please?"

She had a fatigued look on her face and seemed about to dismiss the suggestion entirely, but she paused momentarily and appeared to consider it on a deeper level.

"Actually, yes," she said. "Maybe it's a good idea if you did come along."

★　★　★

Cathryn had taken the Calico Chrysler shopping, but the office was right uptown, so it was only a four block walk.

The straps of Timothy's knapsack cut into his shoulders as they walked, he'd crammed in every last book he could think of, figuring he'd sort it out once they got there.

His mom's office was in the Elmendorf House, one of the older stone houses on Green Street, dating to the late 1600s. Going in was a bonus, even though the law office had been remodeled in recent years. It now had wood paneling and industrial carpeting. Once you were inside, except for the creaky floors and low ceiling, you'd never know you were in a building that was older than the nation, but it was still pretty cool.

Greg Hathaway smiled at his mom as she walked in. His face crinkled slightly when he realized Timothy was right behind her, but he recovered quickly.

"Oh, hey big guy," he said, "coming to help Mom?"

"Yep, coming to help Mom," Timothy readily agreed, a convenient explanation for his presence other than riding Mom's coat-tails to use the office copier.

Greg led them to a desk in a back room where sat a manilla folder with some legal papers in it.

"Well, here they are," he said, tapping the folder. "Just one of each and we should be all set."

It was a thick folder, but really not that thick. Even Timothy had to wonder why this couldn't wait until Monday morning, or why Greg couldn't do this himself since he was already here.

"You can just wait at my desk until I'm finished," his mom said to Timothy.

"I'd rather watch you do it, if you don't mind."

She shrugged, like, suit yourself.

The copier was in a little alcove underneath the stairs where there wasn't much ventilation. It definitely smelled like chemicals. If only he had some kind of test kit so he could sample the air.

One by one, his mom laid the legal papers on the glass plate, shut the lid, waited while the light scanned the paper from underneath, then waited even longer while the printer geared up and slowly spit out the copy.

"What happens if you leave the lid open?" Timothy asked.

"It won't work, the copy won't come out."

"Can we try it?"

"It's bad for your eyes," his mom said.

Timothy couldn't tell if this was one of those mom rules, like no swimming for 45 minutes after you eat, or if this were a real and present danger. He had to remember to jot this down in his notes just the same.

"Oh damn," his mom said, looking at one of the finished copies, then called out, "Greg, it's happening again!"

Greg appeared quickly. She showed him the copy, which was half-faded and unreadable in places.

"Okay," he said, "Let's see if I can work the old Greg magic . . . "

He rolled up his shirt sleeves and popped open the front of the copy machine. Oh man, if only Timothy had the Instamatic with him *now*. Look at all those interconnecting parts.

Greg unlatched a few things, then slid this black tube out and started shaking it like he was making a martini.

"Is that the toner?" Timothy asked.

"Uh, yeah, something like that," Greg said, surprised, "how'd you know that?"

"I'm sort of interested in copy machines at the moment."

"Smart kid," Greg said, after a pause, like he'd almost accidentally said "weird kid" but caught himself in time.

Greg slid the tube back into the machine, reversed the sequence of levers he'd clicked to extract it, then shut the machine. He ran it once himself and had a bit of a self-satisfied look on his face when the copy came out perfectly.

"Voila," he said.

"Thanks, Greg," his mom said, flatly, attempting to neutralize the heroic moment so she could just get on with her work.

"I'll be in my office when you finish," he said.

"Oh, and Greg? Timothy would like to copy one or two pictures for a school report, would that be okay?"

Timothy cringed. Why'd she have to tell him? He figured he'd just slip in there quietly, now he felt like he'd been caught red handed.

"Sure thing, big guy, copy all you like."

Well, that wasn't as bad as it could've been.

"Uh, thanks," Timothy said.

When his mom got to the last few copies, she said to Timothy as she pressed the button, "So, you know how to work this thing, right?"

"Easy peasy," Timothy said.

Taking all the copies she'd just made in both hands, she tapped them sideways on the table like a giant deck of cards to stack them into a neat pile.

"Okay, I just have to file a few things, then we'll get out of here."

And just like that, Timothy was left alone with the IPM copier.

He didn't have much time. He would just have to make a few copies, like he said, and maybe somehow he would learn something along the way.

He popped open the illustrated Tea Party book to the obvious illustration, the one with the patriots in their Indian garb whooping it up all over the deck of the ship.

Placing the book face down on the glass plate, he couldn't get it to lie flat. Even when he pressed down on the cover and heard the spine of the book making a little cracking sound, he still couldn't get the cover to close all the way.

It was now or nothing. He pressed the button and squinted, trying not to look directly at the seductively bright light while it scanned the book, hoping he wouldn't be blinded.

When the copy rolled out, it was kind of dark, and the image got wavy where the original was sewn into the middle of the book. Was there a way to adjust it? There were several dials, but Timothy couldn't tell what they did.

He thought about Steven at school, the kid whose dad had his own IPM photocopier at home. Steven would probably know all about how to lighten up the image, but Timothy couldn't begin to figure it out. Still, even though it was dark and wavy, it was pretty darn cool that he had a photocopy to include in his report. He might be the only kid in class to have thought of this. Except, probably, Steven.

What else should he make a copy of? There was another illustration he'd seen somewhere that he liked, an engraving of the moonlit night. Where had he seen that, was it in his social studies book?

As he pulled the textbook from his knapsack, a small piece of paper fluttered out and onto the floor. Timothy bent over to pick it up—it was the blank late slip he'd scored from the main office at school, the morning he'd been late because he was running errands for the prostitute.

Timothy looked at the slip, then looked at the copier.

Was there ever a purer moment when the universe aligned more perfectly than this?

He peeked out of the alcove to make sure neither his mom nor Greg were coming, then placed the official late slip on the glass plate. The lid closed perfectly. He pressed the button.

When the copy came out, it looked *exactly* like the pass itself. You could not tell the difference.

Timothy hit Copy again. And again. And again.

Gingerly placing the original along with the facsimiles back inside his social studies book, Timothy packed everything into his knapsack and buckled it all up.

This was definitely a time to quit while he was ahead.

Walking softly toward the back of the office, Timothy found his mom crouching in front of a metal filing cabinet, trying to file what she had copied, while Greg hulked over her, speaking in low tones, more-or-less trapping her in the corner.

Timothy didn't like the way this looked.

"Mom," he said, "you ready to go?"

"Oh, hey big guy," Greg said, turning around when he realized Timothy had come in, "just helping your mom here."

His mom used the opening to close the drawer, push past Greg, and get out of the corner.

"I need to get something upstairs, then we're going," she said to Timothy.

Greg watched her walk away. Suddenly left alone in the room with a ten-year-old boy, he tried to make polite small talk.

"So, Timothy, whaddah think of that copy machine?"

"She's a beaut," Timothy said.

The room got quiet again because Greg couldn't quite think of how to respond to this.

Timothy broke the silence.

"So, you know my mom knows karate, right?"

"She does?" Greg said, genuinely surprised at this revelation.

"Oh yeah. She's, like, basically a black belt . . . saw her take down a full-grown man twice her size once, very embarrassing situation . . ."

"I had no idea . . ."

Timothy's mom walked back into the room briskly.

"Okay, we're going."

Greg looked at her like she was a new sort of animal. He said nothing as she and Timothy walked out of the office, and neither did they.

They were halfway home when Timothy started chuckling out loud.

"What are you laughing about?" his mom asked, actually wanting to be let in on the joke to help soothe her nerves.

"Oh, nothing," Timothy said, still snickering, trying to picture his scrawny mom delivering a surprise elbow strike to the face.

CHAPTER 13

t'd been a few days since Charles had called. Timothy figured he could just keep waiting, or he could pick up the phone himself. He no longer needed Charles' calling card, he'd memorized the number.

"Lambeau residence," Charles said, when he answered the phone.

"Lambeau? It's Thunderbird."

"Oh, hey Thunderbird, what's up?"

"What's your 10-20?" Timothy asked.

He thought Charles would be impressed he'd learned the code for *location* in cop talk.

"My 10-20? I'm in my house. Where did you think I was, you just called me here."

"Okay, just checking."

"Anything else?"

"Yeah, uh . . . did you call that kid about the quarry?"

"I sure did, we're on for Thursday, I meant to call and tell you."

Today was only Tuesday, so Thursday was, like, forever from now.

"Why Thursday?"

"He said that's the day the truck comes."

"What truck?"

"I don't know, I just know what he told me. Thursday cool with you?"

"Yeah, Thursday's cool."

"Okay, catch you then."

"Okay, catch you then. Over and out."

"Uh, Timothy?" Charles said.

"Yes?"

"This is a telephone, not a CB, you can just say goodbye."

"Okay, goodbye Lambeau."

"Later, Thunderbird."

Well, Thursday might be two whole days away, but at least it was on the calendar. Meanwhile, what was he supposed to do, keep working on his report for school?

Luckily, a knock came on the front door a few minutes later and saved him from that particular fate. Parting the curtain to look out the window, he saw Crazy Carl and Mark standing awkwardly on his front porch.

"Oh, hey guys," Timothy said, coming out onto the porch to meet them.

Carl was looking all around the porch, at the peace flag, at the beat-up couch, anywhere but at Timothy.

"Say it," Mark said to Carl, stepping on his foot.

"Alright, alright," Carl said to Mark, then looked at the buttons halfway up Timothy's shirt.

"Sorry," Carl said, "you're not a queer."

Somewhere in the back of Timothy's ten-year-old brain, Carl's logic fell slightly short. Like, "So, if I *was* a queer, then it'd be okay if you and your piece of shit brother beat me up?" But he was glad enough to hear Carl's apology. It seemed to release at least some of the pressure inside him.

"It's okay," Timothy said. "Sorry I called you a mother fucker."

"It's okay," Carl said, and smiled a little, like maybe Timothy's apology helped release some pressure inside of him too.

The two boys shook on it.

"So, will you come play whiffle ball now?" Mark said to Timothy with some exasperation. "We never have enough people."

"Yeah," said Timothy, "I'll come play."

The three of them walked down the street to the field behind the Green Apartment Building, where the two or three other kids who were just waiting there killing time said:

"Yay, Timothy's back!"

The game resumed. Since the loss of Robbie's super pinky, the neighborhood kids had gone back to using a regular whiffle ball. Being a hollow piece of white plastic, it never flew much further than the infield, even if you got a solid piece of it. But at least no one would hit it out into the weeds again and bring the game to a screeching halt.

Timothy scored two runs in the first inning, so he felt fairly confident that his presence was valued as something more than just a live body.

After about three innings, some loud yelling was heard coming out of the Green Apartment Building. It was a warmish day and the window was wide open.

Timothy knew it was the prostitute's window, and that it was the same guy that he'd heard yelling on the other side of her closed door the day he was in the hallway with Ken. The same guy he saw walking down the street with the prostitute sometimes.

All the kids in the field froze in place looking up at the open window to see what would happen.

When the guy looked outside and realized a field full of kids were watching him, he put his hands on the sill like he was going to spring out the window and hollered:

"What are you little fuckers looking at?"

He then slammed the window shut and continued yelling.

The kids remained momentarily frozen in place, somewhat terrified that this scary guy just yelled at them. Then Robbie started laughing, so the rest of the kids started laughing too.

Except for Timothy.

He was still trying to figure out why this guy yelling was so deeply upsetting to him, and why was it so strangely familiar?

And then it dawned on him:

It reminded him of his father.

Thursday afternoon, Timothy and Charles rendezvoused at the Stewart's on Route 32.

"I hear the coffee's good here," Charles said.

"That's okay," Timothy said, opting for a Charleston Chew, which he ate enthusiastically to bolster his strength for the coming ride.

Route 32 south was no place for a leisurely side-by-side cruise. Charles led the way, cranking it up to tenth, forgetting that Timothy's banana saddle only had one gear.

"Wait up!" Timothy called, barely loud enough to be heard above the passing traffic.

"Sorry partner," Charles said. He kept it in fifth the rest of the journey. Timothy still had to pedal furiously, but managed to keep up while watching out for passing buses.

They rode just a bit further than Timothy had gone on his own. A few hundred yards past the locked main gate of the quarry, Charles pulled off the road when they reached an old boarded-up garage.

"I thought we were meeting this guy at his house," Timothy said.

"We are, he lives back here."

"He does?"

Back behind the garage they found, not a house, but a beat-up old trailer. It felt like they were in Appalachia or something, Timothy didn't know parts of Kingston like this existed.

What the kid's family lacked in house, they made up for with vehicular assets.

There were trucks, cars, pieces of trucks and cars, and more dirt bikes and go-kart type things than Timothy could count.

"Check it out!" Charles mouthed to Timothy, pointing to an old T-Bird on cinderblocks.

The trailer's screen door slammed open and stayed open because the spring meant to pull it back was dangling in the breeze. Out came an older kid, with a look on his face that would've gone perfectly well with a pitchfork if he'd had one in his hands.

"That you Charles?"

"Hey Dwayne!" Charles called out.

Dwayne approached warily. He had a smudge of motor oil on his face, and was even taller than Charles.

"Who's this kid?" he asked.

"This is my friend who I told you about. His name's Timothy, but you can call him Thunderbird."

"Thunderbird?"

"Don't let the mild-mannered exterior fool you, he's a stone cold killer."

"That so?"

Out of nowhere, Dwayne faked a punch to Timothy's face to see if he would flinch.

Timothy threw his hands up quickly, lightly connecting with Dwayne's fist as he was already pulling it back.

Dwayne searched Timothy's face to see if the faked punch had rattled him or not, then broke into a wide grin.

"Aw, I'm just messing with you, any friend of Charles Lambeau is a friend of mine!"

He put out his big greasy paw and gave Timothy a proper handshake, which Timothy was relieved to accept.

"C'mon, let's go ridin," Dwayne said.

He led Charles and Timothy over to his dirt bike collection.

"I'm gonna take my Yammy," he said, patting his Yamaha 175. "Charles, you can ride the Kawi 100 . . . Thunderbird, how 'bout you take this sweet little Honda 50?"

The 50 was the smallest of the three, just Timothy's size.

"You ever ride one of these before?" Dwayne asked.

Timothy had to admit that he hadn't.

"No problem, I'm gonna give you a quick lesson . . . "

Hopping on his Yamaha 175, Dwayne went through the process of starting it up while explaining it to Timothy in real time.

A whole litany of new terminology was spilling out of Dwayne's mouth. Gas line, ignition, clutch, neutral, gearshift . . . the list went on and on, culminating with Dwayne executing a single deft hop, kickstarting the 175 on the first try. It was instantly so loud that Timothy could barely hear a thing.

"You think you got it?" Dwayne yelled over the noise of the Yamaha.

"Uh, I think so," Timothy called out. He dared not ask for a repeat but, in fact, he didn't understand a thing.

"Okay, hop on."

Timothy mounted the 50. Dwayne left his Yamaha running so he could walk Timothy through it.

"Okay, start by opening up your gas line."

"Gas what?"

"That switch there below your seat . . . that's right . . . now turn the key to start . . . yep . . . now put it into neutral . . ."

Timothy was totally lost.

"That little lever there by your left foot, it's in first now, kick it down to neutral . . . no, squeeze your clutch first, with your left hand, squeeze your clutch . . ."

Timothy did exactly what Dwayne was telling him and, even though it made no sense to him, the process was moving along.

"Okay, now you're ready to kick start it, do it . . ."

With all his weight, Timothy tried the kick starter several times, but just couldn't get it to turn over.

"That's okay, it's probably cold, I'll get it started for you."

Dwayne took Timothy's place, got the Honda started on the first try, then hopped off so Timothy could get back on.

Charles, meanwhile, had had no trouble starting the Kawasaki 100 and was already riding in concentric circles around the dirt patch that functioned as Dwayne's front lawn.

"Okay, squeeze the clutch," Dwayne said to Timothy, resuming the instruction. "Put it in first, yeah, now ease off the clutch and give her just a little bit of gas . . ."

Still not understanding how this thing worked in the slightest, Timothy popped the clutch, immediately causing the Honda to pop a wheelie and spring forward so quickly he didn't have time to think about steering.

Two seconds later, Timothy slammed into the side of Dwayne's trailer, at which point the Honda stalled out and fell over with Timothy still on it, pinning his right leg underneath.

"I said let it out *slowly*, Jeeeesus," Dwayne said, "you ruined our trailer!"

True, Timothy had just put a dent in the side of the trailer, but Dwayne was cracking up, because the trailer already had more dents than a half-price can of SpaghettiOs.

"Don't worry, Thunderbird," Dwayne said, helping to lift the bike off Timothy's leg. "I did the same thing first time I got on a bike. C'mon, let's try again."

In a most brotherly fashion, Dwayne proceeded to walk Timothy through the entire process yet again. This time, Timothy managed not to pop the clutch and, before he knew it, he was chugging around the dirt patch just like Charles.

The smell of oil and gasoline coming off the three dirt bikes filled the air as Dwayne commenced to lead Charles and Timothy back toward the quarry, where they skirted the outer edge of the chainlink fence. It was brambly in places, but there was a clear dirt trail that Dwayne and his pals had obviously been keeping well-worn for years.

Dwayne had told Timothy not to "ride the clutch," which is exactly what Timothy was more-or-less doing, constantly, but he figured this was better than stalling out again.

They came to a stop at a place where the fence had obviously been reinforced recently.

"Hah," Dwayne said, pointing at the patch in the fence. "They keep trying to keep me out, I keep cutting my way back in."

Using the bolt cutters he had bungeed to his mud flap, Dwayne cut a slit into the chain link and peeled it back just enough to squeeze through on his Yamaha. Charles and Timothy exchanged one last cautious glance, then followed Dwayne through the opening and onto private property.

Coming out of the trees atop a sheer rock ledge, the quarry opened up before them. It was a lot bigger than Timothy had even imagined. Part of the terrain down below was flat, open, and dry. The other half was entirely covered in still water, like a giant reflecting pool.

They continued slowly along the top of the ledge until coming to a steep ramp that led down to the quarry floor.

Suddenly letting out a crazy "Wheeooooooo!" Dwayne went full throttle down the ramp then out across the dry half of the quarry floor, leaving a trail of dust in his wake. He rode like a wild man.

"C'mon, let's have some fun," Charles said, then followed suit, likewise taking off like a jackrabbit.

Easing off the clutch, Timothy cautiously made his way down the ramp. He'd heard Dwayne and Charles getting their bikes up to third or maybe even fourth, that's how they were able to race around at such impressive speeds.

Timothy considered trying to shift up to second, but was nervous about attempting anything beyond what had worked so far, so instead he just kept it in first and cranked the throttle.

The Honda 50 complained mightily, begging for Timothy to either shift or ease up on the throttle, but Timothy just kept at it, now on level ground and achieving a high speed of approximately

18 mph, nowhere near what the little speedometer indicated the Honda was capable of, but certainly faster than he was used to going on his banana saddle.

After further displaying his mastery by doing a few donuts and riding a wheelie for a good 50 yards or so, Dwayne rode his Yammy to the water's edge, where he stopped and waved for Charles and Timothy to join him, which they did.

Timothy carefully put the Honda back in neutral, so he was able to let go of the clutch without it stalling out.

"What'd they used to mine here anyway?" Charles asked Dwayne, over the noise of the idling motorbikes.

"Bluestone," Dwayne said. "My pop used to work here. His pop too. Fucking Portland cement, nobody wants bluestone anymore."

This, Timothy thought, began to explain how a place of such epic proportions with so much rock left in it could be left abandoned like this. He looked up at the steep and impressive shale cliffs that seemed such a force of nature. He tried to imagine generations of men, strong as the stone itself, chiseling away, year after year.

"Get a look at this," Dwayne said, pointing into the water.

At first, Timothy saw nothing in the water but the beautiful reflection of a spring afternoon sky. Then, refocusing his eyes, he saw a single barrel floating just under the surface. And then a second barrel, then a third, and then he lost count.

Everywhere he looked, there were submerged barrels as far as the eye could see. The entire quarry was filled with them.

"Holy shit," Charles said, "IPM put these here?"

"They're using it as a freaking dump," Dwayne said.

"Timothy, you getting pictures of this?" Charles asked.

"You want some *real* pictures?" Dwayne said. "Follow me."

Getting back on the dirt bikes, they rode along the water's edge until they came to where it flooded out into the woods at the northern edge of the property. Here the barrels were even more crammed together, and a green ooze could be seen seeping out of them and making its way directly into the brook.

"This is disgusting," Charles said. Dwayne nodded his head in agreement.

Dismounting carefully, Timothy had to get his shoes wet, stepping into the marsh to get close enough, but he made sure to get clear snapshots of where the gunk was coming from and where it was going.

Flashing back to that first day they saw that wispy bit of green foam in the stream, he almost couldn't believe he was actually here seeing this up close.

Dwayne, who was cranking his head around the whole time keeping watch said:

"Oh shit, they're here early . . . they usually don't come till 4:30."

In the distance, a truck was pulling into the quarry.

"They catch us over here they'll call the cops for sure," Dwayne said, "my old man'll have my ass, come on."

Jumping on the bikes, Dwayne and Charles took off immediately and, in no time, were speeding back across the quarry.

Timothy, worried that in a panic he'd stall the Honda and be stuck here, went extra slowly easing it into first just to get it rolling. As before, he red-lined the bike in first gear, the little engine screaming at him, but it just wasn't fast enough.

Up ahead, Dwayne and Charles were on their way up the ramp and in moments would be out of sight. Timothy was going to be out here alone. He'd be the only one to get caught.

"Shit, okay, just do this," he said to himself.

When he squeezed the clutch, the Honda started coasting and losing speed while Timothy summoned the courage to use his left foot to kick it up one. He tenuously let loose the clutch again and, as it shifted into second, the bike beneath him took off, and suddenly he began covering some ground.

Daring to repeat the process, he managed to get it into 3rd and was now really moving. The wind was making his eyes tear, but he squinted and just kept going.

Reaching the bottom of the ramp, he started ascending at a good clip. Then, halfway up the steep incline, the Honda started struggling, wanting him to downshift, but Timothy just kept it in third, beginning to slow substantially but, finally, making it safely behind the cover of trees, just in time to avoid being seen.

Squeezing the clutch and braking simultaneously, he barely managed to stop before bumping into Dwayne and Charles, who were there waiting for him.

"Nice one," Charles said.

Dwayne looked down and saw Timothy's foot was shaking.

"Okay, just kick it down into neutral . . . there you go, now you can let go that clutch . . . alright, good job little buddy."

Dwayne gave Timothy's cheek a clap in a brotherly kind of way.

Leaving the bikes for the moment, they went to the edge of the trees where they could peek out and watch as the otherwise innocuous-looking delivery truck pulled up to the water's edge.

The truck was clearly marked IPM.

"Take some pictures," Charles said.

Timothy took his Instamatic back out and tried pointing it. When Charles looked at him, he realized that Timothy's hands, like his feet, were still shaking from having been holding on to the rattling motor bike for dear life.

"Here, let me get these," Charles said, taking the camera.

Charles crept a little closer and, with a steady hand, took several shots as two guys in coveralls used dollies to unload several barrels, which they rolled straight into the water. They took poles from their truck and poked at the barrels in a well-practiced way until they were completely submerged.

"Damn, will you look at that," Charles said in disbelief. "They been doing that every week?"

"Yep," Dwayne said, "s'why I usually don't even bother coming over here on Thursdays, but for you gentlemen I made an exception."

They continued watching as the men got casually back into their truck like they'd just been delivering bread. They turned it around and drove back toward the gate.

Dwayne spat on the ground and shook his head at the sorrowful sight they'd just witnessed.

"So, Charles," he said, "you guys think you're gonna be able to do something to get'm to clean up that mess?"

"We aim to try," Charles said.

Dwayne wiped his face with the back of his hand.

"That'd be a good thing," he said.

Getting back on the dirt bikes, they angled them out through the slit in the fence Dwayne had cut, then made their way the short distance back to his trailer where they said their fond farewells.

Having tasted speed, Timothy now knew in his bones he'd make it back into Kingston a lot quicker on a Honda 50.

But on the whole, he was relieved to climb back onto his banana saddle.

CHAPTER 14

When Timothy rolled up to the FotoMat, he was no longer distracted by thoughts of secret bathrooms.

"These photos are incredibly important," he said to the gal in the blue and yellow smock.

"I understand," she said.

That is, she understood that all photos were incredibly important. Or at least that all customers thought that they were. She did not, of course, understand that, as far as Timothy was concerned, the ecosystem of Kingston hung in the balance.

"Did you say last time I could get doubles?" he asked her.

"Decided you'd like to share?"

"I might need back ups."

"Always a good idea," she agreed.

She took the film cartridge from him with all the seriousness befitting a hand-off as important as this one.

"Last name was Miller?" she asked.

"Yes, how did you remember?"

"You're a memorable customer."

Timothy tried to read her expression, wondering if she were some sort of IPM spy. Though it was odd that someone should find him memorable, he decided she most likely was not a spy. But if you wanted to spy on people in general, the FotoMat would probably be an excellent place to start.

"Do you need my fifty cents off coupon now?" he asked her

"No, you can give that to me when you pick up your prints."

"Okay then."

"See you in two days."

The photos, along with the water test results, were the single most important pieces of evidence on which Timothy and Charles would prosecute their case, but to seal the deal they needed to find some concrete information connecting the chemicals found in the brook with what was being produced at the IPM plant.

The Kingston Area Library on Broadway seemed a good place to start.

Broadway was another one of those streets along which Timothy had been driven countless times in his mom's car, but this was the first bicycle exploration. It felt more city-like, with countless lunch counters, appliance stores, garages, and four lanes of traffic. He and Charles thought it safest to pedal slowly along the sidewalk rather than mix it up with passing vehicles.

Heading into midtown, they passed a new cast of characters, different from the ones Timothy was familiar with uptown. There was a cigar-chomping man wearing a fedora. A woman carrying an umbrella to keep the sun off her face, even though it wasn't a particularly hot day.

There also seemed to be more black people in this neighborhood.

Just ahead, three black kids in particular appeared to fan out on purpose, to make it harder for Timothy and Charles to get passed. To Timothy, they looked kind of tough.

"It's okay, I know these guys," Charles said, "I go to school with them."

When they came up against the blockade, Charles and Timothy had to stop.

"What's up guys?" Charles said with a smile.

The three kids, who were all about Charles' age, looked incredulously at Charles and the little white kid on the banana saddle bicycle he was hanging out with.

"What's up . . . Oreo," the biggest kid said, which made all three of them start busting up with laughter.

The three boys, still laughing, stepped aside to let Charles and Timothy proceed. After they'd passed, the boys called out "Oreo!" again and continued laughing their way up Broadway.

They'd been riding single file, but Timothy rolled up parallel to Charles so he could talk with him.

"Why'd they call you that?" he asked.

"Never mind," Charles said, seemingly taking it in stride. "I've been called worse than that, I can assure you."

"But what does *Oreo* mean?"

"Chocolate on the outside, vanilla on the inside. I'll explain later," Charles said, he pulled ahead and left it at that.

About a block later, Charles looked behind and turned around when he realized Timothy had stopped for some reason.

Timothy was sitting there on his bicycle, staring at a building.

"This is the place," he said.

"What place?"

"The place that Ken got beat up."

"Oh, that's right," Charles said, seeing the buzzing neon *Oriole Tavern* sign in the darkened front window.

Timothy had had a vague idea that the bar was somewhere along Broadway, but this was the first time he'd come face-to-face with the place.

It was still afternoon, but the door was wide open for business, and the smell of alcohol was radiating out into the street. There were already people in there drinking.

"C'mon," Charles said, breaking Timothy's distant gaze, "we gotta keep moving if we're gonna get to the library on time."

In addition to their stated goal, there was a lot more to look at. On the other side of the train underpass was what had once been the grand municipal center of the city, now fading fast since attention was shifting to the suburbs.

The old post office had been knocked down when they'd built a new one, but the old bus station remained, sitting empty since a new one had been constructed uptown. Even the once-stately City Hall was boarded up, its offices relocated to a more modern building.

There was one old municipal building that had successfully found a second life and appeared to be well-maintained. Charles stopped his bike in front of the old armory to pat the newly placed bronze sign that read:

Lt. Charles Lambeau Neighborhood Youth Center

"That's my dad," he said proudly, spending a dreamy moment to look upward as if his dad were looking down on him right then and there, perhaps equally proud that his son was already following in his footsteps.

"You wanna go in?" Timothy asked.

"That's okay, we'll go in some other time," Charles said, then his tone became cautionary. "Now look, we're coming up on the High School . . . when we ride past, don't stop, just keep going, okay?"

"How come?"

"Just do it."

Kingston High School took up an entire city block and looked like a public high school right out of the movies. To Charles, this place was as big and intimidating as Bailey Jr. High School was to Timothy.

Running the length of the property, dividing the high school's sprawling front lawn from the city sidewalk, was The Wall, a notorious smoking hangout for generations. Timothy and Charles soon found themselves running a gauntlet of secondhand smoke, and various configurations of indolent high schoolers, spreading out across the sidewalk.

The same smoke that was repellent to Charles was strangely enticing to Timothy. He unconsciously slowed to a stop in front of a particularly intriguing circle of glassy-eyed teens who all seemed to be sharing the same lumpy-looking cigarette. It smelled like a skunk.

"You want a hit?" one of them asked Timothy, a comment which caused the one currently smoking to burst out coughing and laughing at the same time, blowing an overwhelming puff of heady smoke directly into Timothy's face.

"Come on," Charles said, doubling back to pull Timothy by the shirt sleeve to keep him moving.

When finally they reached the end of The Wall, they emerged as if from the mists, having finally arrived at their destination.

★ ★ ★

The Kingston Library was actually two libraries.

The children's library was in an old Victorian mansion that'd been donated to the city. Timothy had been taken there for many a story hour by his mom earlier in childhood. Charles had been taken there a lot by his own mother, too, but neither of them had really been inside the other building much.

The Carnegie Library, for adults, stood next door. It maintained a classic look, even if a bit worn around the edges. It was this library building that might have what they were looking for, if only they could find it. They chained their bikes up and went inside.

Timothy, a bit woozy from whatever that guy had exhaled into his face, took a moment to get his bearings.

He was surprised to find it pretty much empty. He thought all libraries had child-friendly, colorful posters saying things like, "READ!" but this was quite the opposite, it was basically colorless and dimly lit. It had a morgue-like quiet about it beyond the absence of voices, like the stacks were filled with dead bodies instead of books.

Heading toward the reference desk in the back, they passed five times as many card catalogues as were in Timothy's school library. This was the Big League.

"The Children's Library is next door," the librarian said to them, barely looking up.

"We're not looking for the Children's Library, ma'am," Charles said. "We need the Library Library."

Timothy snickered slightly, something about the way Charles said Library Library was funny. The librarian, meanwhile, was not amused. Unlike Mrs. Stein at Timothy's school, this librarian was not much interested in helping two kids who, she assumed, were just messing around.

"May I ask what it is you're looking for?"

"We'd like some information about water pollution," Charles said.

"Water pollution . . ." she repeated, her voice trailing off, like the unexpected seriousness of their query was echoing around her head, looking for a place to land. Slowly, she was roused into action.

She came out from behind her desk and led them over to the periodicals.

"We just started getting a magazine called *Ecology Now*. I suggest you start here."

She took the current issue along with a single back issue, laid them out on a reading desk for them, and returned to her librarian duties.

Charles and Timothy took one magazine each and began pouring over them.

Well, Charles was pouring over his. Timothy was more like zoning out looking at beautiful nature photos from national parks. Nice colors, he thought. Then he remembered that this was not what he was looking for, and kept turning pages.

Soon, he came to pictures that were not as pretty. Pictures of erosion, forest fires and . . . a polluted beach with some kind of sludge all over it. Looked promising. Timothy began to read that article in particular. And then, he found something.

"Look here, look here!" he said to Charles excitedly.

"Shhhh," the librarian scolded from her desk, even though there still wasn't anyone in the library except for them.

"Whaddah you got?" Charles whispered.

Timothy pointed to a line in the article and quietly read aloud:

"*The Clean Water Act of 1972 prohibits the discharging of pollutants into US waters without an NPDES permit.*"

"What's an NPDES permit?" Charles said.

"I don't know," Timothy said, "but it's about water pollution!"

They continued to read through the article together. They learned that NPDES stood for National Pollutant Discharge Elimination System. To their great surprise, they also learned that polluting the water wasn't necessarily illegal.

"Wait a minute," Charles said incredulously, "so all IPM had to do was get one of these permits and then they can just dump shit into the water and there's nothing you can do about it?"

Timothy scanned ahead and pointed to another sentence.

"Right here, it says: *If a facility in your area has applied to get an NPDES permit, that company by law must provide notice in the legal section of a major local newspaper.* Why don't we check the legal section?"

This was all unbelievable, but at least it gave them a starting point for further inquiry. Carrying the magazine with them, they returned to the reference desk.

"Ma'am, how do we check the legal section of the *Daily Freeman?*" Charles asked respectfully.

"We keep hardcopies of the *Freeman* on file for one year, before that you'd have to look through the microfiche. Do you know which date you're looking for?"

"Uh, not really."

"Well, we don't categorize the legal section by subject, only by date. You just have to go through all the newspapers one at a time."

"ALL the newspapers?"

This would obviously take forever. But when the librarian saw the boys' faces falling at the impossibility of the task before them, she began to soften. She was pretty convinced by now they weren't here to fool around, even if they didn't know what they were doing.

"May I ask specifically what you are looking for?"

Charles looked at Timothy for permission to proceed, Timothy nodded, so Charles spoke carefully, trying not to give too much away.

"Well, let's just say we read that this Clean Water Act requires local . . . companies . . . to make certain announcements in the local paper," Charles said.

"If they're applying for a permit to dump stuff in the water," Timothy filled in.

"I see," said the librarian. "Give me a second."

Behind the desk were all sorts of official-looking books on a big shelf, books that were so important they didn't even usually let normal people look at them. She took one particularly heavy book off the shelf and began to flip through it purposefully, using her index finger to scan the fine print.

"Okay," she said, "the Clean Water Act took effect on October 18th, 1972 . . . so I would suggest using that date as a starting point and going from there."

She went over to special cabinets that looked like the card catalogs but with wider drawers. Producing a small canister containing a spool of film, she led them over to an odd viewing machine.

"Do you know how to use this?" she asked while threading the film for them.

The machine appeared to be some sort of slide projector with a viewing screen, pretty cool because you got to advance the film using hand cranks, but it looked like it could only display one page at a time.

Left to begin their search, Timothy and Charles quickly figured out that you didn't have to read the whole paper, you could scroll quickly to the legal section on any particular day. The downside was that the print on a single legal page was so small, with language so alien to them, it still seemed like it would take a million years, even with a logical starting date.

With the afternoon ticking away, the level of frustration went up a notch with each fruitless attempt at reading another daily legal section. How many old papers would they have to scroll through like this?

But, it turned out, the librarian's guess was right on target. There, on October 25th, just seven days after the law took effect, they came upon a small notice:

Pursuant to US Code 1251, International Photocopy Machines hereby gives notice of application for NPDES permit regarding the hydraulic discharge of production related byproducts.

The language was so fuzzy it almost didn't make sense, but this appeared to be it, hiding in plain sight. This was the moment IPM whispered to the world they planned to dump something into the water. Or maybe that they already had.

"Can we get a copy of this page?" Charles asked the librarian.

"It will be 25 cents," the librarian cautioned. Twenty five cents was five times the price of a normal copy at the library, and two and a half times the price of a candy bar.

"We'll pay it."

The librarian had to press a few buttons, it was a little more complicated than running a standard copy machine, but in a few moments, on shiny paper, a copy of the legal section came curling out of the back of the microfiche machine.

The librarian looked at the copy before handing it to them. Based on their earlier questions, she took an educated guess.

"Is this the legal notice you were looking for?" she asked, pointing at IPM's listing.

"Yes ma'am," Charles said hesitantly.

"This is very interesting . . . I had no idea . . . how did you think to look for this?"

"We're doing a little research project," Timothy offered.

"Well, this is very good work you're doing, boys," she said. "What's your next step?"

"I guess, to find out whether they got the permit or not?" Charles speculated.

"Yes, that would be good to know, wouldn't it."

Timothy and Charles said nothing further at first. Every bit of progress, it seemed, led to another potential dead end.

"Do you know how to find out?" Timothy finally asked.

The librarian tapped the eraser of the pencil she was holding against her thin lips.

"Give me a minute," she said

The boys followed her back to the research desk, where she was looking at the big book again.

"This is a summary of the US Code which we keep on file," she explained. "It doesn't go too deeply into specifics, but it does say that under the Clean Water Act the federal government maintains compliance history available to the general public . . . let me check one other place . . ."

She retrieved yet another formidable-looking book.

"This is a directory of federal phone numbers," she said. "And . . . you're in luck, there's a hotline for questions about NPDES permits . . ."

She copied the number onto a scrap of paper and slid it across the counter. The boys stood looking at the number with its DC area code as if it were in cuneiform.

"Would you like me to try calling the hotline for you?" the librarian offered.

Charles weighed the risk of saying too much against the merits of having a professional-sounding adult offering to make an important phone call on their behalf.

"This is a highly sensitive subject," he said.

"You can count on my discretion, I assure you."

Charles again looked to Timothy, who was obviously also not feeling equipped to make a consequential phone call to the nation's capital himself.

"We'd appreciate that, ma'am," Charles said.

The librarian dialed the number.

"Hello? Yes, this is Phyllis Ackerman at the Kingston Area Library in Kingston, New York? I have a question about an NPDES request made by International Photocopy Machines here in Kingston . . . Yes, the date would've been October 25, 1972 . . . Yes, I can hold . . ."

While whoever was on the other end of the line was finding the particular file in question, the librarian expertly cradled the receiver between ear and raised shoulder while taking the moment to continue doing whatever work needed doing on her desk.

"Yes?" she said, when the DC person began speaking again. "Okay . . . I see . . . oh, that's very interesting . . ."

The librarian was jotting down notes as fast as she could.

"Yes . . . yes, thank you very much, I would like a printed copy, can you please send it to . . ."

She turned to Charles and Timothy, holding her hand over the receiver.

"Is there an address you'd like the information mailed to?" she asked them.

Charles leaned forward and told her his name and address, line by line, which she in turn relayed to the person in Washington.

"You have that?" the librarian confirmed, then closed with, "thank you so much, yes, you've been most helpful."

After hanging up the telephone, she turned to Charles and Timothy, a fully changed personality, having herself been educated in the process of helping them.

"So, thanks to the Freedom of Information Act," she said, enthusiastically, "you'll be receiving a copy of IPM's NPDES request, along with a detailed description of why the federal government rejected their request."

"They rejected it?" Charles said with surprise.

"They did. It seems IPM applied for a permit to dump production-related byproducts directly into the Esopus Creek, and was denied because the chemicals included benzene and toluene, which are known carcinogens."

This was amazing to both Charles and Timothy, an unexpected view into a world where huge entities run by adults seemed to crash into each other with full force.

"May we please have that piece of paper?" Charles asked.

"Yes, of course."

The librarian paper-clipped the notes to the copy of the legal section and passed it across the desk to them.

"Good luck with your project, boys," she added. "I'm sure a lot of people will be very interested to learn what you find . . ."

★   ★   ★

Bounding down the steps of the library into the late afternoon sun, there was a sense of triumph in their detective work, even if their findings looked more and more grim.

"So, IPM *knew* this stuff was bad, and they wanted to dump it anyway," Charles said.

"And when they couldn't dump it directly, they found another way to dump it anyway," Timothy said.

"I think the time has come to pull our report together, you want me to come by your house tomorrow?"

"It's still under construction."

"Man, you sure have a lot of construction going on at your house . . . okay, come up to mine."

Their bikes unlocked, they were just beginning to pedal their way up Broadway when a cop approached them. Timothy froze, thinking this was connected to their investigation. Obviously, the cops had been spying on them all along. Now that the case was coming together, they were going to come down on them.

"Hey," the cop said, to Charles in particular, "where'd you get that bike?"

Charles looked surprised, but remained respectful and succinct in his response.

"It was a present from my mother."

"Pretty nice present, who's your mother?"

"Mrs. Charles Lambeau," Charles said.

The cop did a double take.

"Oh, sorry Charley, my mistake, I didn't recognize you."

"Quite alright, Mr. McGrath," Charles replied, indicating he had recognized the officer all along, even though the officer hadn't recognized him.

"What are you doing in this neighborhood anyway?"

"We were doing research at the library."

"Oh, good for you . . . can I give you boys a lift home in the squad car?"

"We can make it just fine on our own, thank you."

"Okay . . . be safe."

"You too."

Charles and Timothy watched the cop get in his cruiser.

"You know him?" Timothy asked.

"I know most of the cops in this town," Charles said dryly, watching the cruiser drive off.

For the second time today, Timothy watched Charles remaining perfectly composed in the face of unfortunate dealings with other people, but he knew Charles well enough by now to sense this last exchange had rattled him. Maybe his lower lip was wavering, just a bit.

"You okay Charles?"

"Yeah, I'm fine," Charles said. "Let's just go home."

CHAPTER 15

FotoMat Girl wasn't there this time, instead, there was a slightly pudgy guy with a mustache. He looked managerial but nonetheless didn't seem to know what he was doing, trying to make sense of piles of envelopes. The booth was too small for him.

Timothy stood there for a minute while mustache guy ignored him. Finally, he rapped on the glass.

"Whaddah you want kid?" the guy said impatiently.

"I'm here to pick up my photos."

"Yeah, right."

Timothy held up his receipt. The guy took it, squinted at, then resentfully started rummaging through the envelopes to find Timothy's photos.

"Where's the girl who usually works here?"

"Melinda decided to call in sick today," the guy said, as if anyone decides to be sick.

Hmmm, her name was Melinda.

"Is she okay?" Timothy asked.

Mustache guy didn't bother to answer.

"You sure you dropped off your film at *this* FotoMat?" he said.

"What other one is there?"

"There's the one out on 9W."

"Why would I ride my bike out to 9W?"

9W was a business highway. How did a guy like this get to be a manager?

"Well, I don't know what to tell you kid, I'm not finding it."

Two thoughts crossed Timothy's mind:

One: FotoMat Girl really was a spy and was turning Timothy's photos of the evidence over to IPM at this very moment.

Two: FotoMat Girl was actually sick, the photos were there in the booth somewhere, and this guy was just too lame to bother doing his job to help a longhaired kid.

If it were scenario one, there was little Timothy could do. But if it were scenario two, he just had to figure out a way to push this meathead a little harder. The photos were simply too important to abandon, the investigation was riding on this.

"Look, see what it says here?" Timothy said, sticking the coupon the girl had given him in the guy's face.

"It says 50 cents off."

"No, up at the top, it says Preferred Customer . . . *I'm a Preferred Customer* . . . I come to this FotoMat all the time, and I have never had anyone lose my photos before."

A car pulled up behind Timothy's bike and gave an impatient honk. Mustache guy waved and called "Be right with you" to the car, then said to Timothy:

"Look, kid, I don't know what to tell you, come back tomorrow."

"I'm not going anywhere until you find my photos."

"Listen, you get your little ass out of here or I'm gonna call the police."

Did this guy actually threaten a 10 year old with a profanity? A month ago Timothy might have turned tail and gone home, but a lot had happened in the last month.

"I know half the police in this town," Timothy said, mimicking something Charles had said to him the day before. "You go ahead and call the police and we'll see what happens."

The guy's face actually turned red, his bluff having been called by a hippie kid, but damn it if the kid didn't have a freaking receipt. Like a tornado trapped in a phone booth, the guy tore through the piles of envelopes, making even more of a mess than he'd started with. Finally he held a single envelope in his hands.

"Double prints for Miller?" he asked, catching his breath.

"That's me," Timothy said.

The guy began ringing him up.

"I'll take a replacement roll for 69 cents please," Timothy added, "and don't forget the 50 cents off."

The guy went back and punched in the film plus the discount.

"With tax, that'll be 4.48," the guy said, emotionally spent at this point and just wanting to get this kid out of his hair.

"Okay, here you go," said Timothy, dumping his massive pile of change out on the FotoMat counter.

And this time, it was mostly pennies.

Not wanting to risk spilling these most valuable pieces of evidence onto the city streets and revealing them to prying eyes, Timothy waited until he got home to inspect the photographs.

He opened the envelope carefully . . . yes, here were the countless barrels floating beneath the surface, the toxic sludge seeping

into the brook and, distant but readable, the IPM truck with workers caught in the act of dumping the barrels into the water.

The photos had all come out, every last one.

He called Charles, and Charles' mom answered.

"Hello Mrs. Lambeau, this is Timothy, is Charles there?"

"Hi Timothy, Charles has a baseball game today, can I have him
call you tonight?"

"Yes please," he said, resisting the impulse to add "it's urgent."

When Timothy ducked upstairs to use the bathroom, he could
not help but notice the brand new toilet seat. It was a highly femi-
nine black-and-white collage of naked ladies, but not the good kind,
more like farty old statues from ancient Rome or some such thing.

It made him almost not want to use the toilet, but their house
had only the one bathroom, it's not like he could start boycotting.

When he went back downstairs, he found Cathryn in the living room, painting another window frame deep pink, an ongoing
project.

"What happened to the toilet seat?" he asked her.

"It was getting discolored so I replaced it. Do you like the new
one?"

His mom had stressed upon him the importance of not saying
anything if you didn't have something nice to say, but this was a
strenuous challenge.

"I think I liked the blue one better," he said.

He sat himself down at the dining room table to read the *Daily
Freeman*, and it was a good thing he did. In the local section, it
proved to be a banner news day:

Firstly, there was a prominent article about IPM's application
to the county to expand its facility. The article made it seem like

a win-win situation. More jobs, more tax money flowing into the county coffers. No mention, of course, about more pollution.

The only squirrelly thing was that IPM had apparently hinted they might choose to expand elsewhere in the state if anything happened to bog down the process, so there was considerable pressure on Kingston officials to red stamp everything quickly.

The other article that caught Timothy's attention was much smaller, almost hiding in plain sight. It seemed that Luke Grafton had done something called a plea bargain and had just been sentenced to three years, with eligibility for parole after just a single year.

He was to be transferred to Coxsackie tomorrow at 9am.

Luke Grafton was the one person who could say with utter certainty why he had done what he had done. And, as of tomorrow, Luke Grafton was literally being sent up the river. This would be Timothy and Charles' last chance to question him, if only they could figure out how . . .

Later, at dinner, Timothy's mom said:

"So, you don't like the new toilet seat?"

"It would not have been my first choice."

"Because there's a matching shower curtain we were thinking of getting."

"Are you trying to kill me?"

Timothy's mom allowed herself a small chuckle.

"I suppose we could go with the lavender," she said.

Lavender was not Timothy's favorite either, but it was a step up from dark pink.

"Please," he said.

He took another helping of tuna casserole.

Charles called shortly after supper, while Timothy was still clearing the table.

"I need to take this," Timothy said, stretching the tangled cord almost to the breaking point so he could speak in privacy on the back porch.

"We won, 3 to 2," Charles said.

"Won what?"

"Our baseball game."

"Oh, uh, that's good," Timothy said, happy for Charles, but wanting to cut to the chase.

"Do you play any organized sports, Timothy?"

"Not so much . . ."

"I think baseball would be good for you, I can help you with—"

"I got the photos," Timothy cut in.

"I was going to get to that," Charles said, "but you know, T-Bird, you do need a personal life outside of detective work."

Timothy didn't exactly know this, but he supposed it was something he could work on.

"So, did they come out?" Charles continued.

"They did, all of them."

"Fantastic."

"Did you read the paper today?" Timothy added excitedly.

"No, I just got home in time for dinner, then I called you."

"Go get it, the local section."

Timothy listened patiently as Charles hit some key phrases aloud while speed reading through the IPM article, particularly the part about the race to approve the expansion.

"We need to act now, before this thing gets approved," Charles said. "People need to know what's going on."

"But, we haven't finished the investigation yet," Timothy said.

"We've got photos, we've got water samples, we've got hard info from the Federal Government on its way, what more do we need?"

"I mean, we need to finish the *other* part of the investigation, the *Ken* part," Timothy said. "Read the article on the next page."

Again Timothy waited for Charles to read, but it didn't take long, this was a very short article.

"T-bird, I've been thinking about this," Charles said. "Do you know what objectivity means?"

"Something about objects?"

"Sort of . . . objectivity is the ability to put personal prejudices and opinions aside . . . it's one of the most important skills a detective must develop . . ."

"What does this have to do with the case?"

"Well . . . have you stopped to consider that maybe the reason you're linking the IPM dumping to Ken being killed is because you were friends with the guy?"

"I wasn't friends with him," Timothy said defensively, "I only talked to him the one time, when he told me about the chemicals."

"Then why are you so insistent that we tie Ken's murder in with this case?"

"Because without Ken, we wouldn't have a case," Timothy said.

The phone conversation went quiet for a moment.

"Okay Timothy . . . you want to come over to my house tomorrow and we'll take what we've got so far and try piecing it together?"

Timothy was relieved that Charles wasn't pushing to come over to his house, the girly toilet seat in particular still burned into his retinas.

"That sounds like a plan . . ."

When they got off the phone, happy as Timothy was that Charles' wasn't ruling out the murder case entirely, the article he'd read today still weighed on his mind. If Luke Grafton was being transferred to a state facility first thing in the morning, tomorrow afternoon might be too late.

Timothy went upstairs and retrieved one of the official school late passes he'd photocopied at his mom's office.

The details were hazy, but he began to hatch a plan.

CHAPTER 16

The following morning, Timothy left the house at the usual time. Except when he hit the corner of Wall Street, instead of heading toward school, he made a left toward the County Jail.

His neighbor Christy Vanderbeck happened to be walking to school at the same time.

"You're going the wrong way!" she called out.

"I'm going to the eye doctor on North Front Street," he called back.

Seemed a believable alibi, so long as the daisy chain of neighborhood chitchat didn't wind its way back to his mom.

Purposely skipping school, even for an hour or so, was not something he'd dared do before. Somehow Crazy Carl managed to do it and lived to tell the tale. Then again, Crazy Carl had stayed back once. Or twice. Might be a connection there. Still, Timothy didn't intend to make a habit of it.

To make himself look older and less like himself, Timothy donned his mom's old reading glasses as a disguise. He also used an actual comb to part his hair over to one side and patted it down as flat as he could. He barely recognized himself.

He repeated his alibi to himself as he walked along, just in case anyone should stop him and ask where he was going:

"I'm going to the eye doctor on North Front Street. My mother is meeting me there. We do this type of thing all the time, she works, you know."

Key Man, the guy from the Green Apartment Building with all the keys, walked right past him without saying anything. This was not a surprise since Key Man, to the best of Timothy's knowledge, had never even noticed him.

Or maybe he had? Maybe Key Man had secretly given Timothy a similarly obvious nickname, like Long Hair Boy, and just went about his business? How would you ever know?

Timothy checked his Timex, which he'd given an extra long wind especially for the occasion. The transfer wasn't until 9 and it was just about 8. Where to go?

Ducking to Green Street to get off Wall Street, Timothy caught sight of Tannery Brook behind one of the old stone houses. He realized he didn't really know where the stream led in *this* direction either.

The old houses on this street were pretty much all converted to offices or apartments. One apartment building had a doublewide driveway that looked particularly safe to investigate, so he ducked down it. A window slammed open as he passed.

"I told you to stay outta my garbage!" a shirtless guy yelled at him with crazy eyes.

"Uh, I'm not going in your garbage," Timothy said, "I'm just looking at the brook."

"Yeah, well, just stay the hell outta my garbage!"

The guy slammed the window closed.

Uh, okay then . . .

If Timothy turned tail now, it would seem an admission of guilt
that he had, in fact, intended to rummage through crazy guy's garbage, so he eyed the brook quickly then stuck to the street after
that. One close call was enough. He could more-or-less tell where
the brook was going anyway, at least until Lucas Avenue, at which
point it disappeared into a culvert.

With a bit of time left to kill, Timothy continued to follow what
he imagined was the brook's path to the shopping plaza. There,
tucked away behind the loading docks at Sears, Timothy came upon
the Esopus Creek.

He pocketed the reading glasses so he wouldn't stumble into the
creek as he descended its banks. It was here that he found a drainage pipe unceremoniously dumping the neighborhood brook into
the creek like it was just excess rainwater after a storm.

It was here that he also found Crazy Carl, skipping stones into
the Esopus.

Crazy Carl looked up, surprised to see Timothy.

"What're you doing here?" he asked Timothy.

It'd be a lot cooler to say he was just skipping school, but a devi-
ation might complicate matters, so he stuck with his alibi.

"I'm going to the eye doctor."

"Oh," Carl said, and didn't ask any further questions.

"What're *you* doing here? Timothy asked.

"This is my secret spot. Nobody bothers me here."

Carl had a slight bruise on the side of his head, like someone had
clocked him recently, but Timothy thought it best not to mention it.

Carl invited Timothy to sit on the log beside him, and Timothy
took him up on it.

"If you look close, you can see the fish swimming in the creek," Carl said.

"I think I see one right there," Timothy said.

The two of them continued to sit there, listening to the creek, looking for fish.

"Sometimes I think about how this creek leads to the Hudson," Carl said, "and the Hudson leads down to the ocean, and the ocean leads everywhere . . ."

Man, Crazy Carl was deeper than Timothy had thought. Timothy himself had been thinking about Tannery Brook a lot lately, but not how it connected to the whole world.

The Hudson was on Timothy's mental map because he swam in it, and liked to pretend the triangular rocks he found at Kingston Point were Indian arrowheads. But he had never really contemplated the Esopus much, and here it was, just blocks from his house, hiding behind the shopping plaza.

It had a lazy quality to it, but a quiet strength. It was probably the forgotten lifeblood of the original colonial settlement, now that he thought about it.

Above the gurgle of the Esopus, the Tannery Brook continued to trickle constantly from its drainage pipe, presumably feeding benzene and Lord knows what else to the fish they were looking at.

It's all connected, he thought.

After they'd sat there for a while, he checked his watch.

"Well, I guess I gotta go to that eye doctor appointment now."

"Okay, see ya," Carl said, exhibiting no intention whatsoever to motivate himself away from his log.

"See ya."

Timothy backtracked up to Wall Street and the older buildings with their stores, banks, and offices.

The County Jail was a formidable building located behind the old Court House. Timothy had only dared walk close to the jail a few times. An old stone building with bars on the windows, you could actually hear the prisoners inside sometimes, or at least the sound of the AM radios they listened to to pass the time.

Going right up to the jail while skipping school seemed like going into the belly of the beast. The sheer audacity would bolster his story, like, who would skip school and walk right up to the County Jail?

There was a single oversized spot in the parking lot behind the jail, the same bus was always parked there. It was a small bus, like the ones the special kids rode to school, except this one was painted white instead of yellow, and there were cages on the windows.

Timothy figured this would be the bus that would be taking Luke Grafton off to the state prison.

Alongside the jail parking lot was a separate parking lot for the bank next door. The bank parking lot had a bench with an ashtray beside it, the bank had installed it there so its employees had a place to take breaks outdoors during the warmer months.

Perching himself on this bench, Timothy had a perfect view of the route between the exit door of the jail and the small white bus.

Taking the newspaper he'd brought in his knapsack for this purpose, he held it over his face and pretended to read it, which was paradoxically impossible because the reading glasses were actually blurring his vision.

Peering over the paper, he saw Greg Hathaway and a gaggle of other suited lawyers from *Hathaway, Hathaway and Myers* talking importantly as they made their way across the parking lot. Timothy quickly pulled the paper high over his face again until they disappeared inside the court house.

He was then momentarily startled when a bank teller plopped down next to him on the bench and lit up a cigarette.

"Just sitting here reading the paper, waiting for my eye doctor appointment," Timothy offered by way of explanation before the guy even said anything.

"Sure," the teller said disinterestedly, not really caring about anything beyond his five minutes of personal freedom.

Timothy watched the guy smoking the cigarette out of the corner of his eye to see if he could pick up any pointers. The first inhalation seemed to be of particular importance. It was savored momentarily in the lungs. Then, tilting back the head, the first exhale was a long and slow one, accompanied by a slight whooshing sound through the teeth, as if tension from life's problems was leaving the body along with smoke.

The subsequent inhalations were less singular, more like punctuations of random glances made around the parking lot, looking at birds and passing cars and whatnot. The cigarette was held between index and middle fingers in general, expertly shifted to thumb and middle fingers occasionally so the index finger could be used to tap the ash into the tray.

The teller took one last definitive puff, stubbed out his freedom along with his cigarette, then went back into the bank.

Shortly after Timothy went back to pretending to read his blurry newspaper, the thick exit doors of the jail slowly opened, and out came two sheriff's deputies leading a solitary prisoner with hands cuffed behind him. It was only 8:50, good thing he got here early.

Timothy pushed the reading glasses down his nose so he could see clearly.

Based on his bold exchange with the FotoMat manager the day before, Timothy had thought perhaps he'd developed a magic ability to insert himself into other adult situations, that through sheer force of will he might be able to approach the scene and pop a quick question before Luke Grafton disappeared up the river.

But all it took was one look at the unyielding posture of these deputies, their sheer size, and the sidearms dangling from their holsters. There was *no way* Timothy was going anywhere near them. He shouldn't even be *here*, but here he was, so he continued to watch.

From this vantage point, he could just about see Grafton's face, which Timothy somehow had imagined would be bulging with a killer's venomous rage, that Grafton would be yanking this way and that, trying to bust loose.

But this wasn't what was happening at all.

The short parade was very quiet. Grafton's face appeared, if anything, rather sad and resigned. He was quite a bit smaller than the deputies who were leading him. He didn't pull at all, and neither did they.

As they unlocked the door of the little white bus, Grafton took one last look at the clear blue sky. Then they escorted him on.

The little bus started up, drove away, and that was that.

Whatever secrets Grafton held in his head would be locked away in a state prison 40 miles away. If Timothy and Charles were going to prove that he was somehow connected to IPM, they would have to find another way to do it.

The whole way back to school, Timothy repeated his slightly adjusted alibi in his head.

"I'm just coming back from the eye doctor, I'm just coming back from the eye doctor."

But no one stopped him. It was almost too easy to cut school.

Savoring his own last moment of freedom at the edge of the schoolyard, he stopped to get out his forged late pass. The original had had the imprint of Mrs. Hagen's writing on it, which he'd used as a model to meticulously fill out the bogus pass the night before, except for the time. Checking his watch, he now scribbled 9:15, then slipped in the side door and up the stairs to his classroom.

The room was quiet, devoid of students. Mrs. Brenner was alone at her desk, taking a little break, eating some kind of fruit cobbler she'd brought from home wrapped in tin foil. She wiped her mouth with a paper napkin as Timothy entered the room and approached her desk.

When he handed her the slip, she actually looked at it this time.

"Do you need glasses?" she asked.

"For what?"

"You just came from the eye doctor," she said, holding up the slip.

"Oh, just a routine check-up," Timothy said. She seemed to be buying it.

"You know," she said, reaching forward to tap the bridge of Timothy's nose, where his mother's old reading glasses had left a slight imprint, "wearing glasses is nothing to be ashamed of, if it helps you see the blackboard. I've been wearing eyeglasses since I was your age."

Timothy pictured a little Mrs. Brenner in 1940s clothing but with these same adult glasses she was now wearing as she looked at him.

"Okay," he agreed, though he didn't realize the glasses had made a temporary line on his nose and did not exactly know what she was talking about.

"Well, hurry downstairs now, you should still have twenty minutes of gym class," she said, as if Timothy was in danger of missing the best part of the day.

But the best part of the day had come and gone already.

It just didn't involve going to school.

CHAPTER 17

hen Timothy arrived at Charles' house later that day, he was practically bursting to tell of his adventure.

"It was just like a real stake out," he said, "I saw him with my own two eyes."

"Saw who?"

"Luke Grafton."

"Where did you see Luke Grafton?"

"Outside the County Jail."

"Okay, you need to slow down. Start at the beginning . . ."

Timothy proceeded to tell him everything. About finding how the brook flowed into the Esopus and ultimately to the ocean, about his clever disguise with the newspaper and glasses, about the towering deputies with their guns leading Luke Grafton away in cuffs.

"He was smaller than I thought he'd be, actually," Timothy said.

Charles looked at Timothy like he couldn't believe what he was hearing.

"Timothy, you skipped school to do this? Don't you know that's a oneway ticket to the inside of that jail?"

This wasn't the response Timothy was expecting.

"I thought I was helping the case," he said. "I thought you'd be . . ."

"Impressed?"

"Well, yeah, sort of."

Charles shook his head, his expression bordering between amusement and *What am I going to do with this boy?*

"Well, it was a daring maneuver, I'll give you that," Charles said. "So, solving this case is really that important to you?"

"Don't you think it's important?"

"I do but . . ."

Charles looked like he could go one way or the other, but appeared at least to be thinking it over.

"I'll tell you what . . ." he said, finally. "I've thought of a couple of leads we can follow . . . but if nothing materializes within the next two weeks, we need to go ahead with the IPM case before they get permission to expand the facility . . . can we agree on that?"

Timothy was impressed with the way Charles had cantilevered his argument, he hoped some day he'd be able to make a case like this.

"Yes," he agreed.

"And another thing, no more skipping school, you promise?"

Timothy thought about crossing his fingers. He still had two blank late passes in reserve and the first one had worked like a charm. Still, if he had to choose between role models, Charles was clearly a safer bet than Crazy Carl.

"Well, okay," he said.

Thus agreed, Timothy got out the photos and added them to the other materials they'd already acquired. It was an impressive array, anyone would have to take this seriously.

"I think it's time for some Thin Lizzy," Charles said.

Charles got out the *Jailbreak* LP and put it on his stereo.

Timothy held the album cover in his hands, its artwork depicting the band like superheroes trying to escape from an evil comic strip universe. The music was both crisp and grinding at the same time, rocking Charles' bedroom, with two guitars sometimes soaring next to each other. Timothy bopped his head, and Charles was glad to see that he liked it.

Charles let the whole first side play then, deciding Timothy needed a little more variety, played a few songs off Led Zeppelin III, then added the new Doobie Brothers and some Sly Stone for good measure.

The afternoon flew by, Timothy didn't want to leave, but he still had a bike ride ahead of him. With their investigation advancing and his heart pumping with music, he was heading toward the front door, when Charles' mom ducked into the hallway with a surprise invitation:

"Why don't you join us for supper, Timothy?" she offered.

"Oh, that's okay, I don't think my mom would let me . . ."

"You'll never know if you don't ask," Charles' mom said. "What's your number, why don't I give her a call?"

With Charles' encouragement, Timothy followed her into their kitchen, which had avocado green appliances with matching linoleum. The Lambeaus had a pushbutton phone that lit up when Charles' mom lifted it off the cradle. She punched the numbers quickly and effortlessly.

"What's your mother's name?"

He almost said Denny, like the women called her in Group.

"Denise," he said, and prayed that Cathryn wouldn't answer.

"Hello Denise? This is Carolyn Lambeau, your son Timothy is friends with my son Charles . . . no, nothing's wrong, the boys were just having such a nice afternoon together we thought it might be nice if Timothy stayed for supper . . . "

Timothy imagined his mom would say no because it was a school night, or for some other random reason, but amazingly, the conversation seemed to be going well.

After she hung up the phone Charles' mom turned to the boys.

"Charles, why don't you and Timothy wash up and set the table."

"My mom said *yes*?" Timothy asked.

"Yes," Charles' mom said, laughing that Timothy was so surprised. "I told her it would be no trouble to drive you home after supper."

Setting the table at Charles' house was a lot like back at his house, but different in subtle ways. At Charles' house they used cloth napkins. The glasses were more like goblets, and the silverware had a pewter look to it, like they'd acquired it recently to go with the recent craze for all things colonial.

Timothy began to put a place setting at the head of the table, the chair with the armrests, where he assumed Charles' mom would sit.

"No, my mom sits at the other end," Charles said, moving the place setting to the opposite end, leaving the chair with the armrests vacant.

When they sat down to dinner, they started by holding hands and saying a prayer, another thing they did not do at Timothy's house.

At first, holding hands with Charles and his mom seemed weird, touchy, Timothy's first inclination was to recoil. Yet when he felt the sincerity and commitment in both their grasps, he began to give into it, and it didn't feel so awkward.

"Thank you for bringing our new friend Timothy into our

home," Charles' mom said, "and for the meal and all the other benefits we enjoy."

Charles said, "Amen," so Timothy said it too.

Then, Charles' mom opened the lid of the casserole dish and revealed the most interesting sight: the chicken had *pineapple* on top of it.

"Timothy, may I serve you?"

"Yes please."

She then served Charles, and finally herself.

When Timothy dug into his supper, he could not believe the flavor. It was both sweet and salty at the same time, he'd never tried such a thing. He was almost squealing with delight.

"You like my mom's pineapple chicken, Timothy?" Charles asked.

"It's amazing," Timothy said.

Both Charles and his mom had to laugh at Timothy's enthusiasm, it was like watching someone who hadn't eaten in a week.

By and by, Charles' mom began to initiate a conversation.

"So, Timothy, Charles says you live right uptown?"

"Yes."

"It must be very convenient to be so close to the stores," she said, as if she really thought living in town was a positive thing instead of a negative.

"Yeah, you can pretty much walk to everything," Timothy agreed.

"And what does your father do for a living?"

"Um, my father left home a while ago," Timothy said. "We don't really know where he went."

"That must be hard," Charles' mom said sympathetically. "We can relate to not having a dad around here."

She nodded her head in the direction of the chair with the arm-rests at the opposite head of the table that remained empty.

"It's okay," Timothy said, "I guess you get used to it."

"Has your mother found someone else?"

Timothy paused for a moment before answering.

"No, she hasn't."

On one level, this didn't feel like a lie. As far as Timothy was concerned, the hole in his household created by his dad's absence was still a hole, whether Cathryn had moved in with them or not.

And yet, on another level, although he couldn't admit it to himself, it did feel like a lie.

"I'm sorry, I shouldn't have asked," Charles' mother said, sensing she'd touched a nerve.

"Mom," Charles said, instinctively changing the topic to diffuse the situation, "did you know Timothy knows everything about old stone houses?"

"He does?"

"Well, not everything," Timothy demurred.

"Don't be embarrassed, Timothy," Charles said, "Tell her about how President Van Buren lived right on Green Street."

He felt a little put on the spot, but Timothy was nonetheless touched to discover that Charles had been listening to him carefully and knew more about him than he thought he did.

"Actually, President Van Buren lived up in Kinderhook," Timothy said, "it was his uncle who lived on Green Street. But George Clinton lived there, and he was Vice President, on top of being Governor."

"Clinton was the Vice President?" Charles' mom said. "You know, I grew up in Kingston and somehow I never knew that."

"And George Washington visited the Old Dutch Church once," Timothy added, "but that was when he was still a General, he wasn't President yet."

Charles beamed with a sort of pride, watching Timothy step up and reveal his level of expertise.

"How wonderful to be surrounded by all that history during the Bicentennial," Charles' mom said, "it's like you're right in the middle of the action."

It had never occurred to Timothy that his neighborhood had so many advantages.

"Yeah . . . I was going to do my Bicentennial report on the stone houses, but my teacher wanted me to do the Boston Tea Party instead."

"Do you like the Boston Tea Party?"

"Not as much."

"Well, that seems like a wasted opportunity, doesn't it?"

Charles agreed.

Timothy appreciated their response, it was certainly a welcome contrast to what his own mom had said about how Mrs. Brenner was justified in wanting to push him to do something else.

When it came time for dessert, Charles' mom said, "I had pineapple left over and didn't know what to do with it, so I made pineapple upside down cake, I hope that's not too much pineapple."

Charles' mom was actually *apologizing* for making pineapple upside down cake? This was the best meal of Timothy's life!

After they cleared the table, Timothy was going to ride his bike home, but Charles' mom had promised Timothy's mom and insisted on driving. They had no trouble fitting Timothy's banana saddle in the way back of their station wagon. Timothy sat in the backseat, and Charles rode up front with his mom.

When they pulled down Warren Street, Timothy at first directed Charles' mom to drop him off in front of the Williams' house, the freshly painted one with the matching chairs on the front porch.

Then, up ahead, there was Timothy's mom standing in front of their house waving, like, *This is the place.*

While the moms introduced themselves to each other, Timothy's mom was using her well-practiced *I'm just a regular mom voice.* Through some miracle Cathryn had not come out of the house.

Charles, meanwhile, helped Timothy get his bike out of the back of the car.

"So, that's your house?" Charles said.

Charles was smiling as if the chipping paint, the messy porch and the beater car were somehow invisible or irrelevant.

But if Timothy knew one thing about Charles, it was that he was taking notice of everything.

CHAPTER 18

Rounding the corner after school the next day, Timothy found Warren Street alive with diesel engine noise. Mr. O'Connor's truck was running in front of his house, it looked like it was ready to roll.

Timothy craned his head to look inside the cab, hoping for a chance to try the CB radio or something, but Mr. O'Connor wasn't in there, he was just letting it warm up.

Timothy went inside his own house to grab a snack.

"Mr. O'Connor's truck is running," he announced to Cathryn.

"I noticed," she said.

The framed Georgia O'Keeffe print was actually vibrating against the wall.

Timothy found a rice cake and dumped a pile of sugar on top so it might resemble something like a cookie. Outside, the massive truck's horn blew.

He went running back outside, as did several other kids, and moms too. When Mr. O'Connor pulled out of town, it was a neighborhood event.

"Where you going, Mr. O'Connor?" Timothy yelled over the engine noise.

"Heading out west Timbo!" Mr. O'Connor called with a big smile on his face. "You take care of the street while I'm gone!"

"Will do, Mr. O'Connor!"

Mr. O'Connor put the truck into gear. As he eased it out of its parking space, the truck belched black smoke, which everyone had to fan from their faces with their hands.

He blasted the horn one last time, then waved his left hand out the open window as he drove off triumphantly to pick up his payload then head out to what Timothy imagined was the Wild West.

Everyone waved and called after him, including Mrs. O'Connor of course, who was left standing alone on her front porch.

"You need anything, you just let me know," Mrs. Vanderbeck called over to her as the smoke from Mr. O'Connor's truck began to dissipate.

"Oh, I'll be fine, thank you," Mrs. O'Connor said. "Maybe now I'll be able to get some sleep around here."

There was a neighborhood joke that Mr. O'Connor snored so loud that Mrs. O'Connor actually preferred it when he was gone, but everyone could only imagine how much she missed him, because they missed him too.

Timothy went back inside to finish his sugar-covered rice cake.

The investigation now had a looming two-week deadline, but Charles had baseball practice today, so there was not much that could be done.

He killed some time walking around the block to look at some of the old stone houses with renewed appreciation. He looked at his Timex. It was still only 4:15. What was he going to do with the rest of his free time?

★   ★   ★

Timothy had been looking forward to this particular experiment from the Real Men's Guidebook. It involved creating a small explosion to blow open a padlock.

Sitting at the desk in his room late in the afternoon, he cut the heads off a few dozen match sticks. He was in the process of pulverizing them into potassium chlorate powder when his mom knocked on his door.

"Can I talk with you a minute?"

Timothy covered the gunpowder-like substance with a piece of looseleaf paper.

"Sure, Mom."

She sat down on the bed, took brief note of whatever odd project Timothy was plotting out on his bulletin board, then got down to business.

"I got a phone call at work today from Mrs. Brenner."

"You did?"

"Something about you needing glasses to see the chalkboard?"

Oh shit. Was this where Timothy's alibi worked so well that it was going to wind up getting him busted anyway?

"I think she's calling everyone's mom about this."

"I don't think so, she was pretty specific."

"No, really, she called Brandon's mom, I think she called Steven's mom too."

Digging the hole deeper, would she bother calling other moms to check?

"She did?"

"Oh yeah, it's like a general thing."

Timothy's mom looked skeptically at him.

"You promise me you're not having trouble seeing the board?"

"I promise," he said, holding his hand up, like scout's honor.

"And if you do, you'll tell me so we can see about getting you glasses?"

"I will . . . I actually think it would be kind of cool to have glasses, if I actually needed them, but I don't."

This last line seemed to seal the deal. His mom nodded her head and rose from the bed. Taking a last look around the room as if she were looking for something in particular, she walked to the door.

"One other thing," she said, "have you seen the camera around?"

"The camera? Oh sure."

Timothy eagerly went into his bottom drawer and got it for her. Compared to getting busted for skipping school, admitting he'd borrowed the camera seemed like nothing.

She looked at the blank window on the back of the camera when he handed it to her, and shook it to confirm that it was empty.

"There was film in this camera, what did you do with it?"

Her voice was suddenly more concerned than when she'd been talking about the phone call from Timothy's teacher.

"I had it developed," Timothy said. He reached back into his drawer and handed her the FotoMat envelope.

She opened the envelope brusquely.

"Timothy, this film was not yours to play around with," she said, almost angrily.

She flipped quickly past the first several photos, the ones of her and Timothy on Lake George. When she came to the pictures of her and Cathryn she seemed to breathe a sigh of relief. She smiled as she looked at them, then, holding them up, her voice turned serious again.

"These photos are very important to me," she said.

If she'd been holding their vacation photos, or even the one Halloween photo of her and Cathryn and Timothy, he would have agreed and apologized profusely.

But she was only holding up the photos of her and Cathryn.

He found himself growing angry.

"Why are those ones so damn important?"

"Don't curse at your mother."

"Tell me," he repeated, "what makes those ones so important?"

"If you must know, it's because this was the weekend that Cathryn and I decided that we would be together."

Really? This was more important than the vacation she took with her own son?

"Okay, so Cathryn moved in with us," Timothy said, "why do you have to make such a big deal about it? She's just your roommate."

"She is not just my roommate, Timothy," she said, now speaking as angrily as he was. "She's my partner, we are a *couple* whether you want to accept it or not, and you'd better start welcoming her into this house like she's a member of this family or there will be hell to pay."

Timothy pushed past her, marched down the hallway and flew down the stairwell.

"You get back here, mister," she called after him.

"I'll go where I want," he said, slamming the front door behind him and hitting the street.

★ ★ ★

The schoolyard was empty.

It was suppertime and everyone was at home with their families, except for Timothy, who sat alone on the swing set at the edge of the parking lot, not swinging.

He wished he had a cigarette.

Why couldn't she have held up those photos of Lake George along with the other ones? He'd be home eating dinner right now if she had.

What the hell had happened between her and his dad? Why did he have to leave?

And why did life have to be so unfair?

Somewhere in the background he heard it. The unmistakable sound of a car in desperate need of a new muffler, slowly making its way into the school parking lot.

It came to a stop several feet away from the swing set and continued to sit there, idling.

At first, Timothy did not look up. But it soon became obvious that the car was not going anywhere, and that his solitary meditations, for now, were over.

He rose from the swing, walked over to the Calico Chrysler, opened the passenger door, and fell with some resignation into the front seat.

He didn't say anything and neither did his mom as they drove the three blocks back home.

"verything okay?" Charles asked Timothy.

"Yeah."

"Cause you seem a little down about something."

"Nah, everything's fine."

Charles let it go. He didn't like to be needled about stuff either.

They were pedaling down Broadway again, but not to the Kingston Library. This time, their destination was the Oriole Tavern.

There was no bike rack out front, who would ride a bike to the Oriole Tavern? The scraggly tree by the parking meters would have to suffice.

"Now, when we're inside, you let me do the talking," Charles instructed. "Your job is to keep your eyes and ears open, see what you can find out, got it?"

"Got it."

Staying quiet suited Timothy just fine. He'd never been inside a bar before, much less the Oriole. He had to remind himself that Ken hadn't actually died in this place, he'd gotten in a fight, but it was still enough to creep Timothy out.

Going from the afternoon sun into the bar was like entering a black hole. Aside from the neon beer signs, there barely seemed to be any light whatsoever. The smell of stale beer and cheap vodka nearly overwhelmed them, and the air was so thick with cigarette smoke it was hard to breathe.

"No kids in here," the bartender said, when he realized they weren't just midgets.

"We won't take but a minute of your time," Charles assured him, confidently slapping a brochure on the bar, "we're here representing the Youth Center and we're looking for sponsorships."

There were three or four guys in various states of inebriation sitting around the bar, they all seemed to find this amusing.

"Youth Center, huh?" the bartender said.

"Yes sir, we're going to have full-color banners going all the way around the basketball court featuring the names of all our sponsors. We've got commitments from over a dozen businesses already up and down Broadway."

Charles slid his calling card a little closer so the bartender would see it.

The bartender looked down at the card, then back up at Charles.

"You Charlie Lambeau's kid?"

"One and the same."

The bartender nodded slowly as this sunk in.

"I was real sorry when he passed, your pop was a good man."

"For a cop," the guy on the stool next to Charles said out of the side of his mouth.

"Hey, *I* was a cop," the bartender said to the guy. "Move over and make some room for my friends here."

Disgruntled, the guy slid his beer down two spaces, his butt eventually caught up.

Charles sidled onto his stool no problem, for Timothy it was more of a climb.

"You boys want a soda?"

"Don't mind if we do," Charles said. "This here's my friend Timothy, by the way."

"Timothy, Charles, good to know you. My name's Jack Flanagan."

Jack Flanagan filled two large plastic tumblers with ice, then used the soda gun to fill each one with Coca Cola, all the way to the top. Timothy watched intently as he slid the tumbler toward him across the worn formica.

He waited for Charles to take a sip, then joined right in. This was the single biggest glass of Coke he'd ever drank in his life. It was delicious.

Looking around as his eyes adjusted to the dim light, Timothy now saw that there were little tables alongside the wall with a few people sitting at them. The sole woman in the place looked strangely familiar, then he realized it was the prostitute from the Green Apartment Building. Sitting next to her at the small table was the guy he sometimes saw her walking with, the guy who yelled at her behind closed doors.

"Were you on the force with my dad?" Charles asked Jack Flanagan.

"He was coming in when I was going out, but I knew him a little . . . he was what we call natural police, real instinct for the job."

"You must've seen a lot in your time."

"That I did."

"You ever miss it?"

"Yeah," the disgruntled guy chimed in, "he misses it so much he keeps calling 'em to come visit us."

"That's not funny," said another guy at the far end of the bar, weighing in.

"No offense to your brother," the jokester said to the guy who'd snapped at him.

The offended guy had a reckless look about him beyond the fact that he was drinking. He squinted at the jokester like he had half a mind to grab him by the collar, then just shook his head like it wasn't worth it.

"Fuck face," he hissed.

"Easy Grafton," Jack Flanagan said to the guy, then to Charles and Timothy said, "You'll have to excuse us, it's been a little tense around here lately."

Timothy looked to Charles, who blinked once slowly to indicate he'd just heard the name Grafton too. They both listened attentively to see if more information would be forthcoming, but the room fell quiet.

Jack Flanagan took the opportunity to empty an overflowing ashtray, and do a little general clean-up with a bar rag.

Starting to wiggle atop his barstool from the infusion of Coca Cola, Timothy noticed out of the corner of his eye that the man sitting with the prostitute was standing up and adjusting himself before heading to the men's room.

"I'll be right back," he said to her.

As he disappeared into the back, the guy called Grafton seemed to sense an opportunity. Dismounting his barstool, he sauntered over to the prostitute. Timothy tried to watch without being obvious.

"Looking good today, Lynda," he said to her.

He reached for her, pushing her blouse open slightly. She slapped his hand away without saying anything.

"Heh, heh," Grafton said.

He sat down where the man had been and placed his hand on her knee. She allowed him to leave it there but didn't seem too happy about it.

The man came back from the bathroom faster than Grafton thought he would. He stood up quickly.

"I was just keeping Lynda here company," he said to the man.

"You got money Grafton?" the man asked quietly.

"Now, you know I don't get paid until Friday."

"Then keep your hands off the merchandise."

The man opened his jacket slightly. Whatever Grafton saw inside the jacket made him sober up quickly.

"Okay, take it easy, I was just being friendly."

The man said nothing further, waiting for Grafton to return to the bar before taking his seat again next to Lynda, the prostitute.

Timothy turned his attention back to the bar.

"So tell me again about this banner business," Jack Flanagan was asking Charles.

"It's $300 for a full-sized banner, 150 for a half-sized."

"What are the other bars on Broadway getting?"

Charles referred to his notes.

"The Anchor is getting a half-sized, and . . . looks like Smitty's is getting a full size."

"Smitty's getting a full size?"

"That's what it looks like."

Jack Flanagan mulled it over for a moment.

"Okay, tell you what, you can put us down for a full-size too."

"Thank you very much, Mr. Flanagan."

As Charles got the paperwork in order, the jokester made his way over to the jukebox, dropped a dime, and in a crackly voice, Hank Williams started whining about a tear in his beer.

"Not again, Jesus!" everyone groaned, to which the guy at the box laughed, like he'd tortured the small crowd with this song many, many times before.

When Timothy and Charles emerged from the bar, the sun seemed so bright it almost knocked them over. Their bikes, luckily, were still chained to the excuse for a tree.

Timothy could smell the odor of cigarette smoke still radiating off his own clothing. He'd have to figure a way to sneak into the house and change before his mom or Cathryn caught a whiff of him.

When they'd pedaled half a block or so, Timothy said to Charles, "Lucky coincidence that guy used to be a cop."

"That was no coincidence. I knew before we went in there."

"How?"

"I just know these things," Charles said with a sly smile.

Timothy smiled too. Just when he thought Charles was the coolest guy he ever met, he got even cooler.

"What else do you know?" he said.

"Well, we know that hothead at the end of the bar is Luke Grafton's brother," he said. "Now we just need a way to find out a little more about him."

Timothy thought back to the scene he watched play out at the little table.

"I think I know a way," he said.

★　　★　　★

After school the next day, Timothy stopped at Terri's Deli to pick up a newspaper and a quart of milk.

Back on Warren Street, he stood looking at the Green Apartment Building. Mr. O'Connor had warned him about going back in there. But Mr. O'Connor was currently driving in his big rig, somewhere out on the interstates of America.

The front door was closed but not locked. When Timothy let himself into the front hallway, he noticed that Ken's mailbox was stuffed so full that the mailman had just started piling it on the floor.

He also noticed the padlock on the door to Ken's apartment. The pile of mail and the padlock seemed to confirm Timothy's feeling that, even if no one was talking about what had happened to Ken, there was still a lot left unresolved.

Tentatively, Timothy knocked on the prostitute's door. Maybe she wouldn't be home. He almost turned away, this was probably another bad idea anyway.

Then he heard footsteps padding across the floor to the other side of the door.

"Who is it?"

He thought about this, would she even know him by name?

"Timothy," he said.

She opened the door a crack and looked out.

"Oh, it's you," she said, flatly. "What do you want?"

Her hair was in rollers, she was in the same dressing gown and appeared to be halfway through doing her make-up.

"I brought your milk and newspaper."

"Did I need milk and a newspaper?"

"You did that one morning."

"So I did . . ."

She stared at him a moment.

"You're a little young to be showing up at my door with gifts, don't you think?" she said.

"I just want to talk."

"Talk, huh."

She considered the proposition for a moment, then walked away but left the door swinging open slightly.

"Well, don't just stand there," she called as she headed back to the dressing table in her bedroom.

Timothy entered the apartment. The fake velvet wallpaper made it kind of dark in the living room, particularly with the shades drawn, it wasn't like Ken's modern-looking apartment at all.

There was an old, itchy looking couch. There was a pile of tabloid magazines and a box of tissues on the coffee table.

"You can put the milk in the fridge," she called.

The kitchenette had an old 50s refrigerator that you had to pull like a car door to get open. There wasn't much food inside, just a few stale take-out containers and a couple of big bottles of cheap beer. This explained why she was so skinny, it didn't look like she ate much.

Timothy followed her voice back to her bedroom where she sat in front of the mirror, applying mascara.

"Have a seat," she said.

She was sitting on the only chair in the room. The idea of sitting on a prostitute's unmade bed was scrambling his brain, but there was no place else to sit. He perched birdlike on the absolute corner of the bed.

He was maybe three feet away from the back of her head, but from this angle they could see each other's faces plainly in the mirror.

"Is your name Lynda?" he asked. He didn't want to keep calling her *the prostitute* in his mind.

"It is. And who might you be?"

"Timothy?"

"Right," she said, "you'd said that."

The tone of her voice remained flat, as if she dared not get emotionally involved, even in conversation.

"I saw you in the bar yesterday," Timothy said.

"I saw you too."

"You did?"

"I have eyes, don't I?"

She made eye contact with him in the mirror, to prove her point.

"So," she continued, "what are you and your little black friend up to?"

"We were looking for sponsorship for the Youth Center."

"Please," she said, "you couldn't call the Rotary Club?"

Unlike many other adults, this woman seemed to have the most stone-cold bullshit detector Timothy had yet encountered. His instincts told him it would be best just to level with her.

"Okay . . . we're sort of doing an investigation."

"An investigation?" she almost laughed, "of what?"

"We're trying to find out what really happened to Ken, next door."

The slight smile dropped from her face. She looked in the mirror at Timothy again. When she saw he was sincere, she looked back at herself sadly, and let out a long, audible breath.

"What happened to Kenny was an absolute crime, an absolute crime," she said twice, like it was still echoing in her head.

"Were you there that night?"

"No, thank God. And you shouldn't be going in there either. Bad things happen in that place."

"What kinds of things?"

"Things that someone your age shouldn't be concerned with."

This last statement seemed definitive, like the conversation was closed.

Timothy thought about how measured Charles had been in the bar, careful not to ask too many direct questions. If Charles were here, he never would've painted himself into a corner like this. But this was likely Timothy's only chance, he had to risk prying the door open a little further.

"The guy who . . . approached you in the bar," Timothy said cautiously, "is that Luke Grafton's brother?"

"What do you want to know about him for?"

"I don't know . . . just looking for clues, you know?"

"Look," Lynda said, turning around to face Timothy directly to drive the point home, "you stay away from Kurt Grafton, he's a bad one, do you understand?"

Timothy nodded, like he understood, even if he didn't, exactly.

She turned back to face herself in the mirror and finish putting on her make-up.

"Some people have no morals," she said, as much to herself as to Timothy.

She carefully put lipstick on her lower lip, the puckered up lips with a *smwacking* sound to finish the job. She took one last look at herself then turned from the mirror to face Timothy again.

"So, how do I look?" she asked.

Her painted face was almost unreal, but there was something about her eyes, they were usually so cold and distant, but she seemed to turn them on for a moment as she looked at him directly, and he suddenly understood why men were attracted to her.

"You look . . . very nice," he said, perhaps too politely, which seemed to make her eyes turn a little sad.

Timothy couldn't help but imagine this sadness was connected with the way the man was always yelling at her, with how Grafton's brother had put his hand on her leg and she couldn't seem to do anything about it.

"Can I . . . help you?" he asked innocently.

Lynda smiled wistfully at this. She shook her head like Timothy would never be able to understand.

"You're a silly boy," she said.

She leaned over and gave him a kiss on his forehead.

"Now go . . . I have to finish getting dressed, and I'm not about to give you a free show," she swept her hand toward the door. "Go on, scram."

Timothy smiled at her as he left, as if she'd let him in on a little secret, even if he wasn't exactly sure if she'd told him anything specific that would help the case.

Closing the front door of the Green Apartment Building, he luckily caught his own reflection in the window. He wiped the lipstick kiss from his forehead before anyone else could see it.

CHAPTER 20

The small confrontation between Timothy and his mom was not mentioned again. Of practical necessity, the household returned to its version of equilibrium, or at least a sort of detente.

Besides, it was mac-n-cheese night, Timothy's favorite. Who could be grumpy with a mouthful of mac-n-cheese?

"Pass the creamy salad dressing please?" he asked.

Cathryn passed the dressing once she finished using it. Timothy proceeded to saturate his iceberg lettuce to the point where it blended with the mac-n-cheese, an added bonus.

"You want some lettuce with your dressing?" his mom asked.

"Heh," Timothy said, a courtesy laugh.

"Isn't your Bicentennial presentation coming up?" Cathryn asked.

"Yep, this coming Monday," Timothy said.

He used the edge of his fork to break up a particularly crusty clump of macaroni, the best part.

"Is it something parents are expected to come to?" his mom wondered.

"No, not really, it's just an in-school type of thing."

This was sort of half true. It wasn't a full-on assembly in the auditorium, but Mrs. Brenner had said parents could come, if they wanted to.

"Are you ready?" his mom asked.

"I sure am."

And this really was true. Well, he still needed to finish the concluding paragraph, which Mrs. Brenner said should leave people with something to think about, but he basically knew what he wanted to say.

"Well I'm looking forward to reading it, when you're ready to share," his mom said.

"Me too," Cathryn said.

Timothy nodded with his mouth full. He supposed he might share it with them after the fact, but for now was content to keep it to himself to avoid potential adult nitpicking before his presentation.

The sun was coming horizontally through the back window onto the dinner table like it always did this time of year when the days were getting longer. Timothy noticed how it illuminated the dinner glasses and made little rainbows on the opposite wall. It was kind of beautiful.

"Well, speaking of homework, I have an exam coming up myself," his mom said, referring to the paralegal course she was taking.

"Are YOU ready?" Cathryn joked.

"I'd better be," she said. "Just don't mind me if I bow out of TV watching tonight . . ."

"We'll save some dessert for you," Cathryn said.

After supper, the phone rang while Timothy was washing dishes, his hands full of suds.

Cathryn answered.

"Sure, Timothy's here, just a sec . . . "

Timothy quickly dried his hands and stretched the phone onto the back porch as usual. It was Charles, of course.

"Was that your mom?" he asked.

Timothy thought quickly.

"Yes," he said. It was easier than coming up with a lie that would make sense.

"She sounds nice," Charles said.

"Yeah, she's okay," Timothy said.

"How'd you do today?"

"With what?"

"You said you had a lead you were going to follow up on?"

"Oh yeah . . . I talked to Ken's neighbor today, the one I saw back at the Oriole?"

He deleted for now the part about her being a prostitute. It made a good story, but might've made her seem a less reliable witness.

"And?"

"And nothing, she wasn't there that night. But I did find out Luke Grafton's brother's name is Kurt. She said to stay away from him, he's more dangerous than his brother."

"Kurt, huh?"

Timothy could hear that Charles was holding the phone with his shoulder while he was flipping through the pages of something.

"Looks like the Grafton brothers share an apartment on Furnace Street," Charles said, "at least they did until Luke became a guest of the State."

"How'd you figure that out?"

"My top secret database," Charles replied, "also called called the White Pages."

Why didn't Timothy think of that?

"You think the brother's still living there?" Timothy wondered.

"Only one way to find out . . . you up for a little surveillance?"

"You mean, actually following him or something?"

"Yeah, something like that."

Back at the Oriole, Charles had been paying attention to Jack Flanagan while Timothy had been watching the way Kurt Grafton acted with Lynda, so maybe Charles didn't fully realize how scary the thing he was suggesting was. But Charles had yet to lead him into anything the two of them together hadn't figured out how to handle.

"I am if you are . . ." Timothy said.

Back in the kitchen, he found Cathryn finishing the dishes when he got off the phone.

"I was gonna do that," Timothy said, thinking a guilt trip might be forthcoming.

"That's okay, you do plenty around here," Cathryn said. "Is Charles the new friend you've been hanging out with?"

She'd obviously caught his name when Charles politely introduced himself.

"Uh, yeah."

"He sounds nice."

"He is, actually. He's really nice."

When they settled into watching television for the night, Timothy's mom, as promised, had sequestered herself in the dining room with her textbooks, leaving him and Cathryn alone in the living room.

There was plenty of room on the couch, but Timothy let Cathryn have it and he sat on the floor as usual.

When 9:00 rolled around, Cathryn said, "You wanna watch The Rockford Files?"

Timothy always wanted to watch the Rockford Files, but his mom always wanted to watch something else.

"Don't you want to watch the ABC Friday Night Movie?"

"Nah, I don't care either way."

"You really don't mind?"

Timothy reached over to the TV dial and clicked onto channel 4 just in time to catch the freewheeling harmonica part of the theme song during the opening credits.

Cathryn hadn't stretched out, there was still space where his mom would usually sit.

So, cautiously, Timothy joined Cathryn on the couch. They proceeded to enjoy the show together.

Timothy specified that Charles should meet him in front of the Peter Stuyvesant statue at Academy Green.

"How come Peter Stuyvesant?" Charles asked when he got there, seeing there were two equally prominent statues in the immediate vicinity.

"He's the only one with a peg leg," Timothy said.

"You know, I never would've noticed that," Charles admitted.

"Kinda piratey," Timothy said, "thought you'd like it."

Charles reached into his knapsack.

"Here, try these on," he said, handing Timothy a pair of sunglasses.

"What are these for?"

"You weren't planning on wearing your momma's old reading glasses, were you?"

They were sort of kid's sunglasses that Charles had clearly out-grown, but when Timothy put them on, they did look a lot cooler than the ones he'd worn to the Courthouse stake out.

"Keep them," Charles said, "I have another pair."

Charles put on his own brand-new adult-sized mirrored sun-glasses. Timothy'd never seen a cooler pair of sunglasses in his life.

It was 10am Saturday, no school, the day stretching out long ahead of them.

There was almost zero foot traffic on Broadway today, so they slow rolled down the sidewalk side-by-side, daring the world to get in their way.

One guy did teeter and almost fell into them as they passed. He had wrinkly trousers and no laces in his shoes, seemed he might've still been drunk from the night before.

A few blocks shy of the Oriole, they reached Liberty Street. There was a gas station on the corner where a bunch of kids younger than them were hanging out, nothing better to do.

"Hey Charles!" they all called out to him.

"Hey guys!" Charles called back as he and Timothy turned onto Liberty Street which led them to Furnace Street.

"How do you know those kids?" Timothy asked him.

"I work with them at the Youth Center," Charles said. "They're good kids."

Timothy was glad for the friendly welcome, otherwise Furnace Street might've psyched him out a little bit.

On Warren Street, the Green Apartment Building was the excep-tion, but here was a whole street of green apartment buildings.

Many were uncared for, with multiple mailboxes hanging off the front of each. Guys hung out on the corner. Even the craggy trees looked angry somehow.

Timothy's neighborhood might've seemed rough compared to Charles' in Hilltop Meadows, but this one seemed way rougher.

The sun was shining just the same, and the street was interesting to look at in its way. A few of the houses looked like they hadn't changed much since the Great Depression, and they probably hadn't.

With barely any traffic, they were back to riding in the street. The bluestone sidewalk was in particularly miserable condition here, anyway.

A kid stepped out into the street from between two parked cars, about Charles' age. He looked a little familiar, maybe he was one of the ones who blocked their path on Broadway that one day, but Timothy wasn't sure.

"Yo Charles," the kid said in a low voice.

Charles slowed to a stop, Timothy did too.

"What's up Kyle," Charles said, evenly.

"Nice bike you got there."

"Yes, it is," Charles replied, matter of factly.

The kid, Kyle, reached a lazy hand out and ran his finger along the curving handlebars.

"How 'bout you let me take it for a little spin," he said.

"I don't think so," Charles said, totally keeping his cool.

"C'mon, Oreo, I won't be but a few minutes . . ."

The Kyle kid started to wrap his fingers around the handlebars, as if gently beginning to take possession.

Charles clapped a firm hand over the kid's hand, pushed his

mirrored sunglasses up on top of his forehead, and leaned right into his face.

"Don't underestimate me," Charles said, solidly.

At first, the kid laughed off Charles' formalistic style of speech. But Charles was giving the kid a kind of look Timothy had never seen Charles give anyone before. It was surprisingly . . . deadly.

When the look registered, and the kid realized Charles was not backing down, he started to try to wriggle his hand free, but Charles did not give it back so easily.

"Okay man, you ain't gotta look at me like that," the kid said, "we cool."

Charles let the hand loose and the kid started backing away.

"Yeah, we cool," Charles said straight-faced, demonstrating he could speak the kid's language if he so chose.

Timothy said nothing as the kid looked at both of them one last time before disappearing down the street.

"C'mon," Charles said to Timothy, lightening his tone considerably, "I think it's on the next block . . ."

They rolled up on a brand new Ford Mustang. You couldn't help but notice it, it was the only new car on the block. Charles slowed, looked at the car, noted the address of the building it was parked in front of. This was it. He nodded toward a little alleyway on the other side of the street. It was weedy and overgrown, a perfect place to conceal themselves without attracting much attention.

Pulling their bikes parallel to each other in the alleyway, they faced out into the street, with a clear view of the Mustang and the apartment building behind it.

Charles, on the left as if in the driver seat, let his sunglasses drop back over his eyes. A dog started barking two houses away, the two boys' in their sunglasses turned their heads in unison to see where the sound was coming from, then in slo mo simultaneously returned their gaze to the house across the street.

Their heads began to bob slowly and in sync, as if the whole world could hear the same bad-ass bass line from Thin Lizzy's *Jailbreak* thumping inside both their imaginations.

"We might be here a while," Charles said, reaching into his knapsack, and popping open a box of mini donuts which he extended first to Timothy.

They ate their donuts slowly, unaware in their profound state of coolness of the powdered sugar that was accumulating around their mouths like snowy five-o'clock shadows.

It was a sleepy street, but there were many things to notice. A little baby was crying somewhere, no one seemed to be bothering to comfort it. A woman with a melodious voice was singing as she hung her laundry out on a line from an upper story window. Another woman came walking down the middle of the street pushing a grocery cart she'd obviously taken from whatever supermarket she'd been shopping at blocks and blocks away.

There was also something interesting going on on the corner. Two guys were exchanging a very sly handshake, it seemed to Timothy like something was being passed between them in the process, but he couldn't tell what it was.

"There he is," Charles said, waking Timothy out of what seemed like a daydream.

Kurt Grafton exited the side door of the apartment building, headed out to the Mustang, and looked both ways before opening the door and hopping in.

"That's *his* car?" Charles said in disbelief.

If Grafton was trying to be inconspicuous, this was about to change immediately.

When he started the Mustang, it was loud, and when he revved it purposefully, it got even louder.

The guys on the corner sang out to him cheerfully, seeming to appreciate the sheer volume of the engine. Grafton smiled and held an open hand out the window, as if gladly accepting the accolades for his small feat of automotive noise production.

When he put the car in gear, it seemed to whinny like an actual horse as he turned the wheel to pull out of its parking space, then he began to slow roll along Furnace Street.

When Charles nodded in Timothy's direction, Timothy caught his sugary reflection in the mirrored shades, wiped his face and motioned for Charles to do the same, then they began to follow.

A block later, Grafton slowed to a stop.

"Hang back," Charles advised.

Timothy's coaster brakes squealed slightly as he applied them. They tucked their bikes behind a parked car.

"What's up Anthony?" Grafton called out.

It wasn't exactly hot outside, but this Anthony guy was shirtless as he came off his porch.

Grafton got out of his car, left the door open, again looked around, then opened his trunk. Anthony looked inside, nodded his head, and Grafton pulled out a cardboard box that looked like it maybe had a stereo receiver in it. Keeping it low, he handed it to Anthony, and they did the same sort of handshake like the guys on the corner that made Timothy think money was being exchanged.

Anthony looked both ways, carried the box to his porch and disappeared inside. Grafton got back into his car, put it back in first gear and kept it there as he continued crawling along, rounding onto Liberty with Charles and Timothy following.

Grafton said Hey to a few other people complimenting him on his wheels.

As he inched out onto Broadway, the kids they'd seen earlier at the corner gas station called out to Grafton:

"Gun it!" they said.

Grafton welcomed the suggestion. With a terrifying squeal, he left a track of rubber and smoke three parking meter lengths long. The light on the next block turned red, he ran it anyway and disappeared.

The kids on the corner cheered. Charles took off his sunglasses before approaching them, so he would look more like a normal kid.

"DANG, he got a V8 in that thing?" he asked, to any of them who cared to answer.

"V6, 105 horsepower," said one kid, who'd obviously made it his business to know these things.

"That a 75?" Charles asked.

"76," the kid said, "he just got it three weeks ago."

"Fine car . . ." Charles said, turning his bike around, leading Timothy away from the corner and toward Furnace Street once again.

"You catch that?" Charles asked Timothy.

"What?"

"Sounds like Kurt Grafton went out and got himself a brand new car about five minutes after his brother went away, what's that about?"

They let the question hang there.

Back at Grafton's apartment building, they dismounted. Timothy followed Charles as they tiptoed around back.

"What're we doing?" Timothy whispered.

"Well, we know Grafton's not home, good time to do a little research . . ."

In a busted-up shed next to the back porch, Charles found what he was looking for.

"You take the can on the left, I'll check the one on the right."

"We're looking in the garbage?"

Charles handed Timothy a pair of rubber gloves, like he'd known this was a possibility all along.

"Technically, it would be more legal if we waited till it was out on the curb," Charles whispered, "but I don't want to be out here on trash night."

Timothy remembered how the crazy guy had yelled and accused him of looking through his garbage on that morning he'd skipped school. He had a bad feeling about this.

"You find anything with Grafton's name on it, put it in this bag," Charles said.

"Why're we doing this?"

"You can learn a lot from a person's garbage."

Going through the can was absolutely sickening. There were gnawed on chicken bones, snotty tissues, razor-sharp tin cans, coffee grounds, as well as slimy things with mayonnaise in them Timothy could not identify.

An upstairs window opened. Charles and Timothy froze.

Someone shook out a mop head directly above them. Dust and feathers came floating down, settling in their hair, and adhering to the sticky garbage dripping from their fingers.

The mop was pulled back in. The window closed. The search resumed.

"I found something," Timothy said. It was a ripped envelope with Grafton's name on it.

Charles quit looking in his barrel and began concentrating on Timothy's. They made a quick pile of receipts and bills and whatnot. Hearing footsteps bounding down an inside flight of stairs, Charles stuffed it all in the bag and they got the heck out of there lightning quick before whoever it was came out the back door.

Once they'd put a few houses distance between themselves and Grafton's, they slowed so as not to seem obvious, but did not stop pedaling until they were back on a park bench at Academy Green, not far from the Stuyvesant statue where they'd met earlier.

"Let's see what we've got . . . "

Dumping the pile onto the ground, it didn't look like much to Timothy, but Charles considered each item individually as if it were potentially of utmost importance.

Some of it was junk mail, but there were things that seemed specific. A disconnection notice from the phone company. A receipt from a storage space on Greenkill Avenue, things like that. Then . . .

"Here we go, mother load," Charles said, holding a pay stub.

"Why's that?"

"Look here, now we know where Grafton works, we know his hours, and how much he makes . . . actually, how *little* he makes, for someone who just went out and got himself a brand-new Mustang."

Charles pointed at the figures on the ketchup-stained piece of paper like they were holding gold in their hands.

"Poses an interesting question, especially considering the timing, don't you think?" Charles asked.

"What's that?"

"A guy who doesn't make enough money to keep his phone turned on?" Charles said. "Where'd he suddenly get all that money?"

CHAPTER 21

Timothy spent much of Sunday afternoon putting the finishing touches on his Boston Tea Party project. Using his mom's typewriter was a tedious process because he only knew where half the letters were, plus he had to keep stopping to wait for the Liquid Paper to dry each time he made a mistake.

Finally, when all six paragraphs were finished, he slid the watermarked paper into the brand new report cover binder he'd bought specifically for the project. He added the pictures he'd photocopied at his mom's office, which he jazzed up with colored sticky stars to make up for them being dark and a little wavy.

On Monday morning, he was ready. The day of the Bicentennial Presentation had arrived.

The classroom was festooned with red, white and blue crepe paper. Mrs. Brenner had obviously worked late the night before. She'd also had a janitor wheel in a real lectern, from where the students would give their presentations.

Six or seven mothers had shown up and were sitting in the back of the room, including Brandon's mom, who said hello to Timothy when she walked in. There weren't any dads, they were all at work.

Several students had brought props to help illuminate their presentations. The girl who was doing Betsey Ross brought a handmade cloth star she had stitched herself. She demonstrated the technique by which anyone could fold a piece of cloth in order to cut out a five-pointed star.

The kid doing Thomas Jefferson brought in a copy of the Declaration of Independence. And Drew, from Timothy's lunch table, was wearing a three-pointed hat.

When it came to the reports themselves, Paul Revere's Ride was fairly action-packed, and the Inventions of Ben Franklin had so many curiosities Timothy almost wished he'd picked that subject himself.

None so far had any real zingers, though, nothing as startlingly original as Timothy imagined his own report to be. By the time they were halfway through, Timothy was actually starting to think he had half a chance of winning this thing.

Then Brandon went up to read his report. He came out of the gate pretty strong:

The Battle of Lexington and Concord was singularly important for three distinct reasons. Firstly, it marked the beginning of the armed conflict between the thirteen colonies and Great Britain. Secondly, it gave birth to the image of The Minuteman we still cherish today . . .

But then came the last sentence of his intro paragraph:

Finally, on the level of sheer symbolism, it gave the fledgling American Army its first taste of cohesion.

Fledgling army? Taste of cohesion? Level of sheer symbolism? There was *no way* he did not copy this. He was busted for sure.

But Brandon continued to read confidently, and when Timothy looked over at Mrs. Brenner, she had one leg eagerly crossed over the other, her loose foot bobbing enthusiastically, like it too was cheering Brandon on. She was buying the whole thing, hook, line, and sinker.

The essay continued to flesh out each point laboriously, culminating with a resounding:

The shot heard round the world may not have <u>literally</u> been heard around the world, but it was sure loud enough to rouse the sleeping giant that would soon enough be these United States of America.

The entire class erupted into applause, almost intoxicated by the idea that one of their own had achieved such dizzying heights of prose and patriotism.

"I want to point out how Brandon clearly enumerated his three points in the introductory paragraph," Mrs. Brenner said to the class. "He went on to expand upon each point in its own paragraph. Perfect form. Congratulations, Brandon."

She herself began clapping, which caused the room, including the mothers in the back row, to begin clapping once again.

"Up next," Mrs. Brenner said, checking her notes, "Timothy Miller."

Timothy took to the lectern. It was a little big, but he could still more-or-less see over it.

He had decided against dressing up like an Indian himself, it no longer seemed to go with theme he'd chosen to pursue.

When he'd practiced in his room, he'd held up the glossy binder to show the audience the photocopied images. But Steven with the copier in his house had already dazzled the class with so many perfectly clear photocopies illustrating his report on Washington Crossing the Delaware that Timothy decided to skip it and just launch right in.

He cleared his throat.

We all know that the Boston Tea Party took place in Boston on December 16, 1773. Boston is at 42 degrees latitude, which is a little bit higher than Kingston, so it must have been pretty cold. The Sons of Liberty disguised themselves as Indians, and climbed aboard three British ships all loaded up with tea from China.

Timothy took a breath and looked around the room. Everyone was looking at him and seemed to be following along. So far so good. He continued.

You may also know that the reason that the Boston Tea Party took place was to protest Taxation Without Representation, which meant that the British were taking our money, but didn't let us vote, which is obviously unfair.

He looked over at Mrs. Brenner, who smiled, but was definitely not bobbing her foot. Okay, time to turn up the heat a little.

But did you know this: that John Hancock who organized the Boston Tea Party was a tea smuggler? In the early days, his smuggled tea was cheaper than British tea, so he made a fortune. But when the East India Company cut their prices, their tea became cheaper, so by dumping the tea, John Hancock was actually getting rid of his competition.

A few students looked at each other like the scandal had piqued their interest. Timothy's plan was starting to work.

And another thing, they didn't just dump the unopened chests into the water. The so-called Sons of Liberty took their tomahawks and hacked open all 342 chests of tea and dumped the tea leaves straight into the water. That's a lot of tea leaves. They basically turned Boston Harbor into a giant cup of tea.

He got a few snickers. Keep going, Timothy, you're almost there.

And what about the fish swimming around in the harbor? Most water has a pH level of 7, which is what fish are used to. But black tea has a pH of only about 5, which is different than what fish are used to, and might be really bad for them.

Mrs. Brenner looked like she genuinely didn't know where this was going, but no matter, it was time to go for the kill.

So while we're celebrating our independence this summer, we need to remember that some of the people we think of as heroes are actually environmental criminals. And when it comes to the Boston Tea Party, as far as the fish were concerned, the party's over.

Timothy looked around the quiet room, wondering why it wasn't exploding with applause.

A single girl in the front row, who used to chase Timothy around the schoolyard back in 2nd grade before he had long hair, began to clap furiously, which signaled others to begin clapping. A few of his guy friends actually did call out "Go Timothy!"

"Well, Timothy," Mrs. Brenner said, "that was certainly very *interesting!*"

The mothers in the back row, who were clapping politely, got a laugh out of this.

"Up next . . ." Mrs. Brenner said, checking her list.

The three remaining reports after Timothy's seemed a bit tame in comparison, but were fairly thoughtful and well researched.

At the conclusion, Mrs. Brenner checked the tally of whatever points she'd been keeping on her clip board.

When she announced that Brandon had won the contest, the room again erupted with applause as he went up to accept his Friendly's gift certificate, which he briefly held aloft.

Brandon's mom, on her way out of the room shortly afterwards, made a point of stopping at Timothy's desk and told him personally how much she'd enjoyed his essay.

And Brandon himself was very gracious in victory.

★   ★   ★

When Timothy got home from school, Cathryn was up on a ladder in the living room, painting the upper trim a darker pink than the walls.

"How'd your report go today?" she called down.

"Brandon won for his report on Lexington-Concord."

"But how'd *your* report go?"

"Okay, I guess."

Cathryn came down carefully from the ladder, brush and tin can of paint still in her hands.

"You gonna share it with me?" she asked.

"Nah."

"C'mon, I wanna hear it."

He remained reluctant. Based on the chilly reception at school, he was thinking it must not be very good. But Cathryn had stopped what she was doing to pay attention to him. It seemed rude not to share when she was asking so enthusiastically.

"You wanna just read it?"

"No, you read it, just like at school."

Oscar the cat came into the room at this moment, jumped up on the couch and started looking at Timothy, as if he wanted Timothy to read it too.

Timothy took the report out of his knapsack, halfheartedly holding it up to demonstrate the professional-looking presentation.

We all know that the Boston Tea Party took place in Boston on December 16, 1773 . . .

he began to read, a bit noncommittally, assuming it would be instantly apparent to Cathryn what a dog his report was. But every time he looked up, she had an unmistakable look of admiration on her face, maybe a light glow, even.

This positive reinforcement made Timothy put more and more effort into his performance until, by the concluding paragraph, his delivery was as full-throated as if he were back at the lectern, going for the gold.

"Timothy, you wrote that?" she said.

"Uh, yes."

"That's *amazing.* I can't believe that stupid teacher of yours didn't give you first prize."

It was both surprising and vindicating to hear Cathryn calling his teacher stupid. Maybe Mrs. Brenner really did miss the boat this time.

Cathryn put down the paint and started wiping her hands off on a rag.

"Hey, come on," she said, "we're going to Friendly's right this minute."

"You don't have to do that."

"You're gonna tell me you don't want to go to Friendly's?"

Charles had a game today, so besides worrying about being seen at Friendly's with Cathryn, he really had no excuse.

"Yeah, but . . ."

"Alright then, let's go . . ."

Everyone in Kingston knew the best ice cream was at Mickey's Igloo. But Micky's was only open over the summer, so Friendly's was a dependable year-round favorite.

The waitress escorted Timothy and Cathryn to a prime booth near the window and dropped two menus on the table.

Looking around, Timothy actually saw several other kids from his class out for ice cream, their parents had all obviously had the same idea. Drew was even still wearing his three-pointed hat.

Drew waved to Timothy, so Timothy shyly waved back. He was a little self-conscious about being out with Cathryn, but he quickly saw no one cared, their focus on ice cream easily winning out over all other possible concerns.

"Get what you like," Cathryn said.

Timothy looked down at the dazzling, plastic-coated menu.

"Even a sundae?" he asked.

"Sure."

"Mom never lets me get a sundae."

"I'm not your mom."

Somehow, Cathryn's response had a greater effect than simply allowing Timothy to consume copious amounts of processed sugar.

A small pressure valve was released somewhere inside. Timothy might not have been able to put it into words exactly, but part of the ongoing tension wasn't just who was Cathryn in relation to his mom, but who was she in relation to *him*?

I'm not your mom didn't completely answer the question. But it jumpstarted an adult-sanctioned checklist, at least, of things Cathryn was not.

The waitress returned to their table.

"Do you know what you'd like?" she asked.

Timothy looked around the restaurant at the various kids who'd been allowed to get the most insane super-sized sundaes on the menu. Whipped cream and fudge sauce were exploding everywhere, faces contorting in response to the sudden glycemic spike.

"I'll have a small sundae," he said, sensibly.

"With everything?"

"Hold the fudge, keep the sprinkles," he responded.

The waitress turned to Cathryn.

"That sounds good," she said, "I'll have the same thing."

The waitress took the menus.

A different kid at another table waved to Timothy, he waved back.

"Looks like you know a lot of people here today," Cathryn said.

"Steven did Crossing the Delaware, Ted did the Boston Massacre, Cynthia did . . ."

He gave her the whole litany of Revolutionary subject matter that had earned every consolation prize in the place. She got the idea.

Their sundaes arrived. Timothy ate his whipped cream slowly, savoring one component at a time rather than mushing it all together.

Cathryn went even slower, as if she had ordered more wanting to keep Timothy from feeling self-conscious than because she wanted to eat a dish of ice cream.

"You know," she said, taking a small bite, "if there's anything I can ever help you with, you just have to ask."

"You mean, like homework and stuff."

"Yeah that, but . . ." she paused, as if trying to figure out how to say something delicately, "sometimes you seem like you might be . . . sad about something . . . I'd just hate to think you wouldn't talk to me if there was something I could help you with."

This was starting to get a little uncomfortable. He didn't really want to say anything at all, but somehow found himself saying.

"You wouldn't understand."

"Try me," Cathryn said.

Well, it's not like he could roll one right down the middle of the alley and say *The problem is you*. Besides, that was only part of the problem. The other part was his mom.

Why did his mom seem so . . . *unavailable* . . . since Cathryn had moved in? She was like a different person, and it's not like he was going to talk about this with Cathryn either, the two of them had become such a team, this seemed certain to backfire.

"You just don't know what it's like to have your dad run off," Timothy said, blurting out the one obvious thing that seemed safe to say.

"Actually, I do know. My dad ran off when I was twelve."

This didn't seem to correlate with what Timothy believed to be true.

"But I thought I met your dad that one time," he said, speaking of a single quick and awkward visit to Cathryn's parents' suburban house in New Jersey to pick up some of her stuff.

"That was my step dad," Cathryn said. "He and my mom got married a few years after my real dad left, and . . . let's just say he didn't treat me very nicely."

Timothy had stopped eating his ice cream.

"So, then what happened?" he asked her.

Cathryn kind of shrugged like it was behind her, for the most part. She took a tiny mouthful of her own ice cream.

"So, I left," she said. "I was basically on my own from age 16, until I met your mom. She was the first person who's looked out for me . . . you know, everyone talks about helping other people, but your mom really does . . . she's a really special person, you know?"

Timothy's first thought was that he wished his mom would spend more time looking out for him and less time looking out for Cathryn and women in Group. But this was strange territory. Adults didn't usually lay it on the line like this, so the honesty of what Cathryn was sharing kind of won out.

"How come Mom never tells me stuff like this?"

"She's just trying to protect you, which is not such a bad thing."

"Is she gonna be mad that you're telling me?"

"I don't know . . . she's probably gonna be madder that I let you eat a sundae before dinner," she said, smiling. "C'mon, eat up."

CHAPTER 22

According to Grafton's pay stub, he worked a split shift as a dishwasher at Villa Marsala on Tuesdays. His break between shifts was between 3 and 4, which coincided closely enough with Timothy and Charles' schedule to warrant an investigation.

Villa Marsala was on Smith Avenue, directly across from the new Post Office. From half a block away, the aroma of pizza was already pulling them in like a tractor beam.

"It's 3:15," Charles said, checking his wristwatch as they pedaled along, "we might've missed him already."

As they pulled within sight of Villa Marsala, they could see the Mustang in the far corner of the parking lot. The only other car in the lot at this hour was the beat-up delivery car with the plastic Villa Marsala sign on top.

The Post Office had a convenient bike rack. After locking up their bikes, they crossed the street, then paused on the sidewalk, pretending to look at a faded poster for a lost dog stapled to a splintery telephone pole.

They looked from the restaurant to the car and back again. Nothing was happening.

The smell of the pizza seemed to intensify. Timothy pictured the tomato sauce bubbling up through the cheese like hot lava.

"Maybe we should get a slice," he whispered.

Charles, as if his stomach were not also grumbling at the moment, held up a single finger. The cloak of invisibility he was conjuring required absolute focus.

At precisely the right moment, Charles made his move, walking casually yet catlike across the parking lot. Timothy followed close behind, thinking maybe they'd do a little surveillance first, then get a slice.

Slowly they approached the Mustang. Putting visor-like hands above their brows to cut the glare, they leaned up against glass and looked in. Maybe there'd be a clue in plain sight. There seemed to be a slight grunting sound coming from somewhere.

Then, something in the backseat moved.

Charles and Timothy both jumped back.

"What the fuck was that?" Timothy said, trying to keep up with Charles as they rapidly retreated to the Post Office across the street. Charles shrugged but didn't answer, he didn't know either.

The Post Office was actually perfect because it was such a highly public place. A landscaped berm ran alongside the building, its retaining wall a preferred spot for customers to sit and get organized, either before or after going into the Post Office.

Timothy and Charles perched at the very end of the wall, next to the phone booth and the two outdoor mailboxes. Everyone else was going about their business, not seeming to pay any attention to them.

They each took a textbook from their knapsacks and pretended like they were just doing homework while they were waiting for their moms.

A guy in a suit, who looked like he was on his way home from work, ducked into the phone booth next to them. He didn't bother shutting the door.

"I'm at Villa Marsala, you know what you want?"

He was probably calling his wife, they could hear him loud and clear.

"Hold on, lemme get a pencil . . . " he said.

Meanwhile across the street, the Mustang's door could be observed being kicked open from the inside. A woman emerged awkwardly from the backseat. Shutting the door behind her, she straightened her dress, adjusted her hair and, after looking this way and that, walked off down the street in the opposite direction.

Confused, Timothy looked to Charles, this wasn't what he was expecting.

Charles took out his pencil and wrote on the back of his spiral notebook in small letters:

Prostitute

"Really?" Timothy said in disbelief, looking back at the car.

"So, one half mushrooms and anchovies," the guy in the phone booth continued, "The other half extra cheese . . . "

Barely a minute later, the Mustang's door opened again. Out came Kurt Grafton.

Unlike the woman, who had seemed somehow to be attempting to reclaim her dignity as she put her clothing back in order, Grafton buttoned his black work pants and tucked in his white t-shirt like he couldn't care less.

No sooner did Grafton begin to make his own way across the parking lot, the door to the pizza delivery car opened and some-one came flying out to intercept him. Seemed Timothy and Charles weren't the only ones watching Grafton.

"Now what's going on?" Timothy asked.

"I don't know," Charles whispered, "Delivery guy looks pissed about something."

Whatever it was the guy was trying to get out of Grafton, Grafton tried to brush past him once or twice. Then, when the guy wasn't taking no for an answer, Grafton suddenly snapped.

Pushing him full force, Grafton continued to come at the guy even after he'd flown back five feet and landed on his ass on the hard blacktop. Grafton's muscular arm flexed as he clenched his fist, Timothy was sure he was going to punch his lights out.

But the guy held up both hands like, *okay, okay, take it easy.* He got up and into the safety of his delivery car and exited the scene quite quickly.

Timothy and Charles looked around. No one seemed to be see-ing any of this but them.

Then, like a madman, Grafton suddenly shifted his gaze across the street and came heading straight for Timothy and Charles. There was no time to move or do anything. Both boys instinctively looked down and pretended to be doing their homework, certain Grafton was about to grab both of them by their collars and yell *Why the hell are you following me?*

Grafton stopped two feet away from them. He stood staring at the phone booth.

"So, now Ryan *doesn't* want olives in the salad?" the guy on the phone was saying to his wife. "Since when doesn't he like olives?"

"Hey, I'm expecting a phone call," Grafton said to the phone booth guy.

The guy covered the receiver.

"I'm gonna be a few minutes," he said to Grafton, then back into the receiver, "Just some guy wants to use the phone . . . where were we? No olives, and I take it he still doesn't like onions, anything else?"

Grafton glanced quickly at his watch, growing apoplectic.

Taking a quarter from his pocket, he began using it as a blunt instrument, *clack clack clacking* on the glass of the phone booth repeatedly, like he was going to shatter it.

"What's your problem?" the guy said.

"I said, I'm expecting a call," Grafton said, leaning into the booth right up to the guy's face. "*Get off the phone, dick breath.*"

"Janet, I gotta go," the guy said, hanging up when he realized he was dealing with an unhinged individual.

He almost had to flatten himself to get past Grafton, who was already halfway into the booth before the guy could fully extract himself.

"You need therapy," the guy called back from safely halfway across the street.

Grafton flipped him off then started yanking furiously on the door to try to get it shut, but the phone rang, so he just gave up and left if open.

"Hello . . . yeah, I'll accept, just a minute . . ."

Digging into his pants pocket Grafton pulled out an angry mitt full of change which he started pumping furiously into the phone. Finally, the call came through.

"Yeah, hey, it's me . . . yeah, Mom's fine . . . how you holding up in there?"

Charles pointed to a random diagram in his earth science text-book, bolstering the fiction that he and Timothy doing homework together and not listening in on the phone conversation.

"This job is driving me nuts, I'm gonna fucking lose it, they're fucking riding my ass for twelve straight hours" Grafton was saying. "Yeah I know you're the one on the inside, but I still can't deal with this shit."

Charles took up his pencil again and wrote in tiny letters:

He's talking to his brother.

Timothy stole a glance at the phone booth then quickly back to the textbook before Grafton could see him.

"Look," Grafton said, then started to lower his voice, "I can pull another IPM job, just gimme the info and I'll call the guy myself."

It was almost impossible to keep pretending they were doing homework when they were actually hearing Grafton talk about doing a hit job for IPM with their own ears. Charles reached down and deftly untied his sneaker so he could slowly tie it again while craning his head toward the phone booth.

"Fuck, I gotta add more change," Grafton said to his brother, then to the operator, "Hold on, hold on, hold on . . ."

Frantically pulling change from his pocket, he kept feeding the payphone until he'd hit the required amount to keep the line open.

"Fuck me, where were we," he said, exhaling, then, "Yeah, of course I kept your stuff, it's in storage . . . yeah, I can get the other paperwork when I get the IPM thing, I just can't go till Thursday . . . of course I'm taking your appeal seriously, I've just got another fucking double tomorrow, then a lunch shift Thursday, but I'll go in the afternoon . . ."

Charles took the pencil and wrote: *Thursday afternoon storage.*

"Okay, yeah, sorry . . . yeah, I gotta go too, I gotta be back in there by four," Grafton said, wrapping up the conversation. "Okay, okay, we'll get up there soon . . . "

Grafton hung up the phone with less force than he'd pounded on the glass earlier, like in the process of talking with his brother the hurricane had begun to wear itself out. He hit the coin return button just in case, but Ma Bell wasn't giving anything back, even if he'd paid for two minutes longer.

Resigned to having to go back in for his second shift, Grafton actually looked both ways this time before he crossed the street, then disappeared into the service entrance around the back of Villa Marsala.

"You heard that part about the IPM job, right?" Timothy asked.

"I almost cannot believe he said that," Charles said, "but he did."

"Man, I wish we recorded that," Timothy said.

The two boys continued to sit on the Post Office wall, trying to process what had just happened. Then Timothy pointed to the last note Charles had written.

"Didn't we find a receipt for a storage place on Greenkill?" he asked.

"That's just what I was thinking," Charles said. "But I'm also thinking we may want to think twice about continuing to follow this guy."

"But now we know his next move."

"Thunderbird, have you not been paying attention? This man is *dangerous.*"

"Don't you want to solve this case?"

"I want to see this case solved, yes. But some things are perhaps best left to actual police officers. With guns."

Timothy continued to look across the street at the Mustang while Charles proceeded to put his textbook back into his knapsack. Whether or not the case would resume Thursday had yet to be confirmed, but for today, the chase was over. He packed his own knapsack, then they went to retrieve their bicycles.

They were two blocks away, the smell of the pizzeria long behind them, when Timothy remembered that they'd never gotten around to getting a slice.

CHAPTER 23

ednesday evening was another Group meeting at Timothy's house. One of the women had a friend named Amber visiting from San Francisco. Amber was going to give a slideshow presentation and had shown up early to set up.

"I'm thinking of projecting against that wall over there," Amber said, pointing to the only wall that didn't have a tall bookcase or a window.

"That would work," Cathryn said.

"Can we perhaps . . . move the television?" Amber suggested.

"Sure," Cathryn said. "Timothy!"

Timothy was in the kitchen watching his TV dinner cook through the window in the oven door. The egg timer still had five minutes on it, which left him enough time to disconnect the Cablevision wire so he and Cathryn could wheel the set into the dining room.

Amber then asked Timothy if he felt like helping her set up the slide projector, which he actually did. Getting to run the projector at school was considered an honor, and anything roughly equivalent seemed a.o.k. to Timothy.

Leaving his piping hot TV dinner to cool on a flower-shaped trivet in the kitchen, Timothy returned to the living room and got to work.

Step one: Remove useless Victorian vase from end table. Hide vase in basement and hope Mom and Cathryn forget about it and leave it there permanently.

Step two: Pile glossy coffee table art books onto end table in place of useless Victorian vase. Continue adding books until improvised pedestal appears appropriate height for slideshow projection.

Step three: Borrow extension cord from stereo system for slideshow projector because Amber forgot to bring one.

Step four: Plug in slideshow projector, insert circular slide tray, turn on projector, adjust manual focusing knob.

Step five: Play with remote control for several minutes until Amber says *Thank you Timothy*, and asks you to stop.

Timothy returned to his TV dinner, which had gotten cold, but he ate it anyway, particularly the baked brownie in the middle which was obviously the best part.

The rest of the women began arriving at the usual time.

"Hi Timothy," Cara said, waving across the room.

"Hi," he waved back.

Many of the other women now made a point of saying hello to him by name as well, including Sarah, the female cop with the lethal fighting capabilities, and Anne, who had once upon a time been unfriendly to him.

As the women were half finished with the hugs and started to find their seating pillows, Timothy's mom made a general announcement.

"So, as most of you know, we have a special guest tonight, Amber from San Francisco . . ."

Some light applause.

"Amber's going to be sharing a slideshow presentation with

us put together by the Alice B. Toklas Society, it's about getting involved politically, helping women in the community, and empowerment in general . . . did I get that right Amber?"

"That's about right," said Amber, standing up from her pillow and transitioning into her public speaking mode.

Giving Amber the floor, Timothy's mom inched her way over to Timothy, who was still standing at the edge of the room.

"You heading upstairs?" she asked him.

"Actually, I think I'll just go outside and sit on the front porch," he said.

It was a beautiful spring evening, seemed a waste to sit upstairs in his room.

"That's fine," she said, "by the time the slide show starts, just decide whether you want to be inside or out, okay?" his mom said.

"Yeah, sure," Timothy said, and went out front.

At first, he let himself sink into the old sofa next to Oscar who was already sleeping there. Oscar barely opened his eyes when Timothy stroked his head, he had his own way of making it through Group nights.

Timothy decided a different vantage point might be better to watch the world go by, so he got up and repositioned himself on the front steps.

Mrs. O'Connor was out in front of her house across the street, watering her lawn.

"Hi Timothy," she called over to him.

"Hi Mrs. O'Connor," Timothy called back, "have you heard from Mr. O'Connor?"

"I was just talking to him last night," she said. "He's on a layover in Nevada. Should be back home in about two weeks."

"Tell him I was asking for him."

"Will do, thanks Timothy."

Mrs. O'Connor turned off the spigot and headed inside.

Timothy turned around to check the front window of his house just in time to see the lights going out for the slideshow. Looked like he'd be sitting out here for a while.

The leaves in the trees seemed a darker shade of green than just yesterday, they were definitely inching toward summer. Perfect weather, really.

Looking up the street, he noticed a familiar figure. It was Lynda, walking down the middle of the road, which was typical for Kingstonians, the bluestone sidewalks being the tripping hazard they were.

Usually, Lynda walked facing straight ahead, not looking at anyone. But tonight he could see that she was holding her head down with one hand over her face. Timothy didn't know what to make of this at first. Then he realized she was crying.

Timothy thought hard about this. Lynda would be out of earshot in less than 30 seconds, and gone in little more than a minute. It would be so easy to just let her keep walking and not deal with this.

But it occurred to him, while he remained sitting here, she would still be off crying in her little apartment. Alone. Or worse.

Before he could deliberate further on the subject, he propelled himself off the front steps and into action.

"Lynda?" he asked, approaching her.

Lynda just kept crying softly, changing course just enough to get around him.

"Lynda, are you okay?"

"Just leave me alone," she said, moving her hand from her face just enough so Timothy could see she had a fresh black eye.

He almost let her keep walking, it would have been so much easier. But when he looked back at his house, he knew there was a roomful of women in there watching a slideshow about helping women in the community.

He knew what he had to do.

"Lynda," he called, running after her, trying to get her to stop yet again. "Lynda, come with me, I can help you."

"No one can help me," she sobbed.

"I know who can," Timothy said and reached out his hand. "Please . . ."

Lynda stopped. She looked down at Timothy's outstretched hand.

There seemed to be something so defeated about her that any kind of hope was out of the question.

But maybe it was this same sense of nothing left to lose that allowed her, slowly, to extend the hand that wasn't concealing her face and place it inside Timothy's.

"Come with me," he said, "it will be alright."

Timothy led Lynda up onto his porch and straight inside his house.

"Timothy," his mom said in a stage whisper, "I told you not until after the slideshow . . ."

But Timothy cleared his throat and made an announcement.

"Everybody, this is Lynda," he said. "She needs your help."

Someone turned the living room light on and suddenly everyone saw Lynda standing there, crying, with a black eye.

"Oh my God . . ." someone said.

Instantly, the roomful of women rose to their feet and seemed to envelop her in a collective embrace. At that moment, Lynda allowed herself to weep openly in a way she'd not done once in her entire adult life.

As Timothy slipped alone back out onto the front porch, even though the sounds of Lynda wailing were painful to hear, he knew she was in the right place.

He sat back down on the sofa next to Oscar, listening to a distant siren, and the sounds of his own breathing.

Inside the house, water was being offered, icy compresses were being applied, phone calls were being made. The slideshow was obviously over.

The meeting broke up earlier than planned. As Timothy's mom escorted Lynda, wrapped in an old raincoat, out to their car, Cathryn stopped briefly by the sofa.

"Timothy, we're taking Lynda to the women's shelter, she'll be safe there," she said. "You wait here, don't go anywhere, okay?"

The other women were filtering past on their way to their own cars, but Cara stopped on the porch.

"I can stay with Timothy," she offered.

"That's okay, Cara, Timothy'll be alright," Cathryn said.

"It's okay, I don't mind," Cara said, "I wasn't planning on being home this early anyway . . ."

"Well, okay . . . thanks Cara, much appreciated . . ."

One by one, the cars all pulled away, including their own beater car with Lynda on board, being whisked to safety at an undisclosed location.

"You hungry?" Cara asked.

"A little."

"C'mon, let's get a snack."

Cara and Timothy went back inside long enough to load up two paper plates with assorted chips and cookies. They returned out to the porch and plopped down on the sofa, somewhat close to each other because Oscar refused to budge.

Cara waited until she'd finished crunching on a handful of corn chips, then turned to Timothy.

"You did the right thing," she told him.

Timothy didn't say anything, but he nodded his head as he ate another Mallomar.

Cara set down her snack plate and lit up a cigarette. The sound of the match striking made Timothy look over to her.

He watched carefully as she inhaled. He'd watched several people smoking recently. But this time he wasn't watching the cigarette. He was watching her lips.

"Can I have one?" he asked.

"What?"

Maybe he should make like she'd misheard him. But this felt like another moment to say Yes and double it.

"Can I have a cigarette?" he said, clearly.

Cara laughed at the sheer audacity.

"Your mom would *kill* me if I gave you a cigarette," she said, still laughing.

Timothy thought about asking her simply to fib, but came up with another idea.

"Can I have a puff of yours?" he asked.

Cara continued looking at him like this was a terrible idea. But the night had taken a wild turn, and Timothy had shown remarkable maturity by doing what he'd done.

Almost impetuously, she handed him the cigarette.

Timothy took it awkwardly at first, examining the filter, already slightly brown from tobacco smoke being sucked through it, slightly compacted where it had been lightly clutched between Cara's lips.

He then placed the cigarette with an almost practiced hand into his own lips. He inhaled slowly this time, taking in only as much smoke as he could handle without coughing. He tilted his head back, exhaled with somewhat exaggerated satisfaction, and handed the cigarette back to Cara, who'd been marveling at the whole display.

"Did that satisfy your curiosity?" she asked.

"Yes," Timothy answered, but this was only partially true, because he was still curious, although about things other than Cara's cigarette.

He continued to watch as she resumed smoking.

"Do you have . . . a partner?" he finally found the courage to ask her.

She smiled, happy to see Timothy seemed to be exploring territory he'd refused to consider the first night she'd visited him in his room.

"No," she said, "I don't have a partner."

"Then why do you come to Group?" he asked.

"Group is . . . not just for people with partners," she said.

"Then what's it for?"

How to put this?

"Group is also for people with . . . questions," she said. "People who are processing stuff."

Timothy wasn't exactly sure what this meant, but it seemed like whatever question he was trying to formulate had still not been answered.

"Do you want . . . a partner?" he asked.

Cara made sure not to laugh, because for the life of her, she couldn't tell if he were trying to figure out his home situation, or presenting himself as an option. His curiosity was charming, at any rate.

"Someday . . ." she said.

Her cigarette was almost finished. When she offered him another drag, he took a baby puff before handing it back to her. She took one last small puff herself.

The ashtray was on the floor and she'd been tapping the ashes off casually, but she needed to lean over in order to snuff it out properly. As she did so, her head came close to Timothy. Timothy surprised even himself by using the opportunity to lean in quickly and give a quick, clumsy kiss on her forehead.

Cara was clearly surprised, but made sure to keep her response light, and did not appear to take offense.

"Come on," she said, "let's clean this place up so your mom and Cathryn won't have to do it when they get home."

She rose from the sofa and held the screen door open until Timothy followed her.

Oscar decided to come inside, too.

CHAPTER 24

Charles agreed to one additional stake out on the condition that the situation seemed safe. They met up at Stewart's again because it was only a few blocks from the storage place on Greenkill Avenue.

"Did you bring some means of defending yourself?" Charles asked, which was one of the additional bits of caution they'd discussed on the telephone.

Timothy began to open his knapsack, but paused, first answering the question with a question.

"What'd you bring?"

Charles opened his own knapsack so Timothy could look inside.

"Baseballs?" Timothy asked. There were three of them.

"Mm hmm."

"What good are baseballs?"

"Timothy, batters wear helmets for a reason," Charles said. "My fastball clocks in at an average of 53 miles per hour. You know what kind of damage tightly-wrapped cowhide can do at 53 miles per hour?"

Timothy nodded his head thoughtfully at Charles' reasoning.

"So, what did you bring?" Charles asked.

Timothy opened his knapsack and was about to pull the item out in plain sight, but Charles put his hand on Timothy's wrist and prevented him from doing so.

"A meat cleaver? T-Bird, are you crazy?" Charles said, looking around to make sure no one else had seen it. "You can't go around carrying a meat cleaver."

"You know what kind of damage a meat cleaver can do?" Timothy asked. "A lot more than a baseball."

"That may be true, T-Bird. But, a cop searches my bag and finds three baseballs, you know what I get busted for? Being on my way to baseball practice. A cop finds you carrying around a meat cleaver? That's criminal intent," Charles said. "That's two steps shy of premeditated murder."

Timothy thought back to his alibi the day he'd skipped school.

"What if *I'm* on my way to practice?" he asked.

"Practicing *what?*"

"There've been axe throwing competitions since the colonial days," he said. "I read about it."

"Timothy, nobody is going to believe a ten year old is on his way to an axe throwing competition. Besides, no offense, a guy your size pulls out a meat cleaver? Guy like Grafton's gonna grab it right out of your hands and use it against you . . . "

Timothy had run out of arguments.

"I'll keep it in my bag," he said, somewhat dejectedly.

They saddled up and pedaled up Greenkill.

Their destination was close to the rail yard. A narrow side street led across the train tracks to an old brewery from the days when the small city had made its own beer. Timothy had never been back here before. Apparently they'd converted the brewery to some sort of storage space, because inanimate objects didn't mind so much being rattled by passing trains.

The open gate had a sign reading:

"Gate Closes at 5"

Charles noted that just inside the gate was some kind of sensor embedded in the road so that an exiting car could trigger the gate to open. He subtly jumped up and down on the sensor. Probably they weren't heavy enough to trigger it, but it was only 3:30. They were pretty sure to be out by 5 at any rate.

Charles checked the receipt they'd found in Grafton's garbage.

"D-17," he read aloud, holding the receipt up against the fading numbers painted on the old brick brewery.

Seemed like it should be pretty straight forward, but once they got beyond the first building, they found a rabbit warren of smaller buildings made of corrugated metal. The place had been expanded pell-mell over the years. The alleys between the buildings were maze-like, no straight route leading anywhere.

Even with the number right in Charles' hand, they took a few wrong turns, got slightly lost, but eventually found themselves standing in front of D-17.

Timothy tugged on the padlock. If Charles had nixed the meat cleaver, he probably wasn't going to be too thrilled with the improvised explosive Timothy was also carrying in his knapsack, so he decided not to mention it.

Charles, meanwhile, got down on one knee to check the well-worn tire tracks in the dusty alleyway.

"These are old," he said, "I don't think Grafton's been here yet."

It occurred to Timothy that even though Grafton had told his brother on the phone that he'd been coming to the storage place on Thursday afternoon, he still might not show up. He didn't seem the most reliable person.

But just as they were trying to figure out where they might conceal themselves before he arrived, they heard it: the unmistakable sound of the Mustang, creeping its way through the storage facility.

The sound of the engine was ricocheting all over the place, and they themselves had gotten turned around more than once, it was impossible to know from which direction the Mustang would arrive.

Frantic for a hiding place, Timothy checked a pile of old crates next to Grafton's unit, but there most definitely wasn't room for two boys and two bikes.

Charles, looking quickly at all the other units, noticed the one directly across from Grafton's didn't have a padlock on it. He pulled open the heavy garage-type door as quickly as he could.

Inside was an odd collection of junk, probably cast-offs from abandoned units the storage facility had yet to figure out what to do with.

"In here," Charles said.

There was just enough room to wheel their bikes inside and get inside themselves. Pulling the door down from the inside, Charles jammed an empty beer can underneath to keep the door open a crack, maybe an inch. Trying not to knock anything over in the dark, he and Timothy got down onto their bellies and peeked out.

The Mustang pulled up and stopped just past D-17, so Timothy and Charles still had a strained view across to Grafton's unit. They expected he would hop out of the car at any moment. But he did not.

For whatever reason Grafton remained in his car, he'd yet to cut the engine. In fact, he revved it a few times reflexively.

The tailpipe of the Mustang was right there, almost level with the crack under the garage door, through which Charles and Timothy were trying to breathe.

Each time Grafton revved the engine, a fresh burst of carbon monoxide came pouring under the door and into Charles and Timothy's faces. Charles waved his hand repeatedly, desperately trying to fan the bad air back out through the crack as it filled their small hiding space.

"Try not to cough," he said with a hoarse voice.

But Timothy did start coughing, and so did he. When Grafton finally cut the engine, somehow they were both able to stymie their coughing, but their eyes were still watering like crazy.

The car door opened. From the waist down, Grafton could be observed walking into the scene, still wearing his soiled dishwasher's pants and slip-resistant shoes.

With a jangling keyring, Grafton bent down to unlock the padlock. In the moments it took him to figure out which key and how to insert it, Timothy got his first good look at him in the daylight in fairly close proximity.

His face was pockmarked in places, his hair greasy, and he seemed to have more creases in his forehead than a man his age should have.

Once he figured out the lock, he pulled the door open with considerably less effort than it had taken Charles, and proceeded to pull out seemingly random boxes and pile them in the alleyway for inspection.

He went through one box, then another, then another.

"Shit, where the fuck is it?" he said aloud, unaware that anyone was watching him.

The convulsions in Timothy's lungs from the carbon monoxide had finally abated, but in the rush to conceal himself, he'd lain down uncomfortably interspersed with his banana saddle bicycle. His back was starting to spasm slightly, making him want to adjust his position, but he didn't dare move.

Grafton's search, meanwhile, was growing more frantic. More boxes were being roughly pulled from the storage unit, but he couldn't seem to find what he was looking for.

"Mother fucker," he said to himself, standing there looking at the useless mess he'd just made. He started throwing the boxes back into the unit, seeming to give up the search for now.

Of course, the boxes now didn't fit as neatly as when he'd first arrived, so he started kicking at them to make them conform to the space until he was finally able to yank the door back down and get it closed.

He fumbled with the lock, but managed to get it secured, and pulled hard on it to make sure it held.

He stomped back into his car and was surely just about to slam the car door closed when Timothy, who could not remain still a moment longer, adjusted his body slightly.

Some kind of domino effect occurred, the slight movement of his wedged ankle unmoored a pile of boxes which sent some metallic object on top crashing down onto the concrete pad.

Grafton's car door did not close.

His feet could be observed, slowly, walking back into the picture. Only this time he was holding something: a baseball bat.

"Who's there?" Grafton called out, apparently uncertain from which direction the sound had come.

Timothy and Charles were both holding their breath again, waiting for the door to be maniacally pulled open, their hiding space revealed. Why did he have to listen to Charles? Why didn't he have his meat cleaver gripped tightly in his hand at the ready?

Grafton suddenly took a violent swing at the crates piled next to his unit, where minutes before Timothy and Charles had considered hiding. The crates exploded into splinters. Several mice, who had been hiding within, scurried in all directions.

Grafton could be heard chuckling, as if to be saying to himself, *Oh, it's just a few mice*, but the next moment he called out:

"Next time it's your head, mother fucker," as if he somehow did know someone had been watching him, and the only reason they weren't dead was because he hadn't noticed the unlocked unit across from D-17.

Grafton got into the Mustang and started it up. With a bonus blast of monoxide, he peeled out, leaving Charles and Timothy momentarily asphyxiated one last time until the dust had cleared.

Charles waited until the sound of the Mustang had faded completely before reopening the door so they could creep back out into daylight.

"Damn, that was a close one," he said.

He closed the door of the unit they'd been hiding in. As they slowly pedaled down the alleyway, Charles was trying to figure the way out, but Timothy was looking back at D-17, knowing the final answer to the puzzle remained within, if only he could find it.

The two of them got lost again, finding themselves in the E section instead of on the way out, but they doubled back and soon the exit gate was within their sight.

It was still well before 5, the gate was open, they rolled right through.

The sound of an approaching freight train was growing louder and louder. Looking way down Greenkill, they could see its light still over a block away, its bell ringing, the ground just beginning to vibrate underneath them.

"C'mon, we can make it," Charles said.

They sped up, and got back over the tracks with ten seconds to spare, before the slow moving train rumbled past and cut the old brewery off from the rest of the city.

When they got as far as Stewart's, Charles pulled over in the parking lot.

"Timothy, do you know who Jim Ryan is?" Charles asked.

"He's the Chief of Police, isn't he?"

"That's right. And he's also a close personal friend of my family," Charles said. "If we walk into his office on Monday afternoon and lay out the case we've built against IPM, I know for a fact he will act on it immediately . . . the story will hit the paper by Tuesday and, one way or the other, IPM will be held accountable for what's going on at that quarry."

"What about Grafton?"

"I don't know yet, maybe he was involved, maybe he wasn't . . . but if the guy we're following is a killer like his brother? I think it's high time we leave this aspect of the case to the professionals."

Charles scanned Timothy's face to see if any of this was sinking in then added:

"Why don't we take the weekend to pull together what we have so far, then you and me will head into the station Monday after school, what do you say?"

Timothy didn't say anything at first. He felt like if they couldn't present some hard evidence, when it came to Ken, IPM was going to get away with murder. But he also knew that Charles was probably right, if they didn't get the toxic dump information into the right hands before IPM's proposed expansion was rubber stamped, they were probably going to get away with that too.

"Well, I guess I'll see you over the weekend," he conceded, pointing his bike toward Wall Street, figuring Charles would likely continue riding straight up to Hilltop Meadows at this point. But Charles turned toward Wall Street too.

"Why don't I ride you home?" Charles asked.

Timothy could think of a reason or two, but kept them to himself as they continued together toward Warren Street.

When they got to Timothy's house, Timothy broke the party up quickly so he wouldn't have to invite Charles inside.

"Guess I'll come up to your house tomorrow," he called to Charles, already beginning to carry his bike up the stairs.

Just then, Timothy's mom came out the front door.

"Oh, hello Charles, how are you doing?" she called down to Charles, who was still standing on the sidewalk.

"Fine, Mrs. Miller, how are you?"

"Very well, thank you for asking. How's your mother?"

"She's fine, thank you."

"Glad to hear it."

Timothy was frozen in the middle of this exchange, still standing on the steps holding his bicycle.

"Well, I'd best be going," Charles said.

"Would you like to stay for supper? It was so nice of your mother to invite Timothy that one night."

Where was this coming from? Timothy's mom NEVER invited any of his friends to stay for supper. Of course, this was largely because Timothy never brought any friends home, but this was beside the point.

"I'm sure Charles has stuff to do at home," Timothy cut in.

"Actually," Charles said, "I'd love to stay for supper, that would be lovely."

Timothy's brain was melting like a box of crayons left inside a hot car.

"Great, I'll go inside and tell Cathryn," Timothy's mom said.

"Will my bike be safe out here?" Charles asked Timothy.

"You better bring it onto the porch," Timothy said wearily, "and chain it to the leg of the sofa . . . "

When they went inside the house, Cathryn was at the stove crumpling potato chips into the tuna casserole.

"Cathryn, this is Charles," Timothy's mom said.

"Oh, hello Charles, I think we spoke on the phone once."

"Yes, that's right," Charles agreed, even though Timothy had said it was his mother.

If Charles thought any of this was at all weird—the pink walls, the vintage decor, the unexplained woman at the stove—he didn't betray it on his face for a moment. He just continued smiling like being invited into their home was the nicest thing that had happened to him all week.

"May I just use your phone for a moment?"

"Sure, Charles, it's right there on the back wall."

Charles winked at Timothy in a conspiratorial fashion, even though the plot to torture Timothy was entirely Charles' idea. The galley kitchen had never felt so crowded in Timothy's entire life.

"Hi Mom . . . is tonight still your bowling night?" Charles said. "You wouldn't mind if I stayed for dinner at Timothy's then . . . yes, she invited me . . . great, I'll see you when you get home."

Both Timothy's mom and Cathryn looked over to Charles expectantly.

"All settled," Charles announced happily.

"Great," Timothy's mom said. "Timothy, you want to take Charles upstairs and show him your room?"

"*No*," he said, a little more forcefully than seemed appropriate. "I mean, we'd rather set the table."

"Because I can set the table tonight . . ." she offered.

"No really, Mom, I want to set the table," Timothy insisted. "I really want to show Charles our drinking glass collection."

Timothy's mom's eyes squinted from perplexity. She'd heard some pretty creative excuses for *not* wanting to do chores in her day, but whatever reverse psychology she assumed was at play here was beyond her comprehension.

Timothy led Charles through the swinging door that opened to the dining room.

"It took me a year going to Carroll's to collect these," Timothy said, committing to his stated purpose.

He took the glass tumblers from the hutch and placed them onto the table one by one, each featuring a different cartoon character.

"I collected some of these too," Charles said, going along with whatever.

"You can pick anyone you want. I'm usually Yosemite Sam, but you can use it if you like, I don't care."

"That's okay, I'd prefer Sylvester. That is, if no one objects."

"That should work just fine," Timothy said, placing Sylvester in front of the guest space on the table, and Yosemite Sam in front of his own.

Timothy proceeded to set the rest of the table in slow motion, letting the chore expand to fill the maximum amount of time and space before dinner was served.

"So Charles," Timothy's mom said, shortly after everyone had taken at least one bite of their tuna casserole, "how did you and Timothy meet, anyway?"

"We met at the field right up the street here," Charles said. "I happened by with some other friends of mine and, I guess you could say Timothy and I just hit it off."

Charles smiled across the table to Timothy. As excruciating was the overall experience of having his worlds collide at the dinner table, Timothy was heartened that Charles' first stated reason for their association was true friendship. He managed to smile back.

"And you go to the junior high school?" Cathryn asked.

"I do indeed. It's a fine school, I think Timothy will do very well there."

And so it continued, with pleasantries much like these, Charles all the while exhibiting the flawless table manners Timothy's mom maintained were part of the social fabric that held a family together. In short, despite (or perhaps adding to) Timothy's discomfort, he charmed both his mom and Cathryn.

It seemed like Timothy might get through this alive.

And then:

"Is there a bathroom I could use?" Charles asked.

"It's upstairs," Timothy's mom said.

Please God, no.

Charles took his napkin from his lap and wiped his mouth.

"If you'll excuse me," he said, and headed upstairs.

"He is *so nice*," both Timothy's mom and Cathryn said to Timothy once Charles was out of earshot. They clearly meant to express both that they were impressed with Charles, and with Timothy as well for having scored such an impressive friend.

Dinner was wrapped up shortly after Charles came downstairs. And, although there was nothing like pineapple upside down cake, his mom did produce a fresh box of Freihofer's Chocolate Chip Cookies, whose presence in the house was either an extraordinary coincidence, or proof positive that Timothy's mom and Cathryn were sometimes holding out on him in the dessert department.

"I'll clear the table," Cathryn said, "that way you guys can spend a little time together before Charles has to go home."

"You wanna walk around the block?" Timothy asked.

"Sounds good to me."

Charles waited until they were halfway down the street before he turned and said:

"Timothy, you didn't tell me your mom was gay."

Timothy was so mentally blindsided that such words could come so blatantly out of Charles' mouth, he almost didn't know what to say.

"My mom is not gay," he said.

"Then who is Cathryn?"

"Cathryn is her roommate."

Charles shook his head.

"I saw the upstairs of your house. Cathryn is not your mom's roommate."

"She is," Timothy insisted, "she sleeps in the third bedroom."

"Timothy, that's the guest room, there are macrame pillows on the bed. No one puts macrame pillows on their own bed. Besides, I looked in your mom's bedroom."

"You looked in my mom's bedroom?"

"You don't have to be a detective, there are two sets of slippers in there, one on either side of the bed . . ."

Timothy hid his face in his hands. He could barely bring *himself* to look into that bedroom. The fact that Charles had looked in there and saw their *slippers*? It felt like someone had pried open his chest, like at age ten he was actually going to have a heart attack.

"Timothy, it's nothing to be ashamed of."

"How would you know?" Timothy said. "I know your dad died and everything, but he was a *hero*, not some . . ."

Timothy stopped talking. He had instantly regretted saying anything about Charles' dad, which seemed really out of bounds, but on some level there was truth in what had flown out of his mouth. Not in terms of a loss that couldn't be measured, but a story that could be talked about openly, with pride.

They both stopped walking. Charles thought for a moment about what he was going to say, and when he did speak, it was almost a non sequitur.

"Remember that day those kids called me Oreo?"

Timothy was still looking at the ground.

"Do you?" Charles asked again.

"Yeah, I remember."

"You know why they called me that?"

"No."

"I'll tell you why . . . they were insinuating that I'm black on the outside but white on the inside. They were trying to make me feel bad, but they failed. You know why? Would you like to know who I am on the inside?"

This seemed a rhetorical question, but Timothy said, "Yes."

"I'm me, that's who. I'm the person my dad raised, I'm the person my mom is still raising. And you know something? I love my parents. I'm glad they raised me exactly the way they did. I wouldn't be any other way."

Timothy looked up to Charles.

"Do they call you that a lot?"

"On and off. And, like I said, I've been called a hell of a lot worse by people who think I'm too black, but I'm not even going to get into that . . . the point is, Timothy, you can't spend your life worrying about what other people think of you . . .

"What I said tonight at dinner? I meant it. Yeah, this investigation has been way more interesting than baseball practice, but the best thing about it? has been hanging out with you. And if I could wish one thing for you, it would be the strength not to give two shits about what anybody else thinks of you, because you're a great guy, and I'm proud you're my friend."

Charles reached out and put a brotherly hand on Timothy's shoulder. Like the time Charles and his mom had held his hands when they'd said grace, there was something true, and strong and loving about having the weight of Charles' hand reassuringly resting on his shoulder like this.

Timothy looked up at Charles briefly. His gaze was hard to hold at this moment, his feelings were so raw. He'd heard every word Charles had said, and on one level, he knew that what Charles had said contained some truth.

It would be quite another thing to put this truth into practice.

CHAPTER 25

n Friday afternoon, Timothy found himself walking along Tannery Brook, alone.

There was a lot to think about.

All these tensions he'd been holding. His father leaving. Cathryn moving in. His mother ignoring him. His living room painted pink, his car worse than that . . . the list went on and on . . .

Charles seemed to think that if Timothy would just accept things as they were, everything would somehow be okay. But it wasn't just a matter of accepting current circumstances. It was that the rules had been changed, the rug pulled out from underneath.

It felt right to be angry. Accepting things as they now were felt like defeat.

Having been lost in thought, his eyes came back into focus on the brook. A clump of green foam was trapped among some rocks poking through the water's surface, one of those spots you could really hear the brook gurgling.

Timothy stepped closer. He saw it wasn't just foam, something was caught between the rocks. He had to lean way over but he was able to scoop up . . .

A dead frog.

Timothy wiped the chemical foam from its lifeless eyes. Its dangling little legs dripped water down onto Timothy's sneakers. He looked at the frog a long time. Then to the brook he'd pulled it from. Then over to the Green Apartment Building, standing watch over the field, day in, day out, whether kids were outside playing or not.

Now there were two vacant apartments inside the building that he knew of. He pictured the beer bottles inside Lynda's otherwise empty refrigerator. Who would drink them? And the mail piling outside Ken's door with no one to pick it up. How long before someone just threw it all in the garbage, like Ken had never even existed?

For certain, they needed to wrap up this investigation, to make sure the brook ran clean again. But to give up on Ken now, when they were *this* close to proving the real motive behind what had happened to him?

Timothy knew for a fact there was some kind of evidence, just sitting there, in a box, in a storage facility on Greenkill Avenue. This was his last chance.

All he had to do was make himself go over there, now, and find it.

Back at Timothy's house, his mom and Cathryn were running around, getting ready.

Since the slide show had been interrupted a few nights ago, and since Amber was about to fly back to San Francisco, there was to be a special Friday evening Group meeting, so they could all finish watching the slide show, and have another crack at snacking and socializing.

"Sorry you have to put up with this two nights this week," Cathryn said, piling the books on the end table as Timothy had done previously, making a place for the projector.

"That's okay," Timothy said. "Hey, I think I'm gonna head over to Charles' house, can you just tell Mom?"

Across the room, his mom was occupied with Amber, in the process of moving the TV into the dining room again.

"Sure, have fun," Cathryn said.

It was easy for her to imagine Timothy heading off to a safe place, having met Charles and being so impressed with his character.

Outside, Timothy hopped on his bike and pulled his knapsack over his shoulders.

But he didn't pedal up the hill toward Hilltop Meadows.

He rode instead in the other direction, toward the old brewery on Greenkill Avenue.

He took side streets in case anyone vaguely parental should happen to drive by and wonder where he was going. Also checking to see if Grafton's car was parked at his house would be a sensible precaution.

Pedaling through the midtown neighborhood on a late Friday afternoon, you could almost feel the front porches gearing up to be the site of lazy beer drinking now that the work week was almost over.

Coming up on some kids walking in the street ahead of him, he could already tell they were looking at him like he was in the wrong neighborhood. Veering to avoid them, he almost bumped into a guy he didn't see walking in the street.

"Watch where you're going," the guy said roughly. As he spoke, Timothy realized it was the guy he'd usually see escorting Lynda, now walking the streets angry and alone as if he were still out looking for her.

"Sorry," Timothy said, quickly redirecting his bicycle and moving away.

"Hey, come back here," the guy said, as if suddenly recognizing him, but Timothy kept pedaling, not sticking around to find out what the guy wanted.

He hadn't approached Grafton's house from this direction last time, but when he hit Furnace Street he knew he was almost there. He made his way just far enough to confirm the Mustang was parked in front of Grafton's place, then made a beeline for the storage space.

When he got to Greenkill Avenue, he was glad to put the railroad tracks between him and the angry pimp man he thought might be following him, but he was now in a place desolate enough that it felt creepy in another way.

Approaching the old brewery, the sign reminded him that the gate would close at 5pm. He checked his Timex. It was 4:30, that gave him only a half hour. He would have to work quickly . . .

Cathryn answered the phone when it rang back in their kitchen, thinking it was someone calling to ask about the meeting.

"Hello, it's Charles, is Timothy there?"

"Hi Charles," Cathryn said, "Timothy just left, he said he was going to your house . . . "

Charles had to think quick.

"Yes, that's right, thanks, I'll just see him when he gets here . . . have a good night."

Cathryn went back to carrying snack trays from the kitchen to the dining room.

Charles meanwhile thought to himself:

Why would Timothy say he was coming up to my house?

And then he said aloud:

"Oh shit."

He jumped on his 10 speed and started pedaling into Kingston as fast as his legs could take him.

He kept the 10 speed in top gear the whole way.

Timothy at first did not remember how to get to D-17. The alleyways all looked the same and, for whatever reason, the numbers were not entirely sequential. But after a wrong turn or two, he found the D section and was back where he'd been the day before.

Only today he was by himself, and it was ten times creepier.

The crates that Grafton had destroyed with his baseball bat were still lying here in splinters. No one had been back here in the last 24 hours to clean them up. The tire marks in the dust where Grafton had peeled out were likewise undisturbed by human footprints.

Timothy sat himself down cross-legged in the dust in front of D-17 and examined the padlock. He'd yet to try this experiment at home, but was prepared to try it now. Nothing better than on-the-job training.

Timothy took the plastic sandwich bag from his knapsack and held it up to the light. The potassium chlorate powder he'd made by pulverizing match heads was ready. In his inexpert opinion, there appeared to be enough to blow open the padlock.

Leaning the lock up against the garage door so the bottom was facing up, Timothy slowly sprinkled the gunpowder-like substance into the keyhole, shaking the lock slightly so the explosive powder would trickle into the workings.

He hadn't brought the Real Men's Guidebook with him, but he was pretty sure how to do this, he just needed to whittle the wooden shaft of a single kitchen match to insert into the keyhole and function as a fuse.

The other thing he didn't bring was a pocket knife, but he did have one implement that was incredibly sharp. Holding a tiny match in his left hand, he began to whittle it with the oversized meat cleaver.

With each tiny little chiseling action he felt sure he was about to shave his fingerprints off, ever so delicately carving the small wooden shaft until one end was about the size of a needle.

Setting the cleaver down for now, Timothy tapped the wooden shaft of the kitchen match down into the keyhole, so fragile it seemed it would break, but he managed to get it in just enough.

In truth, he did not know what size explosion to expect. His imagination provided an image of total destruction, the entire unit falling back to earth in flaming chunks after having been blown sky high. But would the Real Men's Guide not have warned him if this were a possibility?

On his feet and prepared to run, he lit a single match. With a slightly shaky hand, he extended the match toward the other match head poking out of the keyhole, but every time he got within a half inch, he pulled it back reflexively as if he were about to get his hand blown off.

He blew the first match out before it could burn his fingers, then he lit another. Finally steadying himself, he extended the lit match, and with a sudden *FFZZZ* the fuse match caught fire and flared up.

Stumbling backwards he ran ten feet and turned to see what would happen.

BAM!

An explosion about as substantial as a firecracker echoed all over the place. Timothy looked around nervously as the sound subsided, then over to the lock, which was smoking.

Walking back over to examine his pyrotechnic handiwork, he was amazed to find that it had actually worked, the padlock had been blown open. Slightly warm to the touch, he jiggled it off the hasp and, just like that, the storage space was unlocked.

Timothy took a deep breath. This was the moment of truth. He reached down, took hold of the knotted bit of dirty rope tied to the handle and, with a bit more effort than it had taken Charles, managed to pull open the heavy garage door.

Behold. Boxes and boxes, piled haphazardly where Grafton had left them yesterday.

Mostly, the boxes seemed to be newish small appliances. Hand-mixers and clock-radios, with a few slightly bigger-ticket items like speakers or home stereos.

There were also the bankers boxes he'd glimpsed yesterday. One of them, he imagined, would contain what he was looking for, even though he didn't know exactly what it was.

He looked at his Timex. It was already 4:42. There was no time to waste.

Quickly, Timothy began removing boxes and placing them onto the ground in the alleyway. This part of the process itself was difficult. Grafton was much taller than Timothy and had piled the boxes so high that Timothy had to reach way over his head to get the top ones down, and some of them were quite heavy.

Once there were a few accessible boxes to choose from, Timothy opened one.

Inside, a nonsensical mess. Receipts, letters, old photographs, all jumbled together like the box had been packed quickly with no sense of order whatsoever. Perhaps the result of a quick clean up of Luke Grafton's personal effects, but no matter the process, if Kurt Grafton couldn't make sense of this, how the hell could Timothy?

He decided to switch tactics and keep taking boxes out instead, maybe something large and obvious would get his attention, though the task seemed impossible as he imagined the storage unit being packed all the way to the back wall with random boxes like these.

But after he'd pulled out a second row of boxes, Timothy was surprised to find that the unit wasn't as packed to the gills as he imagined, there was actually a lot of space in there. It was like Grafton had gotten lazy and kept piling things in front until he couldn't get into the back anymore.

With an entryway cleared wide enough to explore, Timothy struck a kitchen match. With lit match in one hand, meat cleaver in the other, he cautiously tiptoed deeper into the storage space.

It wasn't entirely empty. Curiously, there was an open army cot, along with a battery-powered camping light, an 8-track player with one of those plunger handles on top, and a pile of magazines.

As the match began to burn down, Timothy turned on the electric camping light, which lit the place just well enough to look around. The arrangement looked intentional, as if Grafton at various points had actually been hanging out in here. Why the hell would anyone want to hang out in a storage space?

★   ★   ★

Charles rolled up on Grafton's place not realizing Timothy had been here not twenty minutes earlier. But by this point, the Mustang was not parked out front. Grafton could be anywhere.

Hightailing it out of there, Charles upshifted quickly trying to accelerate as fast as his legs would take him, but found his feet suddenly racing in a circle while the bike beneath him lost speed, not going anywhere.

In his haste he'd shifted more recklessly than the bike wanted him to, the derailleur throwing the chain clear off the gears.

Hopping off, Charles flipped the bike upside down. Taking hold of the greasy chain in one hand, he used the pedal to wriggle the gears forward and backward, gently coaxing the chain until its links were realigned with the gear's teeth and it was spinning properly again.

Flipping the bike back onto its wheels, Charles was just climbing on when a hand clapped down on the handlebars.

Charles looked up to find Kyle, the kid who tried to make off with his bike last week. Only this time, he had his two buddies with him.

"Hey, it's Mr. Tough Guy," Kyle said. "Where's your little white girlfriend?"

Charles looked straight at Kyle, then at each of his buddies who were moving in to flank Charles on both sides.

"I haven't got time for this . . ." Charles said.

★   ★   ★

Deep inside D-17, Timothy looked at his watch. It was 4:52. He should've been out of here already. Hard as it was to admit, he was going to have to give up the search or risk being locked inside the storage facility overnight.

Atop one of the interior piles of small appliance boxes, Timothy spied one last bankers box. Maybe this would be the one, maybe Grafton had simply gotten frustrated and left before he remembered it was back here.

Setting the meat cleaver down for the moment, Timothy stood on the cot so he could reach toward the box. The cot held at first, but as Timothy extended his reach, the cot wiggled beneath him and suddenly collapsed into itself, sending Timothy and various boxes sprawling.

One of the boxes, apparently, landed right on top of the 8-track player, which suddenly started blaring music out of its tinny little speaker.

It took Timothy a moment to get his wits about him and realize what was going on. When he figured which box had triggered the music, he lifted it, and fumbled with the switches on the 8-track until he finally got the thing to stop playing.

The storage space grew silent for a moment. But not totally silent. In the background, Timothy could hear the growing rumble of a singularly distinctive car engine.

The Mustang was pulling into the alleyway.

With nervous hands, Timothy fiddled with the camping light but in his panic could not figure out how to turn it off.

He picked up the meat cleaver and crouched in the corner, his intestines loosening like they were literally going to empty out into his pants.

"What the fuck?" he heard Grafton say as he cut the engine and got out of his car.

He began kicking past the boxes littering the alleyway, then realized that a path had been cleared into the unit and a light was shining out from within.

He reached back into his Mustang for the baseball bat.

"Who the fuck is in here?" he called out, now bashing his own possessions to clear a wider path as he made his way inside.

Petrified, Timothy rose to his feet, holding the meat cleaver aloft, half as if surrendering it, half as if feebly using it to protect himself.

"Who else is in here with you?" Grafton demanded, it seemed unlikely the kid had busted in here by himself.

"No one," Timothy said, shakily.

Then he zeroed in on what Timothy was holding clumsily in his hand.

"A meat cleaver? Whaddah you gonna do with that, huh?"

Grafton stepped closer with the baseball bat.

"Huh?" he repeated, and with a quick flick of the bat, grazed Timothy's wrist just hard enough to send the cleaver clattering to the cement floor.

Timothy's wrist stung, but his heart was racing so fast he barely felt it.

Grafton extended the baseball bat and used it to rake the cleaver across the cement toward himself. He bent over and picked it up.

Setting the bat down, he hefted the cleaver menacingly back-and-forth between his hands.

"You gonna come at me—with this thing?" Grafton said. "How 'bout I chop off your fucking head?"

Grafton begin to hold the cleaver aloft and stepped closer, as if intending to do what he'd just said.

Out of nowhere, a *swoosh* followed immediately by a *thud* was heard, and Grafton was suddenly collapsing onto Timothy, the cleaver again crashing onto the floor.

"Ayy, what the fuck!" Grafton said, holding his head, writhing on the floor in pain.

Using adrenaline-enhanced strength, Timothy managed to wriggle out from beneath Grafton and make his way to the open door of the storage unit, where stood Charles holding another baseball at the ready, in case he needed to throw a second fastball.

"You little fucker," Grafton called, still recovering on the floor inside, "I'm gonna kill you!"

"Let's move," Charles said.

Timothy hopped back on his banana saddle, Charles was on foot for some reason, but running just as fast as Timothy could pedal.

In their confusion, they again took a wrong turn into a dead-end alleyway.

"Fuck, try the next one!"

Their darting eyes could barely scan fast enough to find the exit sign, but Charles finally spied it and redirected them until they came out of the maze of corrugated buildings.

The gate was just ahead of them, but it was well after 5 and closed for the night.

Somewhere deeper in the complex, they could hear the Mustang revving up.

With all their weight they both jumped on the pad, but even together they lacked the tonnage to trigger it open.

"This way!" Charles said, and led Timothy to the spot in the fence he'd obviously scaled to get in here, his own bike waiting in the weeds just on the other side.

The two of them together lifted Timothy's banana saddle up and up, trying to get it over the fence. Timothy looked at Charles up close for the first time and realized he had blood coming down the left side of his face.

"What happened to you?"

"I'm fine, you should see the other guys—keep lifting!"

With a final push, they managed to get Timothy's bike up and over the fence. Charles then linked his fingers together to form a stirrup and knelt down.

"C'mon, move, move, move," Charles said, over the rumbling sound of a train pulling south out of the rail yard.

Timothy stepped into Charles' interlocked fingers, Charles stood and lifted at the same time, giving Timothy the boost he needed to get to the top.

This was the one spot along the fence where the barbed wire had been tamped down, but it still had barbs, one of which caught Timothy's shirt and ripped it as he was pulling himself the rest of the way over, before falling to the ground on the other side otherwise intact.

Left on the inside alone, Charles backed up a few feet to get a running start, then sprang at the fence. Despite his agility, the height of the fence presented some difficulty. He nonetheless managed to use his momentum to make it just high enough to execute a sort of flip which quickly vaulted him up and over and onto the ground alongside Timothy.

They mounted their bikes and began to ride just as the Mustang approached the gate, resting on the pad in the road, growling impatiently as Grafton waited for the gate to open wide enough to pass through.

Charles and Timothy were able to get a precisely one block lead before coming to a full stop at the tracks as an unknowably long freight train lumbered past.

"For the love of fuck!" Charles said.

There were no other roads in or out of the old brewery. You could not go over, under, or around a passing train, whose awesome power would crush a person sure as Grafton would.

They could do nothing but wait.

Behind them, the gate finished opening. Grafton threw the Mustang into gear and began accelerating toward them.

Both Charles and Timothy looked at the Mustang, then back at the train, whose caboose was now in sight as the remaining cars click-clacked past them.

It seemed that Grafton would reach them first. And he did.

Ducking under the gate as a last attempt to distance themselves, Charles and Timothy got within inches of the locomotive behemoth rumbling past them.

Grafton got out of the Mustang and began lurching toward them. Ducking under the gate, he was within feet of either grabbing them or pushing them into the train, when the caboose rolled past, and Charles and Timothy took off like a shot across the tracks.

An increasingly furious Grafton, rubbing the lump on the back of his head, got back into his car and again had to wait for another gate to open before he could move.

Charles and Timothy had bought enough time to get two blocks ahead on Greenkill Avenue. But there were no additional gates that could hinder or save them, and once the Mustang was freed to tear up the road, it caught up with them in no time.

"Split up!" Charles called out.

Timothy cut right onto Wilbur, Charles continued straight on Greenkill.

The tactic worked at first, at least in terms of saving Timothy.

Grafton continued to follow Charles who, through sheer force of will, was able to stay ahead just long enough to fly through a busy intersection, at which Grafton paused momentarily, but was back on his trail in seconds.

With inches to spare, Charles spied an opening in the fence surrounding a field behind the old age home. Charles jumped the curb and flew through the opening. He knew this field from back when he'd gone to George Washington Elementary like Timothy. He knew it would deliver him to a parking lot and through to the next block.

When he emerged on the other side, he figured he'd bought Timothy enough time to escape, so proceeded to zigzag through the intervening streets on his way, ultimately, to the safety of his own suburban neighborhood.

What Charles did not realize was that two moments after he'd given Grafton the slip, Timothy had emerged onto Wall Street not half a block in front of the Mustang, prompting Grafton to change targets.

Timothy, hearing the Mustang approaching behind him, made a quick right just to get away, but this was actually taking him further away from his home.

The Mustang, of course, gunned it and continued to follow.

Timothy managed to stay ahead just long enough to pull into the Gulf Station where he filled up his tires.

"Sal, Sal!" he called, hoping the garage owner would come out and protect him.

But as Grafton came squealing into the station, Timothy pedaled off again, away from the pumps just in time to avoid the Mustang, charging like a bull, *DING DINGing* at high speed as it flew over the wires without stopping.

Sal came out of the station, moments too late, looking both ways, trying to figure out what the heck had just happened.

Timothy, meanwhile, had gotten back on course. Approaching his elementary school, he cut diagonally across the playground blacktop, which was clearly marked "School Buses Only," but Grafton ignored the sign and continued to follow, causing two kids who were playing a late-day pick-up game to grab their basketball and take cover.

Back on Wall Street, Timothy only had two blocks to go, but Grafton was right behind him. He ducked down the alley that ran alongside Terri's Market. He'd never actually been down this alley because it always had the strong, sour smell of rotten meat, and he didn't know where it would lead.

Grafton came to a screeching stop, running into the alleyway himself.

Timothy came to a dead end and turned around to see Grafton running at him. Abandoning his bicycle, Timothy climbed on top of the foul-smelling dumpster and was clambering over a paint-chipped fence when Grafton grabbed him by the foot.

The only advantage Timothy had at this point was gravity. As he fell toward the gravel driveway waiting on the other side, his shoe came loose in Grafton's hand.

Hitting the ground hard, Timothy got up onto his feet immediately and started running. With no bike, one shoe, and a ripped shirt, Timothy had one block to go as Grafton jumped back into his Mustang and came barreling after him.

Rounding the corner onto Warren Street, the Mustang skidded around the same corner just behind him. Almost tripping several times on the uneven bluestone sidewalk, Timothy at last reached his house with Grafton screeching to a stop in the middle of the street right out front.

Timothy raced up the steps of his front porch and threw open the screen door. Grafton, beyond any sense of rationality of whatever, did not pause.

Flying through the front door into the living room, Grafton reached forward and grabbed Timothy by the torn shirt. He was on the verge of throwing him to the floor when he paused momentarily, trying to figure out what he'd just stumbled into.

A roomful of protective women, having just finished watching a slideshow about female empowerment, rose to their feet.

"Timothy, what the hell is going on?" his mom said.

Grafton, whose lizard brain was not going to disengage at this point, seemed to say to himself *Fuck it anyway*. He shook Timothy's body and clocked him at least once in the head before, en masse, the collective force of Group lunged toward him.

Enraged beyond reason, Grafton let go of Timothy and whirled toward the crowd with both fists clenched, hitting with full force whatever got in his way.

Several of the women got clocked in the process, but no one was backing down.

The sheer physical entanglement of the situation prevented Grafton from continuing to swing his fists with full power.

From somewhere in the middle of the Group, policewoman Sarah managed to push her comrades aside to get up front.

"Get the fuck out of this house!" she yelled at Grafton as the other women began to step aside for her, momentarily giving Grafton free range of motion once again.

"Fuck you dike!" he yelled at her, preparing to strike with the full force of his rage.

But Sarah moved more quickly and efficiently than Grafton could.

Executing a single, perfectly positioned throat strike, she sent Grafton crumpling to the living room floor, holding his trachea, making some kind of gurgling noises.

Taking no chances, Sarah capably grabbed Grafton's wrist, getting him into an arm lock. She pushed him face down, pressed him down with one foot, and signaled for one of the other women to throw her her leather bag, from which she pulled a pair of cuffs and an official KPD walkie talkie.

"I've got a Code 30 at 11 Warren Street, requesting back-up . . ."

★   ★   ★

Not five minutes later, three squad cars were double parked out front, flashers lighting up the street.

Women of Group stood here and there, neighbors came out to see what was going on, as two beefy Kingston cops led a cuffed, semi-conscious Grafton out to their car.

Timothy, flanked by his mom and Cathryn, who was holding a compress to his forehead, sat outside on the front steps while the ranking police officer was trying to figure out what happened.

"Now, start from the beginning, in your own words," the officer said, holding his notepad at the ready.

Timothy shook his head.

"I'm not saying anything without my partner . . ."

The officer chuckled slightly and looked to Timothy's mom and Cathryn, who both shrugged their shoulders.

"Your partner?" the officer said. "Who's your partner?"

"Charles Lambeau, Jr.," Timothy pronounced succinctly.

"Oh boy," the cop said with a falling voice, putting down his notepad. "We got trouble . . ."

PART THREE

★ ★ ★

mong those already present around the large table in the conference room at the Kingston Police Department were Police Chief Ryan, Mayor Kroeger, Alderman-at-Large DeMarco, and several detectives that Charles' father had served with when he was on the force.

Charles and Timothy had come with their evidence, and their moms, though Cathryn had stayed home, so as not to complicate matters.

Jack Wallace, Chief of Operations at IPM Kingston, was the last to enter the room.

"Hi Jack," Chief Ryan said.

"Jim," Jack Wallace said, likewise addressing the chief by his first name, taking a seat. "Thanks for calling me."

"Sure thing, Jack," Chief Ryan said. "Okay, I think we're all here. Let's begin, shall we?"

He shuffled a few papers on the table in front of him.

"So, thank you all for coming in on a Saturday, I know there are other places you'd rather be," Chief Ryan began. "I think most of you know Charles Lambeau, Jr. already . . ."

A couple of the detectives at the table chimed in with a friendly, "Hi Charley," to which Charles smiled and politely waved.

" . . . and this is Timothy Miller, Charles's, uh, partner," the chief continued. "I'll be honest, I didn't know what to make of this at first but, I've had a chance to review their collected materials and, frankly, these young men have conducted a thorough and impressive investigation of a situation that's of great local importance . . .

"I think I'd be doing Charles and Timothy a disservice if I attempted to paraphrase here, so . . . I'm going to go ahead and ask them to make their own presentation, if that's what they'd like to do . . ."

Charles looked to Timothy, who nodded for Charles to go ahead.

"Thank you, Chief Ryan," Charles began. "I do believe we'd like to go ahead and present what we've uncovered . . ."

Timothy happened to look in the corner of the room and spied a slide projector sitting on an AV cart. Man, if only he'd known in advance, Foto-Mat girl probably could've turned their photos into a kick-ass slide presentation.

"Ladies and Gentlemen," Charles continued, "Exhibit A is not for the squeamish, but I think you'll agree it immediately draws our attention to the importance of the subject at hand."

This was Timothy's cue to dump the contents of a brown paper lunch bag he'd been holding in his lap.

The dead frog flopped out onto the faux wood-grain of the conference table. Having begun to decompose, it smelled slightly of marine death.

"This frog was found already dead in Tannery Brook just yesterday afternoon. Who was the culprit? A neighborhood cat? A raccoon? A bird of prey perhaps? No . . . the culprit was the water itself."

At this, Charles produced the plastic test bottle with the water sample in it. He plunked it onto the table next to the dead frog with great effect.

"Timothy Miller and I ran a series of laboratory tests in a controlled environment which proved beyond a shadow of a doubt that the water in Tannery Brook contains unacceptably high levels of benzene and other chemicals, which are toxic to both animals as well as humans . . .

"The question, then, how did benzene get into the water? I draw your attention to this map of Kingston, clearly showing the route of Tannery Brook from the old Colonial Quarry on Route 32 to Warren Street uptown, where the sample was taken . . .

"Colonial Quarry for years produced native bluestone, the dust from which would have been about as harmless as dirt flowing into the Tannery Brook . . .

"But these photos, taken within the last month, present quite a different portrait of what's seeping into Tannery Brook at the old Colonial Quarry today . . ."

Charles began passing photos around the table. The photos showed the extent of the barrels floating beneath the surface of the quarry's water, as well as close-ups of particularly corroded barrels, leaking toxins directly into the water.

"Where did these barrels come from?" Charles asked rhetorically. "From the IPM plant right here in Kingston . . ."

Charles then passed around the photos of the van clearly marked IPM, and the men in the process of dumping barrels into the water.

Eyebrows went up around the room, a few pairs of reading glasses came out of shirt pockets.

Mayor Kroeger looked particularly surprised at what he was seeing.

"Jack, is this true?" he stage-whispered down the table.

Jack Wallace did not answer for the time being, patiently waiting his turn to look at the photos, like he was still processing the information like everyone else.

Jack Wallace was the kind of guy who, professionally, was usually cool as a cucumber. He was doing a good job of remaining composed for the moment, but you could tell he was concerned. Very concerned.

"So the question remains," Charles continued, "does IPM know what it is they are doing? Is it their legal right to buy an old unused quarry and dump whatever they like on their own property? Surprisingly, the Federal government does allow this sort of thing to happen under certain circumstances . . .

"But I have in my hands an official Federal document, acquired through the Freedom of Information Act, stating clearly that IPM applied for a permit in 1972 to dump benzene and other chemicals directly into the Esopus Creek . . ."

Charles pointed to the word *benzene* on the document he was holding . . .

" . . . and they were denied a permit on the basis that benzene is a known carcinogen."

Charles pointed to the word *carcinogen* on the document.

"So here we have it in writing, in an official document, that IPM knew that benzene was a carcinogen, but they proceeded to dump it into the waters at the former Colonial Bluestone Quarry anyway . . ."

Charles passed the papers around.

"Please feel free to examine it for yourselves," Charles added, concluding the presentation. "Timothy and I have several copies on file, of course, for our personal records."

Both Timothy's and Charles' moms looked on in utter amazement, both at the detailed work their sons had accomplished without their knowledge, and the utter seriousness with which the City's highest ranking officials were taking it.

The detectives, the Mayor, the Alderman-at-Large, everyone continued to examine everything with great interest, passing it all along until, finally, all the evidence had accumulated in a big pile in front of Jack Wallace, who continued to leaf through it for a moment, then pushed it aside.

"Very interesting indeed," he said finally. "Chief Ryan, can I talk with you alone for a moment?"

Chief Ryan and Jack Wallace walked back into the conference room about five minutes later.

"Mr. Mayor, Mr. Alderman," Chief Ryan said, "I want to thank you for coming in on a Saturday, I think we can take it from here."

"I want an update on Monday," Mayor Kroeger said. "And Tuesday, and Wednesday."

"Yes sir," Chief Ryan assured him, then he thanked the detectives who'd come in on their day off as well. As the men were walking out, they all made sure to say things like, *Nice work Charley, Timothy* . . . etc.

So now it was just Police Chief Ryan at the table with Timothy, Charles, their moms in the background, and the head of IPM.

"Charles, Timothy, I want to thank you for your impressive research," Jack Wallace began. "Truly, you're both a credit to our community, and I appreciate the work you've done . . .

"As head of IPM, I take all this very seriously . . . IPM isn't just an international corporation, we're part of the Kingston community, we're family. If through some oversight it turns out we've somehow contributed to a situation that's less than completely safe for every member of our community . . . then I can assure you, we will resolve this situation quickly, we will resolve it completely, and we will resolve it permanently . . . "

Damn, this guy was good.

"Here is what I'm proposing to do . . . directly after I leave here, I will be calling my board in to meet, today. We will be devising an immediate plan of action and, I give you my word, we will be presenting you with a comprehensive plan within ten day's time . . . and if you find you have any additional concerns, I can also assure you that we will address them most eagerly and work them into our plan . . . does this sound . . . acceptable?"

Timothy suddenly found himself thinking of the boys he ate lunch with every day in the cafeteria, the ones whose dads all worked at IPM. This guy was their dads' boss. No, this guy was their *boss's* boss.

How was it that the boss of the boss of everyone's dad in town was sitting here, asking *them* if his plan was acceptable?

He and Charles looked at each other, trying to decode what they'd just heard and figure out if it was, in fact, acceptable, or if they were being sold a bill of goods.

"The only thing I ask," Jack Wallace added, "is that you let us do our work in good faith, and that we keep it between us, and not bring the press in on it."

It seemed that this was what Jack Wallace was angling for all along, but Timothy found he lacked the confidence in such a high pressure situation to weigh in on this.

Charles meanwhile, seemed to have no trouble jumping back in.

"So, in ten days," he said, "you guys come back to us with a comprehensive plan."

"That's right," Jack Wallace agreed.

"And if you don't have a comprehensive plan in ten days, we go to the press."

Jack Wallace remained perfectly composed. If he didn't adjust his head ever so slightly, you'd never know how hot under the collar he actually was.

While having presented himself as accommodating, he obviously didn't want it to seem that these two boys had any kind of leverage over him, or over the fate of a multi-billion dollar corporation.

But he could not risk equivocating over something that, according to his own terms, seemed perfectly reasonable on the surface.

"You have my word we'll have a plan in place within ten days . . . or you can take it to the *Freeman*."

Charles and Timothy both looked over to Chief Ryan as the authority figure in the room they felt they could trust.

"Sounds good to me," Chief Ryan said, nodding to Jack Wallace, who immediately began rising from his chair.

"Any other concerns, boys?" the Chief added.

Timothy almost held his tongue. The meeting seemed to have gone better than he could have imagined. But he knew that Charles had presented Chief Ryan with some notes on how this all related to Grafton, but the Chief hadn't mentioned this and neither had Charles.

"There's one thing that bothers me," Timothy said, right eye twitching slightly as if channeling Peter Falk.

Jack Wallace made like he was still listening, while continuing to gather his papers. Charles, meanwhile, pleaded subtly with his eyes for Timothy to let it drop, but if IPM could have Ken knocked off before he went to the press, couldn't they do the same to Charles and him?

"Yes, Timothy?" Chief Ryan said.

"How is it that the day before Ken Wilson went to the D.E.C., he wound up dead?"

Jack Wallace stopped moving. He looked from Timothy over to Chief Ryan, like, *What the hell is this kid talking about?*

"I think we should let Mr. Wallace go call his board members," Chief Ryan said, "they've got their work cut out for them if they're going to be ready in the next ten days."

Jack Wallace, glad to be off the hook for whatever this was, said his last goodbyes and exited the room with his copies of the evidence clutched in a manilla folder.

"Timothy and Charles," the Chief said, "why don't you stick around for a few more minutes so we can talk about this . . . "

Timothy and Charles' moms each felt like they had been transported to Mars. They'd been in the room the whole time more-or-less for legal reasons because the boys were both minors, but now that it was down to the boys and Jim Ryan, who was a family friend of the Lambeau's, Charles' mom took Timothy's mom to the break room so they could get a cup of coffee.

"Can I get you guys anything?" Chief Ryan asked Charles and Timothy.

Timothy was actually wondering if the coffee at the police precinct would be any better than at the diner, but when Charles said, "No, we're okay," he decided to keep quiet.

"Timothy, do you know what's meant by fragmentary evidence?" Chief Ryan asked.

The Chief's tone had grown more paternal, Timothy felt he could trust that he was not trying to put him on the spot.

"Not exactly," he said.

"Well, the evidence you fellas presented regarding the quarry? That was solid evidence. That's why I called the Mayor in here. That's why I called Jack Wallace in here. They needed to see this. It's the real deal, and it's going to change lives . . . now, the stuff about Grafton . . . not so solid . . . which is not to say it's not *valuable*, it's just better we leave people like Jack Wallace out of it."

Timothy no doubt had a discouraged look on his face.

"Look, Kurt Grafton's a smalltime criminal, he was on our radar since before we picked up his brother, but you leading us to his storage space actually helped tremendously, did you know that?"

"How did it do that?"

"We found a substantial amount of stolen goods in Grafton's storage space connecting him to all sorts of burglaries. We've finally got enough to build a case against this guy, he's going away for a while."

"But what about Luke Grafton?" Timothy asked. "What about the IPM job we heard the two of them talking about on the phone?"

"I can tell you from our investigation that Luke Grafton sometimes worked as a day laborer over at the IPM plant, that was probably what you heard them talking about. Seems like that's how he and his brother managed to move some high-end copier equipment out the backdoor. We're talking grand theft here, it's significant."

"But what about the timing?" Timothy asked.

"You mean the new car?" Chief Ryan said, pointing to the photo of the Mustang Timothy had included in the evidence. "The Graftons had some money. Seems like Luke was the smart one, always insisted they keep day jobs as a cover, no big expenditures, but the minute he was out of the picture, Kurt couldn't help himself."

"Yeah but, I don't just mean the car," Timothy said, "if there's no connection, why did Luke Grafton attack Ken right before he turned his report in to the D.E.C.?"

Chief Ryan looked at Timothy in an understanding way. He could see the boy desperately needed to find explanations for things that had no explanation.

"Timothy . . . I oversaw this case personally. We are well aware that Ken Wilson was a chemistry student at New Paltz and that he'd identified toxins in the brook by your house. But I can tell you with utter certainty that his assault, while tragic, had nothing to whatsoever with IPM or with the chemicals in Tannery Brook."

"Then . . . why would . . ." Timothy started to ask, but his question trailed off as the case he thought he was building dematerialized in front of his eyes.

"I realize some of this may be . . . particularly troubling to you," Ryan said.

He'd read the report of the scene his officers had come upon at Timothy's house and drawn his own conclusions, but was not going to elaborate further.

"I don't know quite how to explain this . . . there are people in this world who don't understand how other people can be . . . different . . ." Ryan tried to put this delicately. "And sometimes it's easier to hate people who are different than figure out how to accept them . . . I know that's not a very satisfying explanation but, unfortunately, I've seen other cases like this and . . . that's just the way it is."

It wasn't that Timothy didn't know Ken was "different" as Jim Ryan put it. Thinking back to the fight he'd had with Crazy Carl, and similar things he'd heard said over the years, he more-or-less understood what Jim Ryan was trying to say without saying it. He'd known all along that some people could hate other people who were "different."

But that this hatefulness could lead to what had happened to Ken? Jim Ryan could try explaining this five different ways.

Timothy just couldn't believe it.

CHAPTER 27

The ten-day deadline for IPM to get back to them seemed to last forever, particularly as it coincided roughly with the sluggish remaining days of the school year.

Even Mrs. Brenner seemed to be running out of steam. Earlier in the year, she'd changed the bulletin boards regularly, to correspond with seasons and holidays. But it looked like the same fading Bicentennial posters would be hanging up for the duration.

She was showing films in the afternoons with increased regularity, too. She didn't even mind the students ripping lined paper from their three-ring binders to fold into fans, the days growing warmer and the school not equipped with air conditioning.

In the cafeteria, the talk was all about summer plans.

"You hear IPM's gonna have their own fireworks this year out at the Rec?" Brandon asked. "They're gonna be the *best*!"

The other IPM boys all quickly agreed that, if IPM were doing fireworks out at the Rec, they would definitely be the best.

IPM Rec was a country club a few miles out of town for the families of employees. Brandon had taken Timothy out there once or twice, so he knew it was nice.

Talk turned, naturally, to the many days the IPM boys would be spending together, poolside, at the Rec.

"I'm gonna eat french fries everyday," Steve said.

"I am too," Drew said, "and hotdogs."

"The fries at the Rec are the *best*," Brandon agreed.

"Eating french fries everyday gives you cancer," Allen said from across the table.

"Who says?" Steve said.

"My dad," said Allen.

Allen's dad didn't work at IPM, but he was a doctor, which was basically Allen's ace in the hole, when it came down to it.

"I'm gonna eat fries everyday anyway," Steve said.

"Me too," Drew agreed, then added, "and I'm gonna do a cannonball off the high board."

Doing a cannonball off the high board was not likely something Allen's dad was going to say would give him cancer.

"I'm gonna do a flip," Steve one-upped him.

"I'm gonna do a double flip," Brandon said, "and land right in Karen Vandenberg's lap!"

Everyone died laughing at this. At the beginning of the school year, this would have sounded purely icky. But 4th grade had begun to work its magic on a couple of girls in class, and landing in Karen Vandenberg's lap suddenly seemed an almost attractive possibility.

Spending the summer months poolside at IPM Rec was not in the cards for Timothy. Cathryn would probably drive him to Kingston Point occasionally so he could swim in the Hudson, which was fun in its own way, but he still wished he could join the club, or at least the conversation.

Then he found himself asking:

"Do any of you guys know Jack Wallace?"

"Jack Wallace?" Brandon said. "He's, like, the head of IPM."

"Did you ever meet him?"

The IPM boys all laughed at this.

"Of course not, dork," Drew said, "how would any of us meet Jack Wallace?"

Timothy couldn't say anything further, of course, without risking word getting out about the investigation and the shit storm it had just kicked up at their fathers' place of employment.

The laughter about Timothy's ridiculous question continued. Timothy started laughing too.

Only he was laughing at something different than they were.

Even without the benefit of a touchtone telephone, Timothy's fingers could dial Charles' number quickly and automatically at this point.

"Hey Timothy, how's it going?" Charles said.

"Pretty good . . . you hear anything from IPM yet?"

"It's only been four days."

"I know, I just thought I'd check."

Timothy had called the day before, this is more or less what Charles had said then.

"I promise when I hear something, you'll be the first to know, okay?" Charles asked.

"Okay . . . you want to meet at the diner or something?"

"I'd like to, but I'm studying."

"You're *still* studying?"

Since Mrs. Brenner seemed to be running out of things for them to do in 4th grade, he couldn't imagine what Charles could possibly be studying.

"When you get older, you have all these finals," Charles tried to explain. "You'll see when you get to junior high school."

"When're you going to be finished with those?"

"In a week or so."

"Jeez."

Charles let the conversation go silent a few moments before he asked, "Anything else?"

"Guess not," Timothy said.

"Okay, see you soon."

"See you soon."

When Timothy hung up the phone, he left his hand on the receiver momentarily, still trying to decode the conversation. Charles had seemed glad enough to hear from him. Granted, maybe finals were more difficult than Timothy could imagine, but did anyone need to study for two whole afternoons in a row?

Timothy wandered somewhat aimlessly down the street to the field behind the Green Apartment Building. No investigation to conduct. No Charles to hang out with.

Mark and Carl were out there tossing a frisbee back and forth.

"Hey, where you been?"

"Studying," Timothy said.

"Studying?" Carl said. "For what?"

"I don't know," Timothy said. "How come you're not playing whiffle ball?"

"Not enough people," Mark said.

Mark threw the frisbee to Timothy, who clap caught it between two hands. Shifting it into his right hand, he threw it to Carl, who threw it to Mark, who threw it to Timothy again.

After a few throws, the three of them forming roughly an equilateral triangle, Timothy rediscovered the muscle memory to catch and throw with the same hand.

"What're you guys doing this summer?" Timothy asked.

"I dunno," Carl said, throwing a slightly low one to Mark, who compensated fairly effortlessly and made the catch.

"We might go camping," Mark said.

"Where?" Carl asked.

"I dunno," Mark said. "Somewhere."

Carl and Mark both turned to Timothy.

"So what are you doing this summer?" they asked.

"I dunno," he said.

They didn't talk much beyond that. But somehow they managed to keep throwing the frisbee for a good half hour without dropping it.

The next afternoon, Timothy figured he'd give Charles a break and not call. He was probably just going to say he was still studying anyway.

Timothy hadn't consulted the Real Men's Guidebook in a while. Today he pondered the instructions for breaking down a locked door. Unlike the movies, you were not actually supposed to use your shoulder.

He went out into the hallway, closed his own bedroom door, and imagined it was the door to an interior office, say, somewhere deep within the IPM complex.

First step, root your left foot firmly on the floor. Next step, take careful aim at a spot just to one side of the doorknob. Final step, leaning into the kick, drive heel into target.

This final step Timothy executed with approximately half his available strength, which did not open the door but which generated a slamming sound sufficient to reverberate throughout the entire house.

"Is everything okay?" Cathryn called from downstairs.

"Yeah, the wind just blew the door shut," Timothy called back, even though there wasn't much of a breeze today to speak of.

Examining the door, the wood near the doorknob displayed a hairline fracture. Timothy had no doubt that if he were to employ full strength, the door would fly apart and open.

Since this was his own bedroom door, it seemed best to leave remaining experimentation in this area in the realm of conjecture.

Another experiment, using a double A battery to start a fire, likewise seemed like something he probably shouldn't be attempting in the house right now either.

The following day, the *Freeman* reported that a Planning Board Meeting had taken place the previous evening at City Hall.

The Common Council had voted unanimously to give IPM permission to expand their facility.

A formal press conference was scheduled for the following Saturday, which happened to be the first day of summer vacation, and also coincided a little too neatly with the date by which Jack Wallace had promised to deliver his plan for environmental clean-up.

The *Freeman* article included some basic details about the expansion. The groundbreaking was slated for early July of this year. The first of the new buildings would add 50,000 additional square feet of production space, creating almost 200 new jobs immediately, leading to an estimated 500 new jobs over time.

Mayor Kroeger was quoted as saying, "This is a good day for IPM, and a great day for Kingston," as if he hadn't just been informed six days before that IPM was responsible for a toxic spill into the waterways of the City under his watch.

Timothy had to call Charles.

"Did you see the paper?" he asked.

"I'm looking at it right now," Charles replied.

"Were they, like, just bluffing us to buy time?"

Timothy could hear Charles flipping the paper over to finish reading the article on the back page.

"I don't know . . . I mean, we promised not to go public for two weeks, and by that time they're gonna have this big press conference . . ."

"And then it'll be too late?"

"Not totally, but . . . it's kinda hard to argue with 500 new jobs . . ."

It was a hard decision, but Charles and Timothy agreed they needed to stand by their word and wait for Jack Wallace to get back to them, even though they were beginning to have their doubts.

When the subject came up at dinner, his mom, having been at the police station meeting and knowing the backstory, came to roughly the same conclusion that Timothy and Charles had come up with independently.

"Hopefully they'll do the right thing," she said. "Just try not to be too disappointed if they don't."

★ ★ ★

Timothy hadn't ridden his banana saddle since the night Grafton chased him, even though the police had retrieved it from Terri's alleyway and delivered it to his house that same night.

Now it was a beautiful Saturday with not much to do, the bike was calling out to him. The front fender was slightly dented from crashing into the dumpster at Terri's, but beyond this was no worse for wear.

He considered revisiting one of the hotspots related to their investigation, but he found he didn't have much appetite for being out of his comfort zone. He pedaled lazily around uptown instead, familiar turf.

Summer freedom was beginning to wash over him, but it was perhaps more wistful than previous years, with Timothy not really knowing what he wanted to do, and a growing sense that life was a sequence of things given then taken away.

Timothy drifted toward Forsyth Park, as good a destination as any, its few blocks worth of trees not quite forest-like, but dense enough for a little extra oxygen and the sense that you'd gone somewhere.

The path that meandered through the park led up the hill to J. Watson Bailey, so it was only natural that he found himself slow pedaling in front of the junior high.

It was closed now, of course, being Saturday. But Timothy pictured Charles in there, day in, day out, changing classes, doing finals, whatever you did at the end of the year in junior high school.

Timothy tried to imagine going to school there himself, two-plus years from now.

Doing the math, by the time he got to junior high, Charles would be in high school. And by the time he got to high school, Charles would be off in college somewhere.

They would never be in the same school together. Charles would always be several steps ahead. It was only natural that sooner or later, he would leave Timothy behind altogether.

Maybe that was just the way it was going to be.

In school Monday, the kids could barely control themselves knowing this was the very last week. Library was no exception, but there was something about that particular room, the students somehow had the restraint to keep their voices low enough that Mrs. Stein could read them one last story.

"Does anyone remember what a myth is?" Mrs. Stein asked.

Several hands went up and she called on Drew, the boy who'd worn a three-pointed hat during his presentation.

"A myth means it's fake," Drew said.

"Well, that's one meaning of the word myth," Mrs. Stein said, "but a myth is also a certain type of story, which might not be *literally* true, but it might contain a deeper truth that helps people understand something about their lives."

The kids wiggled on their mats, half of them lost already, but she continued just the same.

"Today we're going to hear a myth from the Algonquin people who lived here in New York State, not around here exactly, but not so very far away."

She held the book up for the class to see and announced its title, "The Story of Thunderbird."

Timothy's ears perked up immediately, like she had just said his name, because in a way, she had.

She began to read:

When the people first came to live by the river, they did not know what to eat.

They found the fish in the river to be plentiful. But the river was also home to the Great Horned Serpent, who ruled the underworld.

Great Horned Serpent, they said, we will give you our respect, please allow us to eat the fish from your river. And they offered him various tributes.

The Serpent was well pleased with this, and allowed the people to take fish from the river, and this is how they lived.

Many years passed, the people grew more knowledgeable about life on the shores. They learned to grow corn and beans and squash, and as years passed, they came to offer the Earth Mother more and more tributes, while to the Serpent they offered less and less.

The Serpent grew jealous. When the people weren't paying attention, he rose up angrily from the river. With fire coming from his mouth, he scorched the fields so that the corn, beans and squash could not grow. He muddied the river, so the people could not fish.

The people tried to offer tributes to the Serpent again, but it was too late, he had grown too bitter to hear their words.

Knowing they would surely starve, the people then looked to the sky and called out to Thunderbird, who controlled the upper world.

Now, this was not without risk, because Thunderbird had great destructive power. The flapping of his great wings created thunder, lightning came from his eyes, and his windstorms could be devastating. But he also had the power to feed the earth with life-giving rain.

Thunderbird looked and saw that the Serpent had left his river and was bringing harm to the fields. He swooped down to aid the helpless people.

A great battle between Thunderbird and Serpent began. Thunderbird had Serpent caught in his beak, but Serpent managed to wrap his tail around Thunderbird's neck.

In the upper world, Thunderbird's powers were greater, but below the surface, Serpent had the advantage. When Serpent began to pull Thunderbird into the water, it seemed that Serpent might win. Thunderbird thought only to free himself and return to the upper world.

The people called out to Thunderbird, begging him to keep fighting, but above the noise of battle he could barely hear them.

Then, Earth Mother called out to Thunderbird. She reminded him that it was only because the people had offered her tribute that Serpent had grown so vengeful. If he were left undefeated, he would continue to scorch the earth and muddy the waters, and the people would surely starve.

Hearing this, Thunderbird continued fighting with Serpent. Right before being pulled under, he managed to get Serpent within his talons. Flapping his mighty wings, Thunderbird carried Serpent off to a distant lake.

As he pierced the clouds, rain began to fall, which brought the soil back to life.

> *The corn and beans and squash grew and grew. That year*
> *was the greatest of harvests, and there was much celebration*
> *in the village . . .*

Mrs. Stein closed the book and nodded her head with satisfaction at the power of a good story.

Some kids rolled their eyes, eager to get to lunch and the playground, but Timothy had been mesmerized.

He'd thought that Thunderbird was just another flashy car. But it turned out that Thunderbird ruled the sky. He could shoot lightning from his eyes, and was a protector of the people.

Timothy liked that idea.

After school, Timothy was in his room digging through his bottom drawer when he came upon the envelope of the first roll of film he'd had developed. It was still a sore spot that his mom had only taken the ones of her and Cathryn, but looking at the ones that remained from their Lake George trip, he had a vague idea he should try to make some duplicates to give her so he could keep his own copies.

He popped the envelope into his knapsack and took off on his bike.

Funny, this neighborhood now seemed not so bad at all. Charles' mom was right, it really was close to everything. While kids like Brandon were stuck riding in circles in their suburban cul-de-sacs, Timothy could go pretty much anywhere he wanted.

When he got to the booth, he was glad to see the FotoMat girl, not the chubby guy with the mustache.

"I thought you'd forgotten about me," she said, when Timothy pulled up on his bike.

"How're you feeling?" he asked.

"Fine. Why do you ask?"

"Last time I was here your manager said you called in sick."

"It happens."

"He wasn't so nice."

"One of the benefits of working alone in a booth," she said, "I don't have to deal with him much."

Interesting, Timothy hadn't thought about this. If the paralegal thing didn't work out, maybe his mom should think about working at a FotoMat.

"So, did you have something you wanted to develop," she asked, "or did you just come here to chat?"

"You said can make more regular pictures from negatives, right?"

"You betcha. Whatcha got?"

Timothy took the negatives out of the little side compartment in the envelope and held them up to the sunlight. It was kind of hard to make them out, they were so small.

A car pulled up behind him.

"Sorry it's taking so long."

"Take your time, they can wait."

Squinting at the tiny negatives, he still wasn't sure.

"I'm having trouble choosing," he said.

"You want me to have a look?"

He handed her the negatives. Holding them up to the light in her booth with a more practiced eye, she scanned them quickly.

"These are cute," she said, "how 'bout this one?"

She held her finger by one in particular and handed it back to Timothy. It wasn't one of the ones he was thinking of for a variety of reasons. But then remembered the Real Men's motto:

When that little voice says No, you say Yes, and double it.

This seemed to be one of those moments.

"Okay . . ."

"Great, what size do you want?"

"You can pick sizes?"

"Sure, we can bump it up to 5x7 . . . or, if you really want to go for it, we can do 8x10."

Double it, the voice reminded him.

"Let's go for it," he said.

That evening, the phone rang right in the middle of dinner.

Timothy's mom didn't think much of people who called right in the middle of dinner.

"This better be important," she said.

She rose from the table and went into the kitchen to answer it.

Timothy and Cathryn could clearly hear the tone of her voice going from miffed to quite enthusiastic.

"Why yes . . . yes . . . yes, I think he can do that," she said, seeming to agree to whatever was being proposed on the other end of the line.

Both Timothy and Cathryn had stopped chewing their Hamburger Helper by this point to listen in.

Stretching the phone cord to the max, Timothy's mom came back into the dining room, bringing the phone conversation with her.

"Why don't you ask him yourself?" she said into the phone then, cupping her hand over the receiver: "Timothy, it's Jack Wallace."

Timothy wiped his mouth off lickety-split.

"Hello?"

"Yes, hi Timothy this is Jack Wallace, from IPM, sorry to disturb you during dinner."

"That's okay," Timothy replied perhaps too eagerly, having anticipated this moment, while at the same starting to doubt that it would happen.

"So, I was just telling your mother, we're going to be having a little ceremony at IPM this Saturday to formally announce the upcoming expansion of our facility . . ."

"Yes, I read about it in the paper."

"Of course you did . . . well, we've decided to expand our presentation slightly to showcase the new Environmental Stewardship Program that we're launching, in part thanks to the wonderful research that you were able to provide . . . we'd like to present you and Charles with an award to recognize your achievement, is that something you might be interested in?"

"Yes, definitely," Timothy replied, not attempting to hide his excitement in the slightest by this point.

"It's the first day of your summer vacation, I'm afraid," Jack Wallace said, "maybe you have other plans that day, but the timing of the ceremony has been in the works for some time . . ."

"That's no problem, Mr. Wallace, I'll be there."

"Glad to hear it, and please bring your family too."

"I will, thank you Mr. Wallace."

"No, thank *you* Timothy, good night."

"Good night . . ."

Timothy stood there dumbfounded, then:

"I have to call Charles," he said, "can I call Charles now, or do I have to wait until after dinner?"

"Call Charles," his mom said.

His fingers fumbled on the rotary dial, he was so excited.

"Charles, I just got a call from Jack Wallace!"

"So did I," Charles said, a bit more composed than Timothy, but obviously equally excited.

"We did it!"

"So it seems, Thunderbird, so it seems . . ."

They agreed to talk more later to firm up plans for attending, then Timothy fell back into his seat at the dinner table, still kind of stunned.

"This is great news," his mom said.

"Yeah . . . he said I can bring my family."

"Okay," his mom said without hesitation, "I'll take off work."

Then they both looked at Cathryn.

"I'm very proud of you, Timothy," Cathryn said. "I'll be very happy to stay home and hold down the fort."

Cathryn was smiling as if this was an arrangement that suited her perfectly fine. But Timothy knew her well enough by now. He knew that the smile was masking her hurt feelings at the prospect of being left out.

"No," he said. "I think you should come."

CHAPTER 28

The last day of school had been exciting, but nothing compared to this.

One eye in his bedroom mirror, the other on the diagram in the Real Men's Guidebook, Timothy attempted to tie a half Windsor for the first time.

The necktie was fat, brown, and polyester. Timothy had found it in the back of a closet, his dad must've left it there.

With the thicker end dangling from his neck about a foot lower than the skinny end, he tried to make sense of the instructions. He managed to cross the thicker end over and behind the skinnier end, then looped it successfully through the neckband. But the next steps involved maneuverings that seemed to require a third hand to execute correctly.

On the third try, he finally achieved something resembling a loose knot, but the thicker end was still hopelessly longer than the skinnier end, and was now dangling somewhere near his knees.

Hearing the phone ring, he dashed downstairs, thinking it might be Charles, but from the tone of his mom's voice, he could tell it was Greg from her office.

"I told you," she said, "I have an event to go to with Timothy."

Timothy couldn't hear what was being said on the other end, but it was obvious Greg was putting pressure on her to come in, as he'd done previously.

"I know the Sawyer case is on Monday, I've already cleared it with Evelin, we're covered . . ."

With her free hand, Timothy's mom began unconsciously rubbing her temple, as if to fight back the tension the phone call was inserting into her brain.

"Look Greg, I'm not coming in, I'm going to be with my son, goodbye," she said with finality and hung up the phone.

Her eyes pinched closed, she remained by the phone momentarily, still trying to massage away the headache with her thumb and forefinger.

She looked up, surprised when she realized Timothy was standing there watching her. When she saw the mess of the necktie hanging from around his neck, she began to laugh, grateful to have another channel she could switch to.

"Look at you," she said. "Come here."

Reaching out, she undid the botched necktie, then began tying it for him properly, from the beginning.

"Stand up straight or it won't come out right," she said.

Timothy tried to stand straight and look down simultaneously, so he could see how the hell to tie this thing.

"Your father was never good at this either," she said, "I was always helping him on his way out the door."

This was the first time Timothy had heard her even reference his dad in months. She usually didn't like to talk about him. The fact that she was the one who brought him up seemed to open a window.

"Was he really so bad?" Timothy asked, innocently enough.

Continuing with the tie, she blew a thin column of air out the side of her mouth, as if she had to clear some space to find words to deal with the subject matter.

"Well, your father had a bit of a temper to begin with," she said. "I don't know why I expected him to grow out of it . . . but over the years, he just seemed to get angrier and angrier."

"What was he angry about?"

"Everything and nothing," she said vaguely.

She was to the point in the process where she was looping one end of the brown tie up past his Adam's apple. Timothy tilted his head back slightly and remained silent, hoping his mom would go into greater deal.

"As time went on, he became harder and harder to talk to," she continued, "and I had my own . . . issues . . . anyway, it got to the point where we didn't know each other anymore, and staying together just wasn't an option . . . "

Timothy tried to square this with his fading memories of the man who sometimes laughed when he took him to the park over the weekends, but more often was someone whose way he needed to stay out of when he came home from work, frustrated, banging things around sometimes to the point of breaking them.

"Are you sorry you married him?" Timothy asked hesitantly, afraid of the answer but wanting to know.

She was this close to finishing the necktie, but paused a moment to reflect.

"We were young when we got married, we both needed to get out of our parents' houses, it seemed like the right way to do it . . . maybe it wasn't a good idea."

This small bit of insight almost made Timothy sorry he'd asked, until she added,

"But if your father and I had never married, I never would've gotten you, would I?"

She'd been looking past Timothy a lot lately. But putting the finishing touches on his necktie, she looked right at him. She shook her head in disbelief, as if marveling how much he'd grown this past year and she was just realizing it at this very moment.

"I know this has been a hard year for you. It's been a hard year for me too," she said. "Maybe if I'd done a better job explaining things, it would've been easier on you, I don't know . . ."

She started to turn her head away. Timothy could see her clenching her jaw ever so slightly, like she was fighting to keep her game face on and not start crying.

He'd been keeping his own guard up so long, he couldn't even remember the last time he felt his chest loosening like this, but seeing his mom on the edge of tears had an effect on him, and he had to clench his jaw too.

"It's okay, Mom," he managed to say, "you're doing a fine job."

Hearing him sounding almost like the adult in the situation made Timothy's mom laugh and tear up at the same time. She hugged him hard, and when he hugged back, it was a real hug, his eyes moistening too.

"It's 1:00," Cathryn called in from the living room, "we gotta go."

"Okay, kid," his mom said, pulling herself together. "It's showtime."

★   ★   ★

If arriving at school in the Calico Chrysler was humiliating enough on an average day, the idea of driving it to the IPM ceremony was just plain incomprehensible.

But here they were, piling into their five-different-shades-of-Rustoleum vehicle, heading out to meet the world.

His mom was dressed sort of like she dressed for work. Cathryn was wearing a pants suit he'd seen her wear once when she and his mom had gone to a wedding.

It was a warm day, and the Calico Chrysler of course had no air conditioning, so its windows were wide open on their way out Route 209, blowing all their hair to a point that no amount of combing later could tame.

The IPM facility had a manned guard gate that admitted only one car at a time. Even Timothy's mom had never been out here before.

As they pulled up to the gate in the Calico Chrysler, their hair still wild from the drive out, the guard took one look at them and asked, dubiously, "Can I help you?"

"We're here for the ceremony?" Timothy's mom said, her voice rising at the end almost as if she were asking a question.

"Name please."

"Timothy Miller and guests."

"Oh," the guard said, almost apologetically after checking his notes. "Here, put this in your window and drive right in."

"Thank you," Timothy's mom said, taking the pass from him, "where's guest parking?"

"No, you're not in the guest lot, we've got a space reserved for you in Executive Parking," he said, pointing to the spaces closest to the main building's entryway. "Drive right up front."

"Oh, that's nice," Timothy's mom said, "thank you . . ."

Steering the car to Executive Parking, sure enough, they found an empty space waiting for them with a printed sign on photocopied paper reading *MILLER.*

Please do not dent or scratch anything, Timothy prayed, closing his eyes as his mom maneuvered them in between a glimmering Lincoln Continental and a late-model Cadillac.

Cutting the engine, his mom and Cathryn both patted down their hair. Timothy didn't bother.

"You think we need to lock it?" Cathryn quipped as they got out.

As they walked past the other cars in the executive spaces, Timothy even saw a couple of Mercedes.

When they reached the front door of the building, the person greeting them was obviously somewhat better informed than the guard in the parking lot had been.

"You must be Timothy," he said, welcoming them.

Probably not too many ten-year-olds with crazy long hair expected today, so not much of a stretch, really.

"Hi," Timothy said hesitantly, his own voice sounding odd to him, dwarfed by the imposing environment.

"I have passes for all of you, if you can just clip them to your own clothing, I'll lead you to the conference room . . ."

It's not that Timothy had never walked down a long hallway before, but this hallway seemed exceptionally long, and well-lit to the extent that the air itself almost seemed incandescent.

There was a certain background hum, too, a white noise so

all-encompassing, it felt like the building was some manner of massive creature that had just swallowed them whole.

"Right in here," their guide said, leading them through the open doors of the conference suite.

"Timothy, Timothy!" someone called.

As Timothy jerked his head to see where the voice was coming from, a flashbulb went off in his face, capturing his stunned expression.

"Thanks," the photographer said, "I'm on a tight deadline, just making sure I get a good shot."

The guy's name badge said *Daily Freeman*. Looked like IPM had gone ahead and contacted the press themselves.

"Timothy, welcome . . ."

Timothy turned to find Jack Wallace, extending a warm hand, which Timothy accepted, feeling like he was shaking hands with President Ford himself.

"Hello Mr. Wallace," Timothy said. "This is my mom."

"Yes, hello Denise, we spoke on the phone the other evening . . . and you must be Cathryn."

The guy had done his homework. He greeted both women with equal warmth, no explanation of relationships necessary.

"We have a table waiting for you, right by the dais," Jack Wallace said, escorting them across the room.

There at the table, Charles and his mom were already seated. They rose to greet Timothy, his mom and Cathryn.

Charles' smile was as wide as he'd ever seen it, he actually embraced Timothy in an almost headlock-like hug, he was so excited.

"Can you believe this?" Charles said.

"Uh, actually, no," Timothy said.

Timothy's mom introduced Charles' mom to Cathryn, and the three women fell into polite conversation, leaving Timothy and Charles sitting next to each other looking around the place, taking it all in.

There must've been at least 100 people gathered, the men all in suits, what women were here in conservative skirts and blouses. From the looks of it, these weren't just IPMers, either, but community leaders of all sorts.

Several people around the room were looking over at Charles and Timothy, there was no doubt in either of their minds that they were being talked about.

A uniformed waiter arrived to take a drink order. Charles extended his hand, indicating that the ladies at the table should order first. Charles' mom asked for a soda water, Timothy's mom and Cathryn followed suit.

"And for you?" the waiter asked Charles.

"I'll have a scotch and soda," Charles said with an absolutely straight face.

"Scotch and soda," the waiter repeated with utter seriousness, as if he were actually going to get it for him, though Charles' mom raised a skeptical eyebrow.

"Just kidding," Charles said with a wink. "May I have a Coke, please?"

Timothy thought this was just about the funniest exchange he'd ever heard, could not be topped, so when the waiter asked, "And for you?"

He just said, "I'll have a Coke too."

If the Coke here was even half as good as it'd been at the Oriole Tavern, it would suit him just fine.

And then, snacks started coming.

But these weren't like the snacks on their dining room table on Group night.

There was shrimp cocktail, tiny Swedish meatballs, crabmeat in phyllo dough cups, and some kind of cheese spread with a slight fruity flavor Timothy couldn't identify, but it was delicious.

Jack Wallace stepped up to the microphone.

"Thank you all for coming . . . we've got a somewhat ambitious schedule this afternoon, so let's get started . . ."

The room quieted down almost instantaneously. Jack Wallace definitely wielded a lot more power around here than a substitute teacher.

"When IPM first opened its doors here in Kingston in 1952, we had a five-room office in midtown for twenty employees. Now, five rooms is not a lot of space for twenty employees, and I should know—I was one of them."

The whole room got a big laugh out of this, Jack Wallace's revelation of his own humble beginnings somehow being a real crowd pleaser.

"Anyway, as many of you know, not five years later we'd grown to 10 thousand square feet and 700 employees, a number that would continue to double every five years, bringing us up to over 5,000 on our current team, the biggest single source of jobs this county has ever seen . . ."

The crowd applauded happily, this simple fact alone being worthy of recognition.

"As we embark upon our latest phase of development, we'll continue to put Kingston on the map, bringing world-class copying equipment to a growing market, while growing our workforce to an estimated 8,000 by the 1980s. Where we'll go from there is anyone's guess . . ."

Even more applause. This crowd was ready to go for the ride.

"I'm going to call Burt Thomas up now. He's pulled together a little slide show presentation I think you're going to enjoy, Burt . . ."

At this, Burt Thomas, whoever he was, came to the mic, talked briefly about what everyone was about to see, then someone hit the lights and the slide show began. There was a variety of artist's projections of what the new buildings would look like, interspersed with maps and photos of the existing facility. The shots were all high-contrast with vivid colors. In the outdoor shots, the sun was always shining, and in the indoor shots, the workers were always smiling.

At the conclusion of the slide show, the lights went back up, and a series of additional speakers, including Mayor Kroeger, took turns addressing the crowd, confirming the importance of IPM's growth to the health of the local economy, and a sense of pride and thankfulness that the best darn copy machines in the US of A were being produced right here in Kingston, New York.

It seemed like the congratulatory speeches would go on forever, when Jack Wallace finally returned to the mic.

"I told you we had an ambitious schedule today," he said, pretending to mop his brow.

Again, everyone in the room laughed. This guy could read a shopping list and get the crowd to laugh.

"We do have one final segment of our presentation today, perhaps not directly related to the expansion, but equally important, if not more so . . ."

The crowd simmered down and prepared to pay attention one last time.

"When we began production in the post-war years, it was all systems go, full-steam ahead, without much thought to the environment. Well, times have changed, and IPM intends to change with them, which is why I'm proud to announce the establishment of our Environmental Stewardship Program . . .

"What is the Environmental Stewardship Program, you may ask? It's a new way of thinking about the byproducts of production at facilities like the one here in Kingston. But it's also a concrete new collection of technologies that we'll be employing not only to keep Kingston clean, but Utica, Rochester, and our growing number of locations in the South . . .

"Instrumental in getting this program started was research provided by two community-minded youngsters studying local waterways as part of a school project . . . the incentive they've demonstrated is commendable, it gives us great confidence knowing that with young people like these in our community, our future is indeed in good hands . . .

"Without further ado, I'd like to present Charles Lambeau, Jr., and Timothy Miller."

The crowd started applauding even more loudly than they had for Jack Wallace's jokes. Charles had to nudge Timothy so he would know to stand up.

"Come on up, boys," Jack Wallace said.

It was at this point, coming onto the stage and realizing that all eyes in the room were most definitely upon him, that Timothy began, in vain, to try patting down his hair.

"Charles, Timothy . . . on behalf of IPM, I would like to present each of you with a one thousand dollar scholarship . . . college may still seem a ways away, but it's closer than you think . . ."

Jack Wallace handed both Charles and Timothy certificates with their names printed on them, along with some words about the scholarship and the IPM logo.

The crowd applauded continuously, as flashbulbs went off, Jack Wallace with his hands on the boys' shoulders while they held up their certificates.

"Would either of you like to say a few words?"

Charles looked at Jack Wallace and out at the crowd.

"I would, actually," Charles said.

He stepped up to the mic and began to speak humbly but confidently.

"I just want to say that I wish my dad could be here right now . . . I always thought that him being a detective was just about the coolest thing in the world, but he always made sure to tell me that being of service was the most important thing. Dad . . ." Charles said, looking up, "I hope I'm doing it the right way . . ."

Charles then looked over at the table where his mom was sitting.

"I want to thank my mom, who is the best mom ever, and I'm going to put this scholarship toward the best college there is and make you proud," he said, holding up his certificate.

"Finally, I want to thank my partner, the bravest and smartest and nicest guy I know, Timothy 'Thunderbird' Miller . . ."

Charles turned to Timothy as he said this, making room at the mic while the crowd applauded in encouragement. Timothy had no choice but to approach the mic and try to speak.

He honestly didn't know what to say. This whole thing was like a dream, including the way IPM was making like they were going to clean up the spill all along, and he and Charles had just happened by at the right time to lend a helping hand. This was not something he was going to bring up, especially seeing as Charles had not brought it up himself.

But there was one person that was not being mentioned, and it seemed like if Timothy didn't say anything, it was just going to be swept right under the rug.

"It's true that Charles and I did a lot of work figuring out what kind of pollution was in Tannery Brook," he said, already spelling it out more clearly that Jack Wallace had done.

"But I just want to say that we never would've done it if it wasn't for Ken Wilson," Timothy continued. "He lived up the block from me. He's the one who first figured out that the brook was polluted, so he should get the credit . . ."

People around the room were looking at each other, like, *Who the heck is Ken Wilson?*

"Anyway, thanks to Mr. Wallace for the scholarship, thanks to Charles who *is* the coolest guy I ever met . . . and I should thank my mom too, who's been working so hard to keep our house going . . ."

Timothy looked over to the table. There was only one person remaining who'd yet to be mentioned.

"And thanks to my mom's . . . partner . . . Cathryn, who's always there for me too."

The room gave Timothy and Charles one final round of applause as Jack Wallace conveyed them back to their table and offered the crowd a few parting bits of wit to conclude the presentation.

Back at the table, there were additional proud hugs and congratulations from the moms as the crowd transitioned for some light socializing and networking before things broke up. The photographer from the paper took one or two last shots and was seen running out of the room at lightning speed to make his deadline.

Several community leaders came up to both Charles and Timothy to shake their hands and congratulate them for being such fine young men. It was a little much for Timothy to deal with, and he began to make eye contact with his mom, indicating they should start to make for the door and get out of there.

But Jack Wallace returned to their table before they could break free.

"Charles, Timothy, I thought maybe you and your families might like a little guided tour of the facility—unless you're in a rush."

Jack Wallace was holding two very official-looking hardhats that presumably Charles and Timothy would get to wear as part of the guided tour.

Charles and Timothy both looked at the hardhats, then at each other.

"That'd be great!" they said simultaneously.

As Jack Wallace led the five of them further down the gleaming white hallway toward the mysterious world of photocopier manufacture, he took Timothy's mom aside.

"I understand you're a paralegal, Mrs. Miller," he said to her.

"Ms. Miller," she corrected him.

"Oh, sorry, Ms. Miller."

"And I'll be getting my paralegal certification in the fall."

"Well, Ms. Miller, as you can imagine, we have a fairly extensive legal department here at IPM. I'd like to think I have a good eye for talent and . . . I should tell you, our scholarship program isn't just for young people, we have quite a few lawyers on our team who've worked their way up and earned their law degrees on our dime . . .

"Anyway, we're quite impressed with your family, Ms. Miller," Jack

Wallace said. "I do hope you'll consider coming to work for us in the fall."

Timothy's mom looked over at her son, who was trying to figure out how to get his hardhat over his long hair, unaware at the moment the extent to which he had just seriously scored one for the home team.

"Why thank you, Mr. Wallace, that's an attractive offer," she said. "I will most definitely consider it."

CHAPTER 29

Flying back into Kingston in the Calico Chrysler, the world felt like it had just doubled in size. The residual echoes of the manufacturing plant mixed with the sounds of the road into an abstract sort of symphonic movement.

Above the noise of the wind, Timothy's mom called to the backseat:

"We were thinking about ordering pizza from Villa Marsala, how does that sound?"

Could this day get any better?

"Sounds great!"

Exiting Route 209 and making their way around the traffic circle, as the sounds of the short highway ride died down, Timothy's reflections on what had just happened began to come in for a landing as well.

He was excited about the scholarship, of course, but that reality was eight years away, close to doubling the lifetime he'd lived already. Meanwhile, he still didn't even know what this coming summer was going to look like.

As they drove along Washington Avenue, Timothy saw the sign for Kingston Plaza and suddenly remembered something.

"Oh Mom, can you swing by the FotoMat?" he said from the backseat.

"The FotoMat?"

"There's something I have to pick up."

It seemed like Timothy having a mysterious life of his own was going to continue past this investigation.

"Yeah, sure . . ."

The Kingston Plaza was only a block out of their way. When Timothy's mom pulled up to the booth, FotoMat Girl was there. Timothy noticed that she, his mom, and Cathryn all seemed to share a quick inquisitive glance, as if a secret handshake had just been exchanged with their eyes.

"Something I can help you with?" FotoMat Girl asked.

"I think so . . ." Timothy's mom said, craning her head back around to check with Timothy because she didn't actually know what it was he needed to pick up.

"It's me, Timothy!" he called, leaning up into the front seat so FotoMat Girl could see who it was.

"Oh, I didn't recognize you in a car," she said. "So, this is your car?"

"Yeah," he said kind of sheepishly, admitting at least partial ownership, "this is our car."

"Cool car," she said. "I got one just like it."

Using her thumb, she pointed back to an old Dodge parked just behind the FotoMat. Not the same make or model as the Calico, but similarly multiple shades of Rustoleum.

"Cool car," Timothy said, returning the compliment.

"It works," she said.

"I don't have my receipt with me," Timothy admitted.

"That's okay, you're a Preferred Customer."

"I do have the money," he said.

He reached into his pocket and pulled out a lump of change which he strained to extend past his mom in the driver seat.

"Timothy, you can't expect her to deal with all those dimes and pennies," his mom interjected.

"It's okay," FotoMat Girl said, "I'm used to it."

She took the money and handed Timothy his envelope, which this time was almost the size of a record album cover. He set it aside for now, planning to give it to his mom later.

As they pulled away from the booth, Timothy looked out the rear window.

"Did Charles and his mom just follow us to the FotoMat?" he asked.

His mom looked in the rearview mirror.

"Will you look at that?" she said, as if she was just noticing this for the first time.

"They're still following us," Timothy said as they were chugging along Washington Avenue towards home.

When they turned onto Warren Street, Charles' mom also made the turn. It was clear that they were following them back to the house.

There seemed to be more cars parked on the street than usual, but the spaces in front of Timothy's house were open and waiting.

As they got out of their respective cars, Timothy went running over to Charles.

"What are you doing here?"

"My mom said we're coming over for pizza," Charles said.

"Alright!" Timothy said.

He led Charles up onto the porch and was about to go bounding inside, but Charles blocked him with his arm and physically led him back down the steps onto the sidewalk.

"What are you doing?" Timothy asked.

"Mrs. Miller," Charles said past Timothy to his mother, "I don't want to alarm you, but I believe someone's broken into your home."

"I don't think we have anything valuable enough to steal," Timothy's mom said, trying to make light of it.

"I thought I detected movement," Charles said, "they might still be inside."

"I'm sure it's fine, Charles," she said, oddly unconcerned, urging him back toward the house. "Let's all just go in together."

Back on the porch, Timothy noticed that the drapes were drawn. Charles was right, they never drew the drapes, he might've even seen one of the drapes move. And what was Oscar doing out here? He thought they'd left him inside. But his mom, Cathryn and Charles' mom were all coming up the steps, determined to enter.

Charles assumed a tactically prudent position to the left of the door, indicating that Timothy should position himself likewise on the right.

"On my signal," Charles said. "One, two, three . . ."

Together, the two boys blasted through the door, steeling themselves to protect their mothers, if necessary.

The lights inside the darkened house came on all at once, and at the same time . . .

"SURPRISE!!!"

★　★　★

The room was alive with red, white and blue streamers, balloons, and women from Group, all beaming at Timothy and Charles happily.

"I know we can't compete with the reception at IPM," Timothy's mom said, "but we thought we needed to have a little party of our own."

Timothy felt like if there were any more surprises today he was going to have a coronary, but he was flushed with gratification just the same.

Charles, meanwhile, couldn't stop laughing.

"Who are all these people?" he asked.

"Come on," Timothy said. "I'll introduce you."

Charles' mom may have had a different appearance from the other women, stylistically speaking, but she seemed quite happy to jump right in and socialize, leaving Charles free to make the rounds with Timothy in the packed living room.

"This is Anne," Timothy said, introducing the person that happened to be closest.

"Hello Charles," she said, giving Charles a firm handshake. When she gave Timothy a big hug, he was surprised but glad enough. If you'd've told him two months ago that the woman with the grumpiest eyes in the room would've been hugging him, he never would've believed it.

After she let go of him, Timothy turned to the next person.

"This is Becky," he said, and much the same process repeated itself, handshakes for Charles, hugs for Timothy, until they came to the woman with the lethal striking ability.

"This is Sarah," Timothy said.

"Oh, I know Officer Roberts," Charles said.

"Charles, good to see you," Sarah said, shaking his hand. "Nice work."

"Thank you, Ms. Roberts, much appreciated."

When Sarah hugged Timothy, he made sure it was brief, knowing she could easily get him into a choke hold, even though he was pretty sure this wasn't going to happen.

"So, are you thinking of joining the force someday?" Sarah asked Charles, drawing him into a conversation.

"Well, a criminal justice degree is certainly a strong possibility," Charles began, "but international affairs might position me better, if I decide to pursue intelligence at more of a Federal level . . . "

As Charles was getting deeper into the conversation, someone tapped Timothy's shoulder.

"Do I get a hug too?"

It was Cara.

"Yeah, for sure," he said.

Cara was not particularly tall as far as full-grown women went, but she was still sufficiently taller than Timothy that when she pulled him in for a hug, his face wound up squarely pressed against her bosom.

"We're all so proud of you Timothy," she said.

As she released him, she continued to hold his hands for just a moment then, perhaps thinking of how he'd kissed her forehead, with an almost mischievous twinkle in her eye, she swooped back in and planted a quick one on him before letting him go.

Trying to figure this out in a daze of Cara's patchouli, someone on the other side of him said, "Timothy?"

He turned to face a woman he did not recognize.

"Sorry, I didn't mean to steal you away from Cara," the woman said.

"That's okay," he said, looking around to see where Cara'd gone, but she'd already disappeared into the crowd.

He looked back to the woman who was talking to him.

"You don't recognize me, do you?" she said.

She looked a lot like many of the other women here, natural hair, not too much make-up, a hippy t-shirt. But no, he didn't recognize her.

"It's Lynda," she said, when she saw him struggling to make the connection, "from up the street."

"Oh, sorry!" Timothy said, realizing it was Lynda from the Green Apartment Building, aka Lynda the prostitute, or former prostitute, she certainly did not look that part anymore. Her black eye had healed since the last time he'd seen her.

"I don't know how to say this, these women . . ." Lynda said, holding her hand on her heart, "they're just extraordinary . . . you have no idea how much this has helped me . . . Thank you, Timothy."

"I, uh, I mean," he tried to find the words, then simply said, "You're welcome."

At this moment, Becky came running back into the house holding the *Daily Freeman* over her head.

"Look at the paper!" she said.

Timothy and Charles squeezed their way into the tight circle examining what Becky had just introduced to the party.

There on the front page, hot off the press, was a giant photo of Charles and Timothy standing with Jack Wallace, holding their certificates, his stately hands resting on their shoulders. The headline read:

A New Day For Kingston

The room erupted with chants of "Timothy!" "Charles!" as the newspaper was whisked around.

And then, came an even more important announcement:

"Pizza's here!"

The newspaper article would have to wait. Pizza does not stay hot forever.

As a whole pile of steaming pizza boxes came flying in, people made way to make sure Timothy and Charles could make it into the dining room and get theirs first.

Finally, after being tossed about as if at sea for much of the day, Timothy and Charles went out onto the front porch and fell into each other on the sofa, a wonderfully greasy paper plate of flaming hot pizza burning each of their laps.

"Man, what a day," Charles said.

"You're telling me," Timothy agreed.

"I feel like we haven't talked in a week," Charles said.

"We haven't," Timothy said, not in an accusatory way, it was just a statement of fact.

"Yeah, sorry I had to study for all those finals," Charles said. "Someday, you'll see."

"That's okay," Timothy said.

The two of them stopped talking for a moment so they could stuff some pizza into their mouths.

"So, you think IPM is really gonna clean up that quarry?" Timothy asked.

With all the pageantry behind them, it did occur to him that IPM's plan was light on specifics.

Charles reached into his shirt pocket.

"Well, look what I scored," he said. "Jack Wallace handed it to me in a moment of heightened magnanimousity."

"Is that even a word?"

"You got me," Charles said, "maybe it's magnimity, or something."

"Right. So what does it mean?"

"It means when Jack Wallace was all hopped up on his own generosity, I had the temerity to ask for his card, and he was foolish enough to give it to me," Charles said. "We now have Jack Wallace's private phone number."

"Wow, what're you going to do with that?"

"I propose that *we* allow, say, six months time to pass, then we reconnect with our friend Dwayne by the quarry and go for another little dirt bike ride . . . If there's no clean-up in evidence, Mr. Jack Wallace will be receiving a little phone call, and we'll go from there. Sound like a plan?"

"Sounds like a plan," he agreed.

Timothy was glad to hear Charles thinking into a future that included him. Still, kind of like the college scholarship, six months seemed a long time to wait for another adventure.

Not knowing what else to say on the subject, Timothy asked:

"So, what're you gonna do this summer?"

Timothy figured Charles' summer would involve some fantastic vacation, or perhaps days by the pool of one of the even nicer country clubs some Kingston families belonged to besides the IPM Rec.

"I'm going to be spending a lot of time volunteering at the Youth Center," Charles said. "Summer's a time when they really need me."

Somehow Timothy hadn't thought of this, but it was true, there were tons of kids all over Kingston who would not be going to the IPM Rec or anything like it.

"Actually, Timothy, I've been meaning to ask you," Charles said, "would you like to work with me?"

"Really? What could *I* do?"

"Oh, you could do a lot," Charles said. "There are kids at the Youth Center even younger than you. They could really use a good role model. A guy like you? You could really make a big difference in their lives . . . it's all volunteer, so you won't get paid or anything, but they feed us lunch, usually hotdogs or something . . . plus this way you and I can keep hanging out. What do you think? You can think about it if you want to . . ."

"I don't have to think about it," Timothy said. "I'll do it!"

Charles smiled widely.

"That's great, Timothy. That makes me really happy."

Their paper plates empty except for the grease and residual sauce, the two went back inside to load up on some more pizza.

On their way back in, Timothy noticed the envelope from FotoMat still sitting on the front table where he'd dropped it when they'd first entered the party.

"Go get some more pizza," he told Charles, "I gotta do something."

It took a moment for Timothy to locate both his mom and Cathryn and get them standing still in a single place, he pulled them out onto the front porch so he could have a moment with them.

"There's something I want to give you," he said.

Right before he could hand them the envelope, the sound of a roaring engine came winding down the street accompanied by the massive blare of a loud horn.

It was Mr. O'Connor in his big rig, coming straight off the road after having dropped off his trailer.

"I'm back!" he yelled happily out the window.

Much like Mr. O'Connor's grand departure, his return was likewise a neighborhood event. Kids came from out of the woodwork, cheering, climbing all over the truck happily, like Mr. O'Connor's successful navigation of the country was just as much a triumph for them as for him.

Mr. O'Connor pulled on the emergency brake and cut the engine. Of course, he was blocking traffic, but Warren Street was his street, and for the next hour or so, if anyone had any problem with that, well, they could just take some other street.

"Who wants to help me clean this thing?" he said merrily.

It was true, the rig which had been gleaming on its departure now looked like it had been through hell, but this was nothing a DIY car wash couldn't fix. Hoses came rolling out from all directions. Water started spraying everywhere, people getting wet, but no one cared.

The screen door to Timothy's house was propped open, everyone inside came spilling past Timothy and onto the street. Other neighbors, likewise, came pouring out of their houses to see what was going on.

What had started as a Group party tucked neatly into Timothy's house had suddenly become a mingling of everyone in the neighborhood, it was like a giant spontaneous block party.

Mr. O'Connor, in a moment of exuberance, shot off a few fireworks, which were illegal in New York, but he'd obviously scored them in one of the other states he'd passed through where they were legal.

"Warren Street's gonna have the best 4th of July in Kingston!" he declared and the kids all cheered.

At that moment, the radio in Mr. O'Connor's truck started playing the familiar pulsing chords of a Sly and the Family Stone classic.

"That's my song!" Charles called out.

Apparently, Mr. O'Connor thought it was his song too, because he reached back into the cab and cranked it. Charles climbed up the side of the truck and, like old buddies even though they'd never actually met, he and Mr. O'Connor belted out the chorus to *Everyday People* together.

It was an almost too perfect soundtrack for the festivities on Warren Street at that very moment.

"What were you going to give us, Timothy?" his mom asked.

"Oh, right," he said. "It's just little."

He handed the envelope to her and Cathryn.

They took the photo out and realized what it was.

"This is beautiful," Timothy's mom said. Now all of them were clenching their jaws.

Timothy had decided to enlarge the one photo of all three of them together, in costume, making funny faces the night of the Group Halloween party last October.

They looked like they were having a good time. They looked like a family.

There on the messy porch, the three of them joined in a group hug, which lasted a good long time. It would've made an even better photo if anyone had had a camera.

"I'm sorry I didn't frame it," Timothy said

"I think we've got one inside that will fit just perfectly," Cathryn said.

Water was spraying all over the street from the impromptu car-wash. Timothy's mom disappeared into the house with the photo to find a safe place for it before it could be doused, then she and Cathryn joined the street party.

Timothy was about to climb right up on Mr. O'Connor's truck, but he hung back for a second, just to take in the whole scene:

His mom was talking to Charles' mom. Cathryn and Mrs. Williams were admiring crocuses together. Charles was now singing with Crazy Carl. Cara was listening to Lynda whisper something in her ear. Mr. O'Connor was planting a Times Square style kiss on Mrs. O'Connor.

Everyone seemed to be dancing in the street to the music, and even Oscar the cat brushed up against his own leg, trying to get in on it.

All these disparate elements in his life that he had fought so hard to keep separate, coming together so effortlessly, and it didn't seem to matter one bit.

It was as if his life itself, which had been utterly blown apart for a year or so, was somehow reassembling itself in an unexpected new way, and it was dazzling.

He remembered what Charles had told him about being himself. It had made sense in his mind, yet he hadn't been able to imagine it would ever make sense in his heart.

This was the time.

As the idea of being happy with himself turned into an actual feeling, his belly began to feel a satisfying fullness, and not only from pizza. It felt warm, and secure, and right.

Maybe life wouldn't always be a block party. Maybe every moment would not be this perfect. But he was feeling pretty darn good.

And everything was going to be okay.

SPECIAL THANKS...

To Jen and Elliot for listening as I wrote. To Jason for design and expertise. To Jen for cover art. To early readers Stephen Greco, Victor Bumbalo, Emily Katz, Ellen Tarlow, and Kirsten Bakis. To everyone who read K-76 on Substack. And to Mom, Pat, Jill, and all our friends and neighbors on Warren Street.